CW01189761

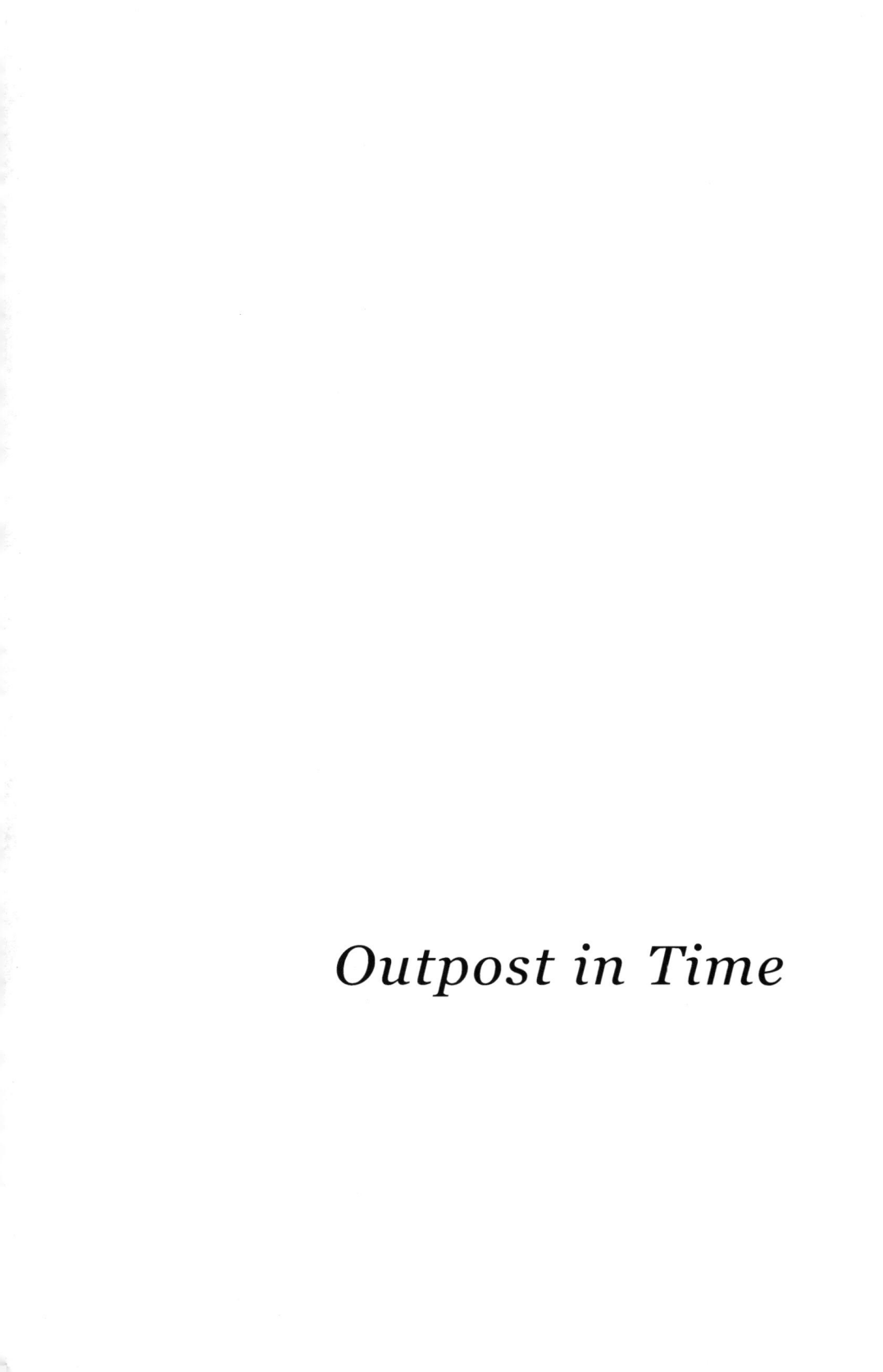

Outpost in Time

Books in the *After Cilmeri* Series

Daughter of Time (prequel)
Footsteps in Time (Book One)
Winds of Time
Prince of Time (Book Two)
Crossroads in Time (Book Three)
Children of Time (Book Four)
Exiles in Time
Castaways in Time
Ashes of Time
Warden of Time
Guardians of Time
Masters of Time
Outpost in Time
Shades of Time
Champions of Time
Refuge in Time
Unbroken in Time

This Small Corner of Time:
The After Cilmeri Series Companion

A Novel from the *After Cilmeri* Series

OUTPOST IN TIME

by

SARAH WOODBURY

Outpost in Time
Copyright © 2016 by Sarah Woodbury

This is a work of fiction.
All rights reserved. No part of this publication may be reproduced, stored in a retrieval system, or transmitted in any form or by any means without the prior written permission of the author, nor be otherwise circulated in any form of binding or cover other than that in which it is published.

www.sarahwoodbury.com

*To Dan, Taran, and Melissa
For sharing the journey*

Cast of Characters

David (Dafydd)—Time-traveler, King of England
Llywelyn—David's father, King of Wales
Meg—Time-traveler, David's mother
Christopher Shepherd – Time-traveler, David's cousin
Callum—Time-traveler, Earl of Shrewsbury
Huw ap Aeddan —David's companion

Geoffrey de Geneville—Anglo-Irish lord (Trim Castle)
Maud de Geneville—Anglo-Irish lady (Trim Castle)
Red Comyn—Scottish lord
Thomas de Clare—Anglo-Irish lord (Lord of Thomond)
Walter Cusack—Anglo-Irish lord (Kells, Killeen, Dunsany Castle)
Richard de Feypo—Anglo-Irish lord (Skryne Castle)
John de Tuyt—Anglo-Irish lord (Castellan of Drogheda Castle)
Aymer de Valence—son of William de Valence
James Stewart—Steward of Scotland
William de Bohun—Anglo-Norman lord
Margery de Bohun—William's aunt (Castle Roche)
Robbie Bruce—Scottish lord
Magnus Godfridson—Mayor of Oxmantown

Niall MacMurrough—Irish lord
Hugh O'Connor—Irish lord (Roscommon Castle)
Gilla O'Reilly—Irish lord (Cloughoughter Castle, Drumconrath)
Matha O'Reilly—Gilla's son
Aine O'Reilly—Gilla's daughter

Prologue

Kells, Ireland
January 1294
Walter

"More wine?" Richard de Feypo gestured with the carafe in his hand.

"Wine will not aid this plan, Richard," Walter Cusack said. "We need level heads and clear eyes going forward."

"It's going to work." Already the most powerful of Geoffrey de Geneville's vassals, Richard was grasping and ambitious, sometimes uncomfortably so. He was also short of stature, with coal black hair and a beaked nose—not the usual physique of a knight. But the size of his brain more than made up for his physical deficiencies, which was why Walter had thrown in with him in the first place.

"Geneville—"

"—is an old man," Richard said. "His mind isn't what it once was. Certainly his body has failed him, and he is distracted by his responsibilities in England. Did you know that he hasn't come to Skryne Castle in five months? He has no idea what I do."

"He has spies." Thomas de Clare, brother to the recently deceased Gilbert, ran his hands through his hair, which was enviably thick and devoid of gray for a man of middle age. He wore it long too, which Walter thought was pure hubris. Walter himself was balding, and while his wife told him that it made him more handsome than ever, he hated every hair he found in his comb most mornings.

"I have turned his spies." Richard had an answer for everything, which was all to the good as far as Walter was concerned. That's why he was questioning him. "I gave you the name of the stable boy he'd bought at Killeen. Did you take care of him?"

"He is dead." Walter's own ambition and his desire to keep both his lands and his head had led him down this path. He would do what was necessary, even if it was unsavory.

"How?" Thomas said sharply. "Nothing that might arouse suspicion, I hope."

"Drowned in the Boyne. It just so happened that he couldn't swim."

Richard nodded. "Then we can move forward."

"What about Valence and Comyn?" Thomas said. "Can you control them?"

Richard was more than confident. "Valence is driven by rage. He can see nothing but King David's corpse on the ground and his head on a pike. You don't have to worry about Aymer."

Walter was pleased to agree with Feypo's assessment. "For Comyn's part, he is motivated by greed. He truly believes we will give him the High Kingship."

Thomas scoffed. "He has to commit far more than five hundred men to our cause if he expects the crown."

"He says he will bring more men if this initial attack goes well," Richard said. "The throne of Scotland will stand with us."

"If so, we will owe Balliol," Thomas said. "You could lose control of this very quickly."

"You will have Thomond so why do you care?" Richard said.

Thomas frowned. "I will care because there are miles of Irish-held territory between Thomond and Dublin. I want to know that you and our other allies will hold those lands, and that you won't balk at a crucial moment—like when you have to kill David."

"The men assigned to him will do their duty," Richard said. "Why wouldn't they?"

Thomas's voice rose, incredulous. "Because he is the return of the great High King Murtagh Mac Ecra come to save the Irish from their oppressors and lead them to the land of milk and honey!"

"That would be King Arthur to you, Richard." Walter rapped his fingers on the table to emphasize his agreement with Thomas. "It's the same tale by a different name, one I learned on my nanny's knee, even if you didn't, and all the peasants believe it. Mark my words, when it comes to it, nobody will want to be responsible for his death."

"My men will be well paid for what they do." Richard moved his hand dismissively. "I anticipate no problems."

Though not completely convinced, Walter grunted his acceptance. David's death was not the minor doing Richard pretended, but it was a small piece of the overall plan, so he was willing to put it aside for now. If all else failed, Walter himself would take care of David. Or Aymer would.

"What of these Irish allies?" Thomas asked. "Surely when it comes to it you don't really intend to include them in the governance of Ireland."

"Of course not. They will fight for us, and then we will isolate them and fall on them one by one." Richard looked from Walter to Thomas and back again. "Is two months enough time for you to prepare?"

"More than enough. I'm already having to hold O'Rourke back. I told you we shouldn't include him in any aspect of the plan until the last moment." Thomas drained his drink and stood. "For that reason alone, I would argue against any delay. Even more, Geneville's health fails daily. With no male heir, if he dies before Parliament convenes, David might claim his lands and give them to the Irish before we even know he's done it. We could be out on our ears by spring."

They all knew David would use any excuse to give away their domains. That was why they were moving at all. The idea that the Lord of Ireland would return their hard-fought lands to the native Irish was an anathema—a betrayal of all that he stood for and they'd fought for. But King David was unlike any king of England who'd gone before him. Which was why they had to act.

"We cannot move sooner. We have to wait until David arrives in Ireland." Richard put one hand on Thomas's shoulder and the other on Walter's. "Now, if there are no more questions, are we agreed? We will see this through?"

The other men nodded their assent. But then Thomas said, "And the king's cousin—this knave who killed my brother and is now hailed as the Hero of Westminster? He truly will come to Ireland as well?"

"I am assured that he will, and he's all yours, Thomas. We win the day, and then you can avenge your brother's death."

Sarah Woodbury

1

Beyond the Pale, Ireland

12 March 1294

Christopher

From Christopher's right, Huw spoke in lilting English. "Who are they?"

Christopher didn't actually say *how the hell should I know?* But his disbelief at being asked that question must have showed on his face, because Huw clapped him on the shoulder and turned to his other side where Robbie Bruce was peering through a pair of medieval binoculars, which (unbelievably) worked quite well. Christopher had already looked through them, so he knew what Robbie was seeing: a dozen ships were sailing up the Boyne River to the town of Drogheda. Given their size, each held at least fifty men and horses. It was a small army. Even Christopher wasn't naïve enough to think that they were here for their health.

"My God," Robbie said. "Those ships fly Red Comyn's banner!"

"You've got to be kidding me!" William de Bohun, the last of Christopher's companions, grabbed the binoculars and yanked them away from Robbie, who swatted at him for doing it but let them go. As far as Christopher could tell, he himself hadn't been good for much during the nine months that he'd lived in the Middle Ages except for teaching his friends bits of American English. William loved the word *kidding* and applied it to almost any situation. Otherwise, he was the most difficult of Christopher's friends to get to know, since most of the time it was impossible to decipher what—if anything—he was hiding beneath his quick banter and pride.

Eighteen seconds into his sojourn in the Middle Ages, Christopher had figured out that he could say goodbye to ever being comfortable again. It wasn't just that the beds were harder here than at home, or that he missed his computer chair, or that he'd ended nearly every day for the last nine months so exhausted he could barely lift his arms. Physical discomfort was the least of his concerns. It was the way everything he had ever thought he knew was not only wrong but likely to get him killed.

He hadn't actually believed that lightsaber fighting with his friends bore much resemblance to sword fighting in the courtyard of a real castle. He'd known before his twelve intensive weeks with Bevyn, David's first instructor, that all that fancy footwork in *The Princess Bride* was essentially useless. But knowing theoretically that one hundred percent of the point of fighting was to get the enemy on his back and drive a sword through his midsection, and understanding that fact, were two entirely different things. Bevyn hadn't much cared what Christopher had to do to win either—as long as he won.

It was almost worse that Christopher had killed Gilbert de Clare with his car that very first day—that very first second—of his arrival in the Middle Ages. Because of it, everyone accorded Christopher a certain amount of respect he didn't deserve. Unlike the guys he'd started hanging with here, each of whom had killed at least one man, Christopher had never killed anyone on purpose.

But as he crouched with his three friends behind the stone wall that made up the border of some poor farmer's field, he had a sinking feeling—to go along with the way his boots had sunk into the mud caused by the endless rain—that he could soon find himself equal to his friends. In fact, the opportunity to do so might be staring him in the face right now, whether or not Christopher was ready for it.

As Christopher gazed through the late afternoon rain to the Boyne River, his stomach curdled at the implications of Red's arrival, and his hand reflexively clutched the St. Christopher's medal around his neck. The medal had been hanging from the rearview mirror of his car when he'd driven into the Middle Ages. Since St. Christopher was not only Christopher's namesake but also the patron saint of travelers, storms, bachelors, and (bizarrely) toothache, he figured wearing it meant he was covering most of his bases. He hadn't even been Catholic back at home, but here, it was the only Christian Church available. Everybody was Catholic and wore one talisman or another all the time.

"Gentlemen, we should move." James Stewart tapped Christopher's shoulder. He spoke with a Scottish accent that had taken

Christopher's ear ages to decipher, but once he had, he found himself mimicking it. James Stewart was the kind of knight that Christopher aspired to become, right down to his loose-hipped, long-legged stride. He was muscled but thin, smart, good-looking, and rich. He was also soft-spoken, but Christopher had noticed right off that when he did speak, people listened. So, Christopher backed away as James wanted, while at the same time keeping his head below the level of the wall.

James was here because David had asked him to keep an eye on Christopher, essentially as a chaperone, which effectively meant that he was William's and Robbie's chaperone too. When he'd first heard about it, Christopher had wanted Rupert, his time-traveling journalist friend, to come along too, but he was in Dublin setting up Ireland's first radio station—and he could barely ride a horse. Rupert had helped Christopher survive some of the harder moments of the last nine months, as one of the few people who understood what it was like to be here accidently. Christopher missed Rupert's humor and the way he had a sarcastic comment for every occasion.

David was in Ireland too, but as the King of England and Lord of Ireland, he was too busy playing politics to run around with Christopher. He'd spent the last three weeks talking with Ireland's barons, trying to find a way to get them to stop fighting each other all the time. So far, however, nothing he or anyone else said seemed to be working. Christopher figured that James had agreed to keep an eye on him because he was sick of all the talking and had jumped at the chance of gallivanting around Ireland for a few days.

William was the last to leave the wall, but after another long look through the binoculars, he hustled after the rest. "What does Red Comyn want? Why has he brought an army to Drogheda?"

James answered without looking back. "I have no idea." Through some sixth sense, which was one of the things Christopher hoped one day to have for himself, James found a path that would bring them closer to the town walls, while at the same time keeping them somewhat hidden from any watchers who might be braving the rain.

None of them had to ask who Red Comyn was, not even Christopher. Before taking him to Ireland in the company of William and Robbie, David had given Christopher a longwinded lecture about noble families and his companions' place in them. Not only were William and Robbie cousins, both descended from William Marshal, the great knight (and Earl of Pembroke AND King of Leinster), but Red Comyn, Robbie's sworn enemy, was too. William was even a true heir to the throne of Scotland. William teased Robbie endlessly about that fact, though he hadn't put in his claim when it mattered.

David had explained to Christopher at great length how, in the Avalon timeline, Robbie had murdered Red in a Scottish church about ten years from now. And then David had immediately made Christopher swear not to tell Robbie about it. Christopher had to admit that sometimes his cousin's lectures were impossibly tedious, but they had a way of sticking in your brain. For example, he now knew that Robbie's killing of Red had prompted Red's family to engineer the capture and eight-year imprisonment of Robbie's future wife, Elizabeth de Burgh. He even could tell you that Elizabeth, who was only ten years old today, happened also to be the daughter of the Earl of Ulster and the niece of James Stewart's Irish wife, Gilles. Christopher took a moment to rub his head. How did David live with all of that swimming around inside his brain, knowing what his friends' future could hold?

The five companions reached the spot where they'd left their horses cropping the grass amidst a stand of trees that screened them from the battlements of Drogheda's town walls. Christopher was a far less experienced horseman than the others, but of all the skills that he'd had to learn in the last nine months, riding was the one he'd taken to most easily. He had no trouble keeping up with his friends on horseback. In fact, he was already a better rider than Huw, who hadn't been born to it either, despite being medieval. Admittedly, Huw wasn't part of the gang because he was a great swordsman or rider. He was here for the same reason James was: to keep an eye on Christopher.

The others viewed Huw as a servant, but the idea of being waited on that way was weird and uncomfortable to Christopher, so he'd settled on treating Huw like what he was—his cousin's friend, who occasionally helped him put on armor. The best thing Huw did for Christopher, however, was to steer him through the blur of names and faces in the castles and countries David visited. Christopher had no memory for names whatsoever, but Huw did, and his voice had been a constant whisper in Christopher's ear about who this lord was or that lady, and he never hesitated to tell Christopher exactly how he was supposed to behave in polite company.

This region of Ireland consisted mostly of farmland and pastureland. Drogheda, where Comyn's ships were docking, was twenty miles northeast of Trim Castle, where the Irish Parliament was meeting. Drogheda was as far as James had intended for them to travel today, and they'd planned to spend the night either at the castle or in the guesthouse of the Dominican monastery, located on the north bank of the Boyne River at the highest point of the town.

With Red Comyn's arrival, that plan wasn't going to work, since there was no way they were letting Robbie Bruce spend the night anywhere near where a Comyn was staying.

The castle lay on the south side of the Boyne River, but the town had been built on both sides with a bridge across the Boyne connecting the two halves. Massive stone walls twenty feet high surrounded the whole thing, and the towers were three times higher than that.

According to James, only English people lived in the town. When the barons from England had conquered this part of Ireland, they'd kicked all the Irish out and made them live in the countryside, though they still had to tithe to the conquerors. Back in Avalon, after King Edward had conquered Wales, he'd done the same thing to the Welsh, effectively making them foreigners in their own country.

In fact, according to Aunt Meg (who rivaled David in her ability to tell you everything about everything), England had used the same tactic over and over again throughout the world. Here in Ireland, the Boyne River acted as the boundary between land that looked to England for authority (called the Pale) and land that was either entirely under Irish control or claimed and fought over by both sides. A big reason David had chosen this moment to come to Ireland and get the peace process going was because it had reached a point in the last year where the warfare never stopped.

Everybody was fighting everyone else, regardless of their ancestry. It was like every lord had delusions of grandeur and was trying to carve out a mini-kingdom for himself.

"We need to find out what Comyn plans before we return to Trim Castle," Robbie said.

"Robbie is right," William chimed in. "We can't go back now!"

William and Robbie were always ready for anything that involved risk. Robbie was older than William, and therefore a little bit wiser, but the two of them together were what Aunt Meg called *a potent combination*. More to the point, they acted first and asked questions later.

Christopher was still waiting for James to answer. He was their leader, so in the end it wouldn't matter what any of them wanted because they would do what James said. After another few seconds of silence, however, Christopher gave in to his impatience. "How worried are you?"

"If I were, would it help?" James gave a sharp shake of his head. "I'm worried, which is why we're going to do as Robbie suggests and find out everything we can about why Comyn is here so we can tell your cousin."

"We really are?" William said. "How?"

"We could find a way inside the castle to listen in on what they're plotting," Christopher said. "Hide in a hay cart like it's the Trojan Horse."

William and Robbie, both of whom knew Greek mythology, nodded vigorously.

Then Christopher's brow furrowed. "Though, now that I think about it, it would probably be easier just to ride down to the dock. Even if Comyn is here to cause trouble, it isn't as if he's going to attack us—especially you, James. You're the Steward of Scotland!"

"I'm sorry to say that I can't agree with either plan," James said. "If Comyn is making a play for power in Ireland, letting you anywhere near Drogheda could make you a pawn in his game."

Christopher blinked. There it was again—the special status he had simply because he was David's cousin. Christopher had been thinking that either he or Huw should be the one to sneak into the castle in a hay cart because nobody would recognize them. He regularly forgot that David was the *King of England,* the most powerful man in Europe. Not even the pope could tell him what to do. There was no way James was ever going to let Christopher do anything even slightly risky. He was lucky James had thought the ride to Drogheda was a walk in the park, or they wouldn't have come.

"Does this mean that Comyn is conspiring with the castellan of the castle?" William said. "John de Tuyt is supposed to be loyal to Geoffrey de Geneville!"

There was a grim set to James's jaw. "Maybe he still is."

"But—" William was struggling with the implications. "That means Geneville—" He broke off, unable to finish the thought.

"Might not be faithful. Yes." James was projecting strength and calm, which was good because Christopher certainly wasn't feeling either. Christopher had met Geoffrey de Geneville over Gilbert de Clare's corpse that first day at Westminster Castle. He was one of the barons David trusted, and Christopher got a sick feeling in his stomach at the thought that Geoffrey might no longer be a friend.

"We should confront Red now." Robbie's eyes lit with an inner fire.

Christopher decided that he didn't care if he came off as ignorant again. "It makes no sense at all that Red would ally with Geneville. Even I know that he and Red have nothing in common. Red doesn't even have any lands in Ireland."

"Like me, his wife does, so he does." James glanced at Christopher. "King David has made no secret of the fact that he doesn't approve of his barons' rule of Ireland. If they're afraid that he might force them to give up their lands in favor of their Irish rivals, they might see the advantage of enlisting outsiders such as Red Comyn—men who aren't loyal to King David and never will be."

"Cousins will be pitted against each other! Brothers too!" William looked horrified, showing for once that he wasn't as jaded as he pretended to be.

James softened his tone. "They already are, William. That's why we're here." He motioned that everyone should close in around him. "Let's not jump to conclusions. While it is my assumption that

Comyn is up to no good, he could have sailed to Ireland as part of the Scot delegation to the Irish Parliament. Or even if Red isn't here innocently, this may be some kind of internal affair that doesn't affect us."

Robbie scoffed, a sound James ignored, instead studying each of the young men in turn. "Robbie and I will ride towards the town and see if we can get a better view of what is happening on the dock. Huw and William will go along the river on foot since the terrain there is no good for horses. I want to know if anyone in Comyn's party disembarks before reaching Drogheda."

William opened his mouth to say something—knowing him, probably to argue—but James flicked out a hand to him before he could. "We need to know if it is truly Tuyt who greets Comyn, and if more men are coming. If Tuyt has an army too, or they are allied with other lords, it will change what King David does. Meet back here in an hour." He pointed a finger at Huw. "No shooting. Keep those arrows in your quiver."

Huw grinned, but he nodded. He wasn't a knight and didn't wear a sword. Instead he wore two sheathed knives, one long, one short, secured by a belt at his waist, and he held his great bow in his left hand. That left his right hand free to reach the arrows on his back.

Finally, James turned to Christopher. "You will stay with the horses."

Christopher didn't even bother to complain. He'd known that staying behind would be his fate before James had opened his mouth. James would have insisted that it wasn't because he didn't trust Christopher but because *someone* had to stay with the horses. But it showed Christopher yet again that his rank counted only when people were being polite. When push came to shove, Christopher was a newbie, not medieval, and unreliable.

He couldn't keep his annoyance from showing, and his voice came out belligerent. "What you haven't said is why Tuyt would conspire with Comyn in the first place. He isn't a great lord. He's just the castellan. None of these lands are his."

"Tuyt's ancestors sailed to Ireland with Strongbow at the very start of the conquest," James said. "He has never known any home but Ireland."

And with James simple explanation, Christopher finally understood why Ireland was such a problem: it had become home to these former Englishmen as much as it was to the Irish who were here first. Christopher missed *his* home at times so much his belly ached with it. Nobody here was going to give theirs up without a fight.

2

Trim Castle, Ireland
David

David's fondness for battlements went beyond access to a long, life-threatening fall, though he was pleased to see that Trim Castle lay in one of the Boyne River's sinuous curves. The river flowed roughly north to south on the castle's east side as it wended its way northeast to the Irish Sea. Because of the precariousness of the castle's location, a second river, on the west side of the castle, had been diverted as a further defensive measure, such that the castle was completely surrounded by water.

David didn't want to time travel anywhere. In fact, just thinking about it made his stomach churn. Now that he had a wife and children, he was repelled not only by the idea of leaving them here alone but at deliberately risking his life to do so. The fact that he *had* done so multiple times had him questioning his own sanity. For this trip to Ireland, he'd left them behind in Wales at Dinas Bran. Lili wouldn't have enjoyed the politics and the posturing of the last three weeks. She would definitely be having more fun with Anna and Bronwen than with him here.

And yet, the daily routine of being King of England—and now finally following through with some of his commitments as Lord of Ireland—had him longing for the freedom and anonymity of Avalon. Here, he couldn't take a step, make an offhand comment, talk to someone, or make any kind of decision at all without it being examined, dissected, and discussed in absurd detail. He was rich and powerful, but he was also the object of jealousy, intrigue, and adulation. He could be objective enough about himself to acknowledge that he now wore a mantle of authority like an extra layer of skin, but much of the rest he could have done without.

Then again, the last few times he'd been in Avalon, he'd been treated like a kid, and he'd never managed to remain anonymous for more than a few hours before being hunted. So ... no solution there either.

Outside of the time travel potential, battlements also tended to be good places to talk, which was what he'd been doing last year with the King of France when Gilbert de Clare's men had attempted to assassinate them both. That happened also to be what Callum, David, and Dad were doing at the moment—hopefully without the assassination attempt. From the moment they'd set foot in Ireland, Callum had been one hundred percent about security, but David was prepared to jump with his dad if someone tried to do them in.

The rain continued to fall—at the moment more like a super heavy mist than actual rain—and a few drips were managing to make it through the timber and hide roof that covered this portion of the battlement. With Callum protecting the far end of the wall-walk, nobody could overhear them.

In most castles, the gap-toothed battlements weren't exposed to the elements all the way around their perimeter. Lengths of them were usually enclosed to protect the defenders from enemy fire, with roofs made of wood and hide. During a siege, the hides were soaked in water so they wouldn't burn easily, though that clearly wasn't a problem today. The coverings were logical, really, but not obvious to the modern observer since anything not made of stone had long since been destroyed or decayed away.

Trim Castle itself was the largest castle in Ireland, with a stunning hundred-foot-tall white-washed keep that could fit three Aber Castles into it, red tile roofs, and a five-hundred-yard-long curtain wall with ten D-shaped towers. It was also Geoffrey of Geneville's seat in Ireland. His son had died in 1292, however, leaving him no heir except for a granddaughter, Joan, who was only eight years old.

"It isn't that I'm ready to give up," David had been saying to his father, "but everybody's talking past each other, and nobody will listen to anyone else." He himself had not yet participated in the Parliamentary meetings themselves, not wanting to be perceived as overbearing. It was Dad who was facilitating the meetings. David confined himself to speaking to lords individually before and after the talks, campaigning for peace in the shadows.

"The Irish love to argue," his father said dryly, "and the English are a close second."

David snorted laughter, as he was meant to. "You did warn me. I should have pressed harder for them to come to Aber or Caerphilly."

"To the people here, the world ends at the Irish Sea, and anything beyond it is *here be dragons*. It wasn't always the case."

"Your prejudices are showing, Dad." David leaned into one of the crenels and looked out at the rain and the lush landscape beyond it. He'd been warned before coming that it rained a lot in Ireland. It rained a lot in Wales and England too, but there was a lot and there was *a lot*. His parents had arrived only a few days ago, not wanting to try Anna's patience by leaving their five-year-old twins in her hands for too long, but David had been here for three weeks. While it didn't rain all day, it did rain every day. No wonder the country was so green and everyone so argumentative.

Admittedly, as he'd said to his father, the Irish had a great deal to be angry about, and even though David hadn't had anything to do with the initial conquest of Ireland a hundred years ago, he was the Lord of Ireland now. They blamed him.

"It would have been less of a security risk," Callum said from the end of the walkway without looking at David. That would have required him to stop surveying the bailey.

"If Trim isn't safe, no place is. You can't protect against everything, particularly treachery from the inside," David said.

"I can try."

David turned back to his father so Callum wouldn't feel like he was mocking him. Which he wasn't. He agreed that security was of paramount importance for everyone. That was why every man's credentials were checked twice before they entered the inner ward: once at the outer gate and once past the barbican. Not that anyone would have an ID card, but any man not in a lord's private retinue had to be personally known to Geoffrey de Geneville's captain or vouched for by someone he did know.

Weapons were the big problem, since every lord, knight, and man-at-arms carried a sword on his hip. No weapons were allowed in the great hall, which was swept daily for hidden stashes, and no lord had been allowed to bring more than ten men with him to Trim. That way, they wouldn't have a repeat of what happened in France.

These regulations applied to David and his father too. Relations between David and his barons were strained enough without David turning Trim into his personal armed camp, and none of the lords would have come at all out of fear of being taken hostage or killed outright. Even Geoffrey de Geneville had complied with the rule, dispersing all but thirty men of his garrison, who were required for the most basic security of Trim, to Skryne Castle where Geoffrey's wife, Maud, was staying for the week. Callum had circumvented the rules by sending most of the servants, stable boys, and craft workers to Skryne too and replacing them with David's men in disguise.

Dad was rubbing at his chin as he looked out on the countryside with David. "I'm not sure some of these men know how to live without fighting. Someday they might be willing to talk, but it isn't today."

"They've been fighting a long time, and the grievances on both sides are many and justified." David let out a sharp sigh. "I know you and Mom just got here, but maybe we should go home."

Dad shook his head. "We can't go home. Leaving would show weakness and truly make things worse. The only way you can go home now without some kind of treaty or settlement is if you intend to return at the head of a massive army. Those you couldn't subjugate you would kill, and then the remainder would have to listen. You have the resources to do it too, which is the *only* thing that is keeping these men at the table."

David stared at his dad. He hadn't seen it. Maybe his father had known this all along and had assumed that David knew what he was doing, but he himself hadn't put two and two together: the men of Ireland were only sitting down to talk because they thought David was holding a sword above their heads. It hadn't been his intent, but now that his father had pointed it out, it was obvious that's what they thought. And really, that was David's own fault. He'd gotten the Scots to talk by threatening them with what would have been a ruinous war—why not the lords of Ireland?

From the other end of the wall-walk, Callum nodded to someone in the bailey below, and then he raised a hand to David and his father. "My lords, it's time."

Dad looked at David apologetically, "Son—"

David shrugged. "I know. I know. You have to go." And then he added under his breath, "I hate being the bad guy."

"You aren't the *bad guy*." Callum had followed up his warning by moving closer. "You're about as far from being the bad guy in Ireland as could be imagined. You're the most powerful man in the world, and still, the people love you." He shrugged. "It's just the nobles who are terrified of you and what you might do next—to them, for them, or with them."

David laughed and felt the tension easing out of him. Then he sobered and shook his head. "If only they knew the truth."

"They do know the truth," Dad said matter-of-factly. "That's why they fear you. Most men either don't know what is right and just do what they personally want, or they do know and do what they want anyway. It is just as Nicholas de Carew said years ago before King Edward's death: nobody knows what to make of a man like you. And they are afraid of what they don't understand. The idea of someone who doesn't act in his own self-interest is so strange that you come off as unpredictable. You aren't attending the conference yourself because you want the justiciars to be able to express themselves freely without feeling like you are looming over them. But it hasn't worked. They see me not as a mediator but as your mouthpiece. You can't escape your authority."

David laughed again, though this time it was mocking. "King Arthur: returned, worshiped, loathed, and resented all in the same breath. If I were they, I would resent me too. In fact, when we were in their shoes, we *did*."

"We won too," Dad said.

"Don't I know it." David shook his head. "I could walk away today if war wasn't the inevitable result."

"If what your father says is true, then war is still the most probable result. The most reasonable proposal I've heard so far from the English side is to partition the country—" Callum broke off to laugh, "—and we know how badly that turns out."

"Meanwhile the Irish demand that the English give up their lands," Dad added, "which is never going to happen."

Callum nodded. "Though they don't know it, it's a thousand-year-old argument."

Frustrated, David ran both hands through his hair, which was still wet from the rainy walk to the battlements. "Clearly, we need a Nelson Mandela solution, but he isn't here to offer one up. You can see why I resisted the legend for so long. Being the return of Arthur—this Mac Ecra to the Irish—is not all it's cracked up to be."

Dad sighed and pulled up the hood of his cloak. "As usual, I have no idea what you two are talking about, but I think this is where I come in." He glanced at David. "I know why your predecessor preferred war to peace."

"Why?"

"Less talking."

David laughed and sent his father on his way.

Callum, however, didn't go with him, instead moving closer and looking out over the landscape with David, towards Irish-controlled lands farther inland.

"Before you do anything rash, I'd like to make a case, if I may." From an inner pocket of his coat, Callum brought out a stoppered bottle and then two small cups. He set the cups on the stones of the crenel, poured red wine into each of them, and handed one to David.

David accepted the wine, though he swirled it around in the cup without drinking. "What case is that?"

"For the continuation of the monarchy." Callum looked over the rim of his cup at David.

David laughed under his breath. "Who said anything about abolishing the monarchy?"

"You have, numerous times. If not in so many words, you've implied it. I think you've been thinking about it a great deal since we arrived."

David sighed. "You're not wrong." He gestured with the cup, indicating the world at large. "I would give anything not to be in this position."

"I would argue that there will always be somebody in this position, and there's nobody I would rather have in it than you. There's a place, even in a modern government, for a leader who stands outside the political process, who isn't answerable to votes, and who can make decisions based on conscience. You have only to look at any modern political structure to see that something like this is needed ... and you know as well as I do that right now in this world and in Avalon, democracy is not working."

"Democracy has always been messy—"

"It isn't working. It can't work when the populace is uneducated and the entire process is being hijacked by powerful men who see openness and honesty as weakness. I don't care which century they're from."

David pressed his lips together, not wanting to argue, but feeling stubborn at the same time. "That's easy for you to say, Callum. We're the ones in power here."

Callum added gently, "At the very least, you have to acknowledge that Ireland isn't England. Children don't go to school. It's every man for himself. Worse, many Irish don't view their country as one entity, and Geneville is right when he says that without us, the Irish kings will descend into open war again—as they have for thousands of years."

"They would be governing themselves," David said.

"No—the most powerful and brutal would be governing everyone else. That might have been acceptable at one time, but are you going to turn your back on the fatherless children and the raped mothers and daughters that result? As king, you have the chance to make things better here."

"Should one man really have that much power?" David said.

"He should if he's you."

David drained his drink in one gulp. It was a seductive argument, but a dangerous one. "And if he isn't me?"

"The monarchy is bigger than one man. You can't make a decision like this based on how you feel."

David laughed again. "I can, actually, since I am the king. That's the problem. But just say, for argument, that I don't disagree. I am the last person to make such a case, since I directly benefit from it—as do you. Us being here in Ireland is no different from when Edward tried to conquer Wales."

"That's where you're wrong. Wales had your father, and he kept order among his barons. Ireland has no such leader."

"They had high kings up until 1169," David said.

Callum scoffed. "I've been reading up. I know you have too. Murtach MacLaughlan, despite swearing an oath of truce to the Bishop of Armagh, had the King of Ulster blinded. Murtach was killed by Rory O'Conner, whose entire career consisted of burning and pillaging the lands of other Irish chieftains. The O'Neills and the O'Briens were no better."

David couldn't pretend he didn't see what Callum was getting at. "I have no Irish blood."

Callum made a *pfft* sound of disgust. "Don't give me that. Through your father, you are descended from the great High King, Brian Boru, not to say Murtagh Mac Ecra. You couldn't have a greater claim if you tried."

"The people don't want me. I can't waltz in here as the savior and expect everyone to fall at my feet."

"A few powerful barons don't want you. The Burghs, Butlers, and Fitzgeralds are fully supportive. And, as I said, the common people love you. King Arthur was Irish. You should have learned that by now." He accompanied this last statement with a wink.

David was officially annoyed. Callum had systematically picked away at his finely conceived thesis. "You sound just like my father."

"That's because your father's right."

3

Drogheda

James

James glanced towards the town's battlements, wishing he could see beneath the covering roofs to the guards inside. More than any place James had ever lived, and that included Scotland, Ireland was a land of war. Town and castle defenses were maintained daily. A castle was kitted out properly or it fell. Except for short sections, each length of battlement was covered, so attackers couldn't see how many men defended, and crossbowmen or archers (if present) were protected from missiles fired from the ground. And from the rain.

He thought again about Christopher's suggestions and, to his own surprise, decided to take one of them and simply enter the town through Drogheda's east gatehouse, the Great East Gate, one of ten such entrances into the city. As the brother-in-law to the Earl of Ulster, he had every right to be here. Still, in their approach to the gate, James and Robbie endeavored to keep to the trees and drew their cloaks closely around themselves. They were riding horses, however, so there was no mistaking that they were men of worth, and the guards could see their swords along their left sides. In some parts of Ireland, men could be cut down for less.

Even if he couldn't see them, he felt the eyes of the garrison on him and Robbie. From now until they left the town, they would be vulnerable to attack or arrest. The town would have crossbowmen within their ranks, and James's only consolation was that archery itself was not practiced here with the same dedication as in Wales—and now England, thanks to David. They shouldn't have Huw's equivalent up there.

None of the lords who'd crossed the Irish Sea with King David had brought more than a handful of retainers with them, and the contingent of two hundred Welsh archers, without whom David never traveled, had been left behind in Dublin with the ships. David wasn't here to conquer anyone. He was here to talk, and he had been very careful from the start to ensure that *that* was the message he was sending.

In addition, David had been deeply wounded by Gilbert de Clare's betrayal. As a result, most of the soldiers serving David were, in fact, Llywelyn's. David had lost Justin, his captain and companion, to Clare's treason, along with a host of other loyal men, and though he continued to move about England with a full complement of guards, he hadn't yet rebuilt his *teulu*.

While James should have brought his ten men from Trim, he'd left them to augment the force under Callum's command. He hadn't done so at Callum's request, but rather because James had seen the concern, not to say fear, in Callum's eyes when he spoke of the castle's security. There were too many lords at Trim who'd spent too many years at each other's throats not to fear for the safety of the king in such a company.

"Whose side will Gilles come down on?" Robbie said.

"Mine." James was glad that Robbie had chosen that moment to talk. It made them look more natural. "But she's also going to want to choose the side that will allow her to continue to live in Ireland and allow her brother to keep his lands." He was sure of that if he was sure of anything.

Although he was only thirty-four years old, James had already lost two wives before marrying Gilles, which had turned out to be by far the best decision of his life. She was smart and capable—and utterly lovely with her thick auburn hair, wide hazel eyes, and white skin. She was also the sister of Richard de Burgh, the Earl of Ulster, who was one of the most powerful lords in Ireland. Her Irish looks had come from her grandmother, who'd been an O'Brien and the daughter of the King of Thomond.

As the guard bowed and admitted them to the town of Drogheda, James acknowledged to himself that his vested interest in the governance of Ireland was well on the way to causing him something of a problem. Even now, with Red Comyn meeting with John de Tuyt, James found himself torn by his competing interests: a desire to remain in Ireland—one shared by all the other English barons; hatred of the Comyns and the impulse to act in every way directly opposite to them; and loyalty to David. The last was, on the surface, an absurd position for a Scottish nobleman to be in. By rights, James should have no obligations to David at all. Scotland owed nothing to England's king and, while Gilles had been born into an Anglo-Norman-Irish family, when she'd married him, she'd become a Scot.

But, by God, he loved Ireland. He hadn't expected to. Up until they'd spied Comyn's ships, today had been a great day for the simple chance of exploring the country unencumbered by his normally weighty responsibilities.

While Scotland was beautiful, and he knew every rock and tree of Strathgryffe, the Stewart ancestral lands in lowland Scotland, every morning that he woke to breathe Irish air was a good morning. He was glad that peace had come to Scotland, but he could have lived without it. Ireland, on the other hand, was a gem in the middle of the sea, and he hated to see one blade of grass trampled by the marching feet of fighting men.

But he knew, regardless of what he'd said to the others about not jumping to conclusions, that the presence of Red Comyn at Drogheda's dock meant the country was about to be torn apart again. He could not countenance that, not now that he had a son of his own, born late last year, to think of.

And it was that knowledge that had James suddenly straightening his shoulders and urging his horse directly towards the bridge across the Boyne. He ignored Robbie's whoop of surprise and kept going. Robbie expected James to always pursue the most conservative action while Robbie argued for the opposite. The whole world knew that nobody was more measured in his thoughts and actions than James Stewart. And yet, ignoring the startled shouts from the townspeople he passed, he cantered the last yards to the river gate and then across the bridge.

Comyn and Tuyt saw him coming, of course, and their soldiers spread out by instinct, though it was absurd to think that two men, no matter how well armed, were any kind of threat. Whether because John de Tuyt recognized this fact or simply because James and Robbie were known to him, by the time James was halfway across the bridge, Tuyt had waved a hand to tell his men to stand down.

Once in the middle of the bridge, James tried to get a better look at Comyn's ships, which were docked downstream of Drogheda's armada of river boats. Unlike Red's seagoing vessels, these were flat-bottomed in order to navigate the fords along the Boyne River, which was navigable all the way to Trim Castle, twenty-five miles upstream.

Established at a narrow section of the Boyne River, Drogheda's location allowed the town to exact a tax on any vessels small enough to fit under the bridge, while the goods from ships like Comyn's, which couldn't sail upriver (because of the bridge and the shallow riverbed), would have to be transferred to boats rented from the town. All in all, it was a very profitable scheme for Geoffrey de Geneville, the overlord of these lands.

James trotted his horse the last yards to the far bank of the Boyne and then slowed to a walk before reining in near Comyn and Tuyt. The gray stone castle loomed behind them on its motte. As on the other side of the river, the town walls ran all the way down to the riverbank, enclosing an area three hundred yards wide east-to-west and twice that distance from the Boyne south. Down by the river, the wind blew less strongly, and thus the rain wasn't quite as forceful as it had been on the hill to the north of the town. Still, James waited until the last moment to push back his hood.

If Tuyt had recognized James from a distance, he hadn't said anything to Comyn, because Red startled—and then glowered at James. "What are you doing here?"

"I could ask you the same thing."

Comyn's eyes went past James to Robbie, who was just reining in. The young man's eyes were alight, but he kept his mouth shut, for which James was grateful. James was the Steward of Scotland, but Robbie was the heir to an earldom and the descendant of the great King David of Scotland. The fact that he was currently James's squire said nothing at all about his pride or self-restraint. Or his ability to curb his emotions.

"I have come to inspect my wife's lands in Ireland." Comyn's father-in-law was William de Valence, who had been executed five years ago after attempting to overthrow David. William had bestowed his Irish lands on his daughter before his death, which meant that David hadn't confiscated them, and Red was within his rights to inspect them.

In point of fact, however, William de Valence had been a great deal more than just a rebel baron, having been an uncle and close confidant to King Edward and one of the most powerful men in England—before his actions had compelled David to bring him down. That should have been a lesson to Comyn—and to every baron who sought to go against the King of England. But Comyn wouldn't be the first baron who'd learned the wrong lesson from Valence's downfall. For some men, rather than realizing that a man went against David at his peril, he instead saw the flaws in Valence's machinations and told himself that not only was his strategy far better, but that he was cleverer than Valence and would succeed where Valence had failed.

James had no doubt that Comyn believed himself to be such a man. "For that you need five hundred men? You brought an army to Ireland, Red."

"I am a loyal subject of the Lord of Ireland," Comyn said. "You have no cause to doubt me."

James rubbed his chin as he looked at his old enemy. A little over a year ago at Christmastime, Comyn had allied with his brother-in-law, Aymer de Valence, to orchestrate the murder of an ambassador from France. By sheer chance, James had been in attendance, thinking to speak to David regarding other matters and riding with the ambassador out of convenience. Instead, he'd found himself a prisoner. He'd been rescued by Callum, David's right-hand man and the Earl of Shrewsbury. In the aftermath of being caught, Red Comyn had professed regret at what he'd done.

David had forgiven him, hoping he was genuinely penitent. It seemed Red hadn't been, or at least he wasn't now. The king had thrown Aymer in prison, though he was free now too by the hand of Gilbert de Clare, who nine months ago had been one of those men who thought he was smarter than everybody else and had made a play for the crown. In the aftermath of Clare's defeat and death, nobody knew for certain where Aymer had gone, though James suspected that he'd found a haven in his sister's house in Scotland. Or maybe in her lands in Ireland. With Comyn looking at him now, backed by a fleet of vessels packed with men and horses, the latter case seemed likely.

And very dangerous.

With that thought, James laughed inwardly at the way he'd questioned his loyalty to David a moment ago. Not only did he owe David for his life but, so far, everybody who'd gone against the king had failed utterly. Who was James Stewart to doubt? "Wexford is far to the south. What are you doing here?"

"The winds blew us off course. You know how temperamental the Irish Sea can be. I hope to rest and resupply here, and then we will sail south in the morning." Comyn had an answer for everything.

"See that you do." Abruptly, James turned his horse, jerked his chin at Robbie, and headed back the way he'd come. Their horses' hooves thudded on the wooden bridge, a match to James's pounding heart. With each stride of his horse, James feared to find a bolt between his shoulder blades. But even Comyn didn't have the temerity to direct his crossbowmen to shoot. He might be plotting treason, but if so, killing James and Robbie in cold blood was not the way to begin.

They were soon out of bowshot and riding back through the town, though until they were through the east gate again, James feared at any moment to be stopped. They were not, however, and Robbie held his tongue until they had ridden some distance from the gate. "Why did you do that? I thought you were going to discover the truth of why he was here? We need to know what he is planning! We would have been far better off speaking to townspeople in a tavern."

James laughed—at and to himself. "I acted on impulse, and I am a fool."

That shut Robbie up for a heartbeat, but then he canted his head and studied his mentor. "For once, you did what I might have done. And I would have been just as foolish. I'm sorry if my enthusiasm pushed you into it."

"Thank you, Robbie." James didn't know whether to laugh again or curse. "Still, all is not lost. Now he knows we're watching him. My thought, if I had taken the time to think it through, is that Comyn will be more hesitant about implementing whatever it is he has planned and will genuinely sail south as he told us he would. Whatever he's here to speak to Tuyt about—or action he intends to take with him—could be deferred."

Robbie chewed on his lower lip. "I wish we had some idea of what that was. He could be marching on Trim tomorrow."

"He could," James agreed. "Perhaps we should find shelter nearby for the night and see what he does."

"Or we could hasten back to Trim to tell King David that Comyn is here."

James grunted his assent, pleased that Robbie was sounding remarkably like James himself. Maybe the boy really would eventually learn temperance.

"Or is it something else?" Robbie said. "Is he here to distract King David from some venture in Scotland that Balliol has planned?"

James shook his head. They were nearing the spot where they'd left Christopher. "We have just invented a war out of whole cloth on no evidence but a dozen ships."

Robbie glowered. "Comyn is up to something. Of that I have no doubt."

They reached the little glade, but instead of reuniting with the others, saw only William, who was loping from one side of the clearing to the other, calling Christopher's name. Then Huw dashed headlong into view from the opposite direction, shaking his head and cursing.

William bent back his head and shouted at the sky, "You've got to be kidding me!"

Both turned towards James and Robbie as they reined in.

"Where's Christopher?" James said.

"We can't find him," Huw said.

James twisted in the saddle. "This *is* the right place. Perhaps he moved the horses for some reason?"

"He moved them all right—" Huw pointed to the ground where a dozen hoof prints and boot prints were clearly visible in the soft earth, "—but maybe not of his own accord. I fear someone took him—and the horses."

The complexities of the politics of Ireland were immediately pushed to the back of James's mind. Christopher was King David's cousin and in James's charge—and yet, absurdly and unexpectedly,

James had lost him. He cursed under his breath at his folly for leaving him alone, even knowing how inexperienced he was. Christopher's inexperience was, in fact, why James had left him behind.

"He has to be close by." Robbie was still disbelieving.

Huw shook his head. "If he is, I don't know where."

"Blame can wait," James said. "Christopher is missing. That is all that matters now. Can you track the prints?"

Huw jerked his head in a nod. "I should be able to."

"Then let's get going," James said. "We're nearly out of daylight, and I would prefer my next audience with King David to be about the arrival of Red Comyn, not to inform him that I've misplaced his cousin."

4

Drogheda

Red

As he watched Robbie and James ride out of sight, Red took the name of the Lord in vain.

"We could go after them. Arrest them," John de Tuyt said, ignoring Red's blasphemy.

"To what end? It would give the plan away too soon. Feypo wouldn't thank us for that." Red cursed again. "But it's damn bad luck that Stewart knows I'm here."

Tuyt put a hand on Red's shoulder. "We have a good plan, and it's going to work."

"So Feypo says," Red said sourly.

"You are having second thoughts?"

Red scoffed. "Of course not."

What he didn't say was that up until he'd seen Stewart and the Bruce heir right in front of him, he'd been having a series of second, third, and fourth thoughts. Now that Red was actually here in Ireland, it seemed impossible that Feypo's plan was going to work. It had too many moving parts and relied too much on everything going perfectly—and their opponents being far less clever than Red knew James Stewart to be. In his experience, barons of whatever stripe did not by nature cooperate well. That they had held the conspiracy together for this long was something of a miracle.

And yet, the sight of Robbie Bruce still had the power to raise Red's hackles, and he put aside his doubts. If James Stewart and Robbie were here, it was at David's behest. Swinging around, Red refrained from spitting on the ground in his distaste of that alliance. He knew full well that he'd been lucky to escape the kind of treatment David had meted out to Aymer de Valence two Christmases ago. Red had been forgiven. He'd even intended to adhere to his agreement.

The High Kingship of Ireland, however, was too great a prize to resist, especially once John Balliol, the King of Scotland and Red's uncle, urged him to consider it. While it was possible that John hoped to distract Red from his own claim to the throne of Scotland, that didn't discount the value of what Feypo had offered Red. Ireland was a richer land than Scotland, which explained why the English had hung on to it so tenaciously. Red's advancement in Ireland also could put Scotland in a more powerful position vis a vis England. David was far too strong a king for Scotland ever to be comfortable with him as a neighbor.

Red nodded at Tuyt. "We must prepare. And my men must eat and sleep. We had a rough crossing."

"We have been stockpiling food for just this occasion. Of course, soon we will have all the resources we need."

Again, Red didn't scoff openly, but inside, he found himself thinking, *we'll see about that*. Tuyt was a typical arrogant Anglo-Irish-Norman, sure of his pedigree and happy to stand on the shoulders of those who came before him, while still claiming that his achievements were entirely his own doing. Red didn't like it. But he set it aside. Instead, he waved a hand and got his captain working to unload the ships at the dock and transfer the supplies onto the river boats that would take his army upriver to Trim. It was a relief to stand on solid ground after the journey from Scotland, and he happily walked the short distance to Drogheda Castle at Tuyt's side.

Drogheda's original wooden fortress, located on a motte, had been replaced by a new stone keep, as had the castle walls. And, because the town's walls conjoined the castle's, craft halls were located in the town itself rather than inside the bailey. The latter, though large, contained only the stables and barracks.

Red followed Tuyt into the hall, where a meal had been prepared for him and his captains. The bulk of his men would spend the night outside the castle, ready to march at a moment's notice if required. He almost considered doing as he'd told Stewart he would—getting back into his boats and sailing along the coast for Wexford. There, he could join up with Aymer, who, while not exactly trustworthy in the general sense, could be trusted not to betray Red. But the thought that Stewart was on his way to David even now to tell him that Red was here had the power to make his stomach burn.

Tuyt handed him a glass of mulled wine, and Red took a sip, telling himself to remain calm. James Stewart knew nothing, David was completely occupied with Parliament, and by the time he heard of Comyn's arrival and decided to do something about it, it would be too late.

Red raised his cup, convinced again that this time, he'd chosen the right allies and the right side.

"To a new Ireland!" Tuyt said.

They both drank.

5

Beyond the Pale
Christopher

Christopher woke with his head hanging down the side of a horse. His wrists and ankles were tied, his limbs felt numb, and every step the horse took felt like someone was beating him in the stomach and ribs. He was pretty sure he'd been bashed on the head by the medieval version of a baseball bat.

Panic rose in his throat, but something told him not to show it. Instead, he took in a wavering breath. He had no idea how long he'd been unconscious, but it was long enough for the rain to have stopped, and he seemed to be okay, aside from what felt like a massive lump on the back of his head. Hopefully, being upside down was most of the reason that his head hurt so much, since all the blood had rushed to it. He carefully twisted his body, using only his stomach muscles (hooray for the zillion sit-ups he'd done this year!) so that he arched upwards and could see over the top of the horse next to him. His horse was one of at least ten, each ridden by a soldier.

It was only then, at Christopher's movement, that the man closest to him shouted a warning. Christopher couldn't understand anything he said, which meant that he was probably speaking Gaelic. Practically everybody Christopher had encountered in the Middle Ages could speak at least two languages, and often three or four. In Ireland, it was Gaelic, English, and French. Christopher's French wasn't terrible these days. He couldn't read it at all, but he could get by, at least when his English friends were speaking it. Gaelic-accented French and English were harder for him to understand, and it was almost refreshing to hear straight Gaelic, because he didn't have to pretend that he had the least clue what anyone was talking about.

At the warning, the leading riders looked back and then pulled up. The reins of Christopher's horse were attached to the saddle horn of the horse in front of him, which had allowed the whole company to ride instead of walk. As soon as the horse in front stopped, Christopher's horse stopped too.

Now that he was conscious, there was no way he was going to ride like this anymore. Before any of his captors could dismount and stop him, Christopher wriggled his body backwards and slid off the side of the horse. His feet hit the ground, but because they were tied together, he instantly overbalanced. He would have fallen if a man behind him hadn't been right there to catch him.

This man spoke in Gaelic, but this time, instead of a warning, his tone held laughter. He said something to the others, and they laughed too. Christopher hated being the subject of anyone's jokes, but even though they were speaking Gaelic, he thought that their tone wasn't so much mocking as genuinely amused.

Then the man who'd caught him pulled a knife from his waist. Christopher's heart leapt into his throat, but the man laughed again, bent down, and sliced the bonds that bound Christopher's ankles.

Christopher's next impulse was to run, but a second later, another man coming up behind him placed a heavy hand on Christopher's shoulder and spoke in accented English. "If you swear not to try to escape, we will let you ride. If you run, we will catch you and tie you tighter." He canted his head. "Or kill you."

Christopher nodded. He might not know much about much, but that sounded like a deal to him—and the fact that he'd been offered it implied (Christopher thought) a kind of respect. Before, when he'd been upside down, he'd been no better than a piece of meat. Now they were treating him like a man. He was their captive, but getting himself off the horse had earned him a measure of respect. It had been fear and instinct that had made him do it, and it was startling to discover that he'd done something right. For once.

Another man held the horse's bridle while the man who'd spoken English steadied Christopher so he could mount. Because his hands were tied in front of him (rather than behind), he just managed it, though his captors still left his horse's reins attached to the horse in front. They'd taken his sword too, so he had little chance of fighting his way out, but his situation was way better than before. Even though it was night, now that he was in the saddle, he could see something of his surroundings.

He was on a road—at home it would have been a wide trail, but here people would call it a road—made of dirt, of course, and wending its way through pasturelands and stands of trees. Stone walls lined the road on either side. Huge puddles were everywhere, which the riders seemed mostly to be ignoring, preferring to trot right through them rather than go around, which would have meant jostling other riders or waiting for others to go first and riding single file.

Even though he'd already interacted in some way with half of the men who'd captured him, Christopher was struggling to tell them apart. They all had beards, wore encompassing cloaks and hats pulled down low over their eyes to keep out the weather, and had swords or axes belted at their waists. From the way they spoke, along with the breeches, long belted tunic, and vest that every man wore under his cloak, Christopher was pretty sure that they were all native Irish.

That puzzled him, since it made no sense that an Irish band had abducted him. He had no value on his own whatsoever, and if they'd kidnapped him in order to get to David, which had to be the reason they'd taken him, Christopher couldn't think what they wanted. Didn't they know that if David was on any side in this whole mess it was theirs? On top of which, David wasn't going to change his policies to save Christopher no matter how much he loved him. Because politics were so personal here, caving to threats or demands would make David look weak. And that would open the floodgates to more people doing more terrible things.

Which meant, all in all, that even if Christopher didn't have a chance to escape right now, he needed to get away as soon as possible. No way was he going to put David in such an awful position simply because Christopher had been stupid enough to get himself captured.

Then Christopher bit his lip as more implications of his captivity occurred to him: if the men who'd abducted him knew who he was, had they deliberately targeted him? Had they followed him from Trim, or had they simply come upon him in the course of doing something else and taken advantage of the opportunity presented to them? The second possibility seemed unlikely, but so did the idea of James Stewart not noticing that they were being followed.

Or ... almost worse, the company had learned of James's plans to take Christopher to Drogheda and had lain in wait for their opportunity to abduct him. They must have laughed and laughed when James had obliged them by leaving Christopher alone. Christopher felt sick at the thought—and he'd been feeling bad enough already. His head hurt, and he was dizzy.

Up until this point, he'd been trying to tell himself that he really was okay, but now that he was upright, he was pretty sure that the man who'd hit him had given him a concussion. He'd never had one before, but one of his friends had, and he'd had to stop playing soccer for the rest of the season. Now wasn't the time to need to lie down. Christopher blinked his eyes to clear them, and he hoped that his blurred vision was due to drips from his wet hair rather than because of the giant lump at the back of his head.

As it turned out, by the time he'd regained consciousness, they hadn't been very far from their destination, which appeared to be a wooden fort on a rise overlooking waterlogged pasturelands and fields—or that's what Christopher thought he was seeing by the light of the men's torches. That they hadn't had far to go was probably why his captors had gone so easy on him. But at this point, given how crappy he was feeling, Christopher didn't particularly care about why. It was way better to ride through the gate upright than upside down.

When they came to a stop in the fort's courtyard, there was enough light from the torches the men carried to see something of their surroundings. Ahead of him lay a two-story building that at first he thought was a barn and then realized was the great hall. A bunch of smaller buildings, including a stable, lined the wooden fence surrounding the property (belatedly, he remembered that the proper word for this was palisade). It had rained on and off all day, so the ground was churned up and mucky, and when anyone stepped off the stone path that led between the front door of the house and the gatehouse, they stood three inches deep in mud.

As everyone dismounted, rather than ask for help, Christopher leaned back in the saddle, swung his leg over the horse's head, and dropped to the ground, hands still tied in front of him. He'd practiced the move a thousand times because he thought it was cool. He had no idea that he would ever need to use it. Unfortunately, dropping off the horse like that jarred him enough to hurt his head again, even with the squishy mud to cushion his landing.

Christopher's suave dismount put him a few feet from the leader of his captors, who'd been talking to one of the men who'd come out of the hall to greet the company. A second later, the English-speaking man pushed at Christopher from behind, and Christopher walked forward towards the house. It still looked an awful lot like a barn, and for the Middle Ages, it was huge. Christopher hadn't yet spent much time outside of English-controlled lands, so he hadn't seen any Irish who weren't ruled by Englishmen. But whoever lived here seemed to be doing just fine for himself.

A moment later, Christopher found himself pushed through the doorway into a large hall, nearly as long as the hall he'd taken Gwenllian to at Bryn Mawr College before he'd come to the Middle Ages. The ceiling was thirty feet high at least, and an eight-foot-wide loft, edged by a railing, went all the way around the interior walls, giving the hall a rudimentary second floor. Stairs on both the right and left led up to the loft, and a big fire was burning in the center of the room, with the smoke heading for a hole in the ceiling.

Upon his entrance, the dozen people on the main floor stopped what they were doing and stared at Christopher. One man, who'd been leaning against one of the posts that supported the loft, straightened and took a step forward. As he did so, everybody else seemed to fall back slightly. The man had red-brown curly hair and blue eyes, looked to be about Callum's age, and was dressed in what even Christopher could tell was an expensive blue tunic that exactly matched the color of his eyes. It made him stand out among his men, most of whom wore one shade or another of yellow.

"I am Gilla O'Reilly," the man said in accented English. "You are Christopher, David's cousin, yes?"

Up until that moment, Christopher hadn't decided whether or not to confess to who he was. If he admitted that he was David's cousin, they could use him as leverage against David, but if he lied, they might kill him because they'd abducted the wrong man, and he was useless to them. So Christopher gave in to his instinct to tell the truth. "Yes."

Gilla swept out a hand and said something in Gaelic to the onlookers, laughing as he did so. The other men in the room laughed too, and several women came to stand on the balcony and look down upon them. Maybe that's where they were banished to while the men talked. Though, judging from the small children in sleeping gowns who were rubbing their eyes beside their mothers, it might just be that people slept up there.

Gilla gave a last chuckle, pulled out the knife he kept at his waist, and came closer. He held the blade point down as if he intended to stab Christopher, but, like the man who'd cut the rope around Christopher's feet, all Gilla did was slice though the bonds that held his wrists.

"Come. The man who killed Gilbert de Clare is welcome in my home. I will drink with the Hero of Westminster."

6

Beyond the Pale
Christopher

Christopher groaned inwardly, but he didn't contradict Gilla, since being the Hero of Westminster appeared to be the only reason he wasn't spending the night in a cell.

Gilla swung his arm in a sweeping arc, which seemed to imply that everyone was included in the invitation. Several of the women and children came down from the loft, and all of the men, including those who'd abducted Christopher, found seats either at the table or on benches or stools around the fire, chattering all the while in Gaelic.

A servant came up to Christopher and took his cloak to hang before the fire. He also shed his mail vest and underpadding and was given an undershirt and tunic like the other men in the hall were wearing. Christopher kept his pants, which were mostly dry, and his boots.

Gilla, meanwhile, put a hand at the back of Christopher's neck and guided him to a bench next to a teenage girl, who twisted in her seat to look up at him. She had red hair the same color as Christopher's own, green eyes, and a spray of freckles across her nose—and looked so much like an older version of his little sister that he just stared at her and had no idea what to say. She stared back at him too, and it occurred to him that if she looked like his sister, then he might look like her brother. And maybe that was another reason Gilla had cut his bonds.

Gilla spoke to her in Gaelic, and though she replied to him in the same language, her eyes remained fixed on Christopher. As Gilla said something else, for a second she had the same look Christopher's mother always got when she was irritated, but then she nodded. Gilla patted her shoulder before moving to the head of the table, a good eight seats away. For a few seconds, Christopher had thought he was going to be the guest of honor, and he was relieved not to be interrogated by Gilla right away.

The girl, meanwhile, eyed him warily, and scooted over on the bench a bit more than necessary to make room for Christopher to sit down beside her. Though she could be anywhere from fifteen to twenty-five years old, now that he was looking right at her, he thought she might actually be close in age to him.

Pretending to be relaxed, though that was the last thing he was feeling, he smiled. That seemed to make the girl even more worried, because her eyes widened for a second, and Christopher's smile became a little fixed. But then she pressed her lips together in an almost-smile and grew much more business-like. She poured wine into a cup and set it between them, indicating that they would share it, and pulled a trencher from the stack in the center of the table. Setting it in front of the cup, she started piling food on it.

Christopher had thought from the start that trenchers were the kind of thing that should have caught on a long time ago in Avalon among people worried about the environment. After a meal, you didn't have to throw them away like paper plates or use any water washing them. Instead, you could eat them, give them to an animal, or compost them.

Right now he was looking at roasted mutton, onions, some other vegetables he was pretty sure he wasn't going to like, and three tiny potatoes. Potatoes had been introduced to this world a few years ago from Avalon (of course), and since the first crop had come in, every lord who crossed David's threshold came away with a bag of potatoes, having been told to plant them. They'd obviously made it to Ireland, but too recently to be as common as they already were in England.

The food was a great distraction, and it meant that Christopher didn't have to look directly at the girl. Finally, she broke the silence. "Don't be afraid of my father."

He almost laughed. That Gilla was this girl's father explained a lot. She spoke perfect English with just a hint of lilt that reminded Christopher of how Lili, David's wife, talked, though Lili's accent came from Welsh.

"I gather your father makes a habit of abducting cousins of the King of England?" Christopher was trying really hard to sound sophisticated—or like David might—and he thought the wording had come off just as he intended.

It really might have too, because, for the first time, the girl looked at him—really looked at him—and with less derision than interest. "Why do you say that?"

"Because you're so calm about me being here."

She bobbed her head. "Himself didn't abduct you. They did." She gestured across the table to where some of his captors were sitting. One of them was the man who spoke English, and he raised his eyebrows at the girl, since it seemed he had overheard.

Christopher frowned, understanding by context that the girl was referring to her father when she said *Himself*. He shook his head. "They're his men. They were acting on his orders."

"Maybe." She glanced at him. "Are you responsible for the actions of every one of your men? Is David responsible for yours?"

"Touché." Christopher didn't have any men, but he didn't think right now was a good time to say so, especially since he felt like he'd been holding up his end of the conversation really well so far.

The girl laughed unexpectedly. "What do you mean by that?" But before he could answer, she added, "I'm Aine, by the way." She pronounced the name 'awn-yeh'.

"Christopher." He held out his hand to her, thinking they would shake.

"So I understand." She looked at his hand, still laughing and clearly puzzled, but when he didn't lower his hand, she touched her fingers quickly to his. Then she looked at him curiously. "Aren't you going to answer?"

Christopher stared at her, confused. Then he remembered that she'd wanted to know why he'd said *touché*. Before his French lessons had begun, it had been pretty much the only French word he'd known, though he and his friends had used it all the time. "It comes from sword practice," he said, deciding instantly that *fencing* would be another word she wouldn't know. "If one fighter touches another's body with the weapon, that's a point or a score, and you're supposed to say, *touché!*"

Aine gave him a dark look. "So you said it to me because you scored a point?"

"No, because you did."

That seemed to please her, because she looked down at the trencher with a smile hovering around her lips. She still looked a ton like his sister, but she was pretty, and he hadn't spent so much time with pretty girls lately that he wasn't happy to please this one or keep her talking to him.

He tipped his head and worked on channeling David again. "You said that I don't need to fear your father. Given that I'm here against my will, why would you say that?"

She shrugged. "If Himself was going to have you killed, he wouldn't have let you sit at his table."

"Because of the Irish rule of hospitality?"

She laughed again. "No, because it would be a waste of good food."

Christopher stared at her. Even with the laughter, he was having trouble figuring out whether or not she was joking.

Once again, she glanced at him out of the corner of her eye, and when she noticed the concerned look on his face, she smiled, put down the spoon, and turned directly to him. "If my father was going to kill you, he wouldn't have had you sit by me."

Christopher looked away from her to stare at the food she'd loaded on the trencher. He was feeling even more queasy now and didn't want any of it, but he stabbed at a piece of mutton anyway to cover his uncertainty. The conversation continued to swirl around him, a confused mash of Gaelic, and he chewed and forced himself to swallow. Unfortunately, by looking away and eating, he'd killed the conversation, so after a minute, he decided that he should be the one to try again. "If your father didn't order his men to abduct me, why did they? What did they hope to gain?"

Aine frowned. "Do you hold yourself so cheaply?"

Christopher opened his mouth to reply, thinking to say *of course not*, but then he thought better of it. He didn't feel like exchanging any more barbs with this girl. "Are you saying that your father will want a ransom for me? This is about gold?"

She gave a brief shake of her head. "I—" She pressed her lips together, perhaps thinking better of her frankness.

"Or are you saying that I'm here so your father can make King David do something he doesn't want to do?" That was Christopher's worst case scenario, but the one he'd assumed was true from the start.

Aine scoffed. "David wouldn't."

That was an odd response. She should have been defending her father's honor, not David's. "I know that, but why do you?"

"We—" She stopped again, her face flushing. Then she took a sip of wine, swallowed, set down her cup, and cleared her throat before answering. Her color had cooled a bit by then. He couldn't figure out why she would be embarrassed until she said somewhat stiffly, "David is an honorable man."

Christopher paused, noting how she again had said David's name without including his title. He'd noticed people doing that since he'd been in Ireland. And yet, it didn't seem to be out of disrespect. More, it implied that they knew him so well that they didn't need to clarify who he was by calling him *King David* or *Lord David*. He was just *David*, because there was only one.

"Yes, he is." He considered mentioning that David was married, but thought maybe changing the subject was a better idea. "Aren't we on Geoffrey of Geneville's lands?"

"Oh no." She shook her head. "Not here."

That didn't do anything to help Christopher's understanding, but he was glad he'd gotten her to speak straightforwardly again about something.

"Then where are we?" The clearing where he'd been captured was on a ridge north of the Boyne River. Admittedly he didn't know how long he'd been unconscious, but it wasn't as if they could have thrown him in the back of a car and driven for an hour.

"East Breifne."

Again, that wasn't helpful, but Christopher nodded knowingly and took a stab at his location. "That's west of Drogheda?"

"Northwest." Aine had been taking a drink from their shared cup, and she swallowed and put it down. "Twenty miles. The closest village is Drumconrath."

Christopher let out a breath. A horse could easily canter ten miles an hour but couldn't maintain that pace for two hours. It had been growing dark when he'd been captured, roughly five o'clock in the evening, and his internal clock told him that it was past nine now. That made sense. Even if the company had been mounted, with him thrown over the horse's withers, upside down and unconscious, it could have taken them more than four hours to go the twenty miles they'd had to ride.

Mostly, people here kept track of time by the position of the sun and went to bed at night when they were tired. They slept a lot in winter and less in summer. With the spring equinox coming up, night and day were getting near to even. While time and counting time didn't mean the same thing to medieval people as it did to him, it still took the same amount of time to ride from point A to point B here as in Avalon. It also meant that the people in the hall were awake kind of late. Maybe they'd been waiting for the company to return.

"What's your father going to do with me now that I'm here? What did he say when I came in that made everyone laugh?"

"Are you afraid they were laughing at you? I assure you they weren't. He merely explained that a man sprung from such ancient roots deserves the benefit of the doubt."

"Ancient root?"

"From the line of Mac Ecra, the man you call Arthur." She leaned into him and lowered her voice. "I confess I wasn't entirely truthful with you before. My father also said that he found having you here useful because he could learn more of David by observing you."

Christopher looked down at his food. "So in that sense, David is responsible for the behavior of his men—or at least will be judged by it." He was beginning to understand why David hated the legend that had grown up around him. They created an impossible ideal in people's minds, which could never be lived up to.

Aine looked at him again, half-laughing. "Isn't it enough to know that you'll live, Hero of Westminster?"

Out of nowhere, the rage that had been building inside Christopher for the last nine months threatened to overwhelm him. He was tired of being useless and mistaken for a killer. His hands clenched into fists, and his jaw tightened, which was the only way to hold back the seventeen angry replies that clogged his throat.

To be captured and helpless—and the object of this girl's amusement, even if it wasn't malicious—was one straw too many. Since he'd come to the Middle Ages, he'd pretty much done what he'd been told. He'd learned a lot, but he'd been dragged from France to England to Wales and to Ireland in David's shadow, all the while being known solely for the death of a man he'd killed by accident in the first seconds of being here.

Aine must have sensed the change in him because she stopped picking at her food and looked at him closely, without the half-mocking smiles she'd been directing at him up until now. She put a hand on his arm. "I'm sorry. No, it isn't enough, and it wouldn't be for me either."

Christopher took in a shaky breath and let it out.

Then Aine added, "Please don't try to fight my father's men. You have no weapons, and you cannot win."

"It might be worth it to try." It was a bravado reply, but he'd spoken it through gritted teeth and without managing yet to clear the anger from his face. He really did know better than to fight or to try to escape from a hall with thirty armed men looking on, but Aine didn't know that.

Looking worried—even a bit like she'd suddenly found herself next to a rabid dog, Aine glanced towards Gilla, who was sitting at the head of the long table. He'd been talking continually to his men, but for the first time that Christopher had noticed, Gilla looked steadily down the table at him. Then he nodded, which prompted Aine to grip Christopher's wrist. "You can have your answer if you want it. Himself is ready to speak to you."

Christopher pressed his lips together, not trusting *himself* to say anything, and stood. Aine came with him, still holding his wrist, which felt odd. It wasn't as if he couldn't have wrenched himself away, but it wasn't like she was holding his hand either. Maybe wrist-holding meant something to the Irish culturally—or maybe she thought by holding on to him, she could prevent him from leaping at Gilla and biting his neck.

The thought actually made Christopher laugh inside, and he relaxed a little. Objectively, the day had gone downhill from the moment they'd spied Comyn's men sailing up the Boyne River. Ending the day in a cell would pretty much round things out perfectly.

At Christopher's and Aine's approach, Gilla scooted back his chair so it was kitty-corner to the table. He waved a hand, and the two men who'd been sitting closest to him on either side of the table stood up and left. One went out the main door, and the other took Christopher's seat farther down the table.

"Sit." It was an order, and Christopher didn't feel as if he was in a position to disobey—or had a good reason to. He sat in the chair Gilla indicated, and Aine let go of his wrist to sit opposite him, somewhat behind her father, since Gilla had turned his chair towards Christopher's side of the table.

"My men tell me that they captured you at Drogheda. What were you doing there?"

Again, Christopher wracked his brains for a reason not to answer truthfully and didn't come up with anything. "Watching Red Comyn sail his ships up the Boyne."

Gilla's mouth fell open slightly, and he turned to speak in Gaelic to Aine. She nodded and answered. Gilla looked back to Christopher. "My men have been scouting the area for weeks. We've known John de Tuyt has been up to something, but our spies have not been able to discover what." His eyes narrowed. "They didn't say anything about Red Comyn."

Christopher was pleased that he'd hit a home run at his first at bat. "Maybe they should have been paying better attention to the dozen ships at Drogheda's dock instead of abducting me." He knew he was coming off as belligerent, but he couldn't help it. He was angry—at himself for getting captured and Gilla's men for doing the capturing. "What in particular have you seen Tuyt doing?"

"He's been meeting with an odd variety of men—and more than just Saxons."

"Comyn is a Scot." Christopher understood that the native Irish referred to all foreigners from England as *Saxons*, regardless of their actual ancestry. Whether Norman, English, or Welsh, they were from across the sea, and that's all the Irish cared about.

Gilla lifted one shoulder. "I meant Irishmen." Then he raised a hand and snapped his fingers to someone behind Christopher. A servant hustled forward and poured a cup of burgundy-red wine for Gilla and then two additional cups for Aine and Christopher. As Christopher accepted the cup, he realized that he was being treated like a man rather than an appendage to David.

"Who are we talking about?" Christopher put the cup to his lips and drank. As he did so, yet another of David's lectures—this one about drinking in moderation—cycled through his head. David needn't have worried about Christopher overdrinking today, that was for sure. If he ever needed a clear head, it was at this moment.

"My men named a MacMurrough from the south, an O'Rourke from the west, and one of the O'Brien cousins. They met with Tuyt and the lord of Kells, Walter Cusack, who has always believed he should have more power than he does."

None of the names meant anything to Christopher, but he nodded knowingly anyway. "So the question is, what do all of these men have in common? What would make them gather at Drogheda, and what role, if any, does a man like Red Comyn have to play in their plans?"

Gilla stared hard at Christopher. "You see it too."

Christopher didn't. He'd been feigning wisdom and had no clue what all this added up to. He tipped his head to one side and waited for Gilla to tell him what he was thinking so he didn't have to invent something that was probably wrong.

Gilla obliged by answering his own question. "They're planning something—something big—something dangerous and possibly treasonous." He clenched his right hand into a fist and pounded it once onto the arm of his chair. "And I wasn't invited to the table."

7

Beyond the Pale

James

Huw set off after Christopher. Those same men had taken the horses too, so Huw kept to his feet, somehow capable of a ground-eating trot that rivaled what the horses could do. Remaining on foot made it easier for him to make sure they were going the right way too. The other three took turns riding the two remaining horses.

They rode down from the ridge and then picked up a road, which took them almost directly northwest of Drogheda. It had been nearly dark by the time they discovered Christopher was missing, and because of the cloud cover, they were forced to light a torch. Huw couldn't have continued to follow after dark without it. Fortunately, the way was relatively plain.

The companions had started out several miles behind the kidnappers, but ten miles from Drogheda, they caught up. The moment the flare of the kidnappers' torches shone in the distance, James called a halt. Both groups had crested a rise at the same time, on opposite sides of the valley that lay between them.

"What are you doing?" William hadn't slowed immediately and had to retrace the ten yards he'd outpaced James. "They're getting away!"

"Now that we've found them, we have to let them go," James said. "If they were a smaller band, I might consider getting ahead of them farther down the road and ambushing them, but they outnumber us three to one."

"Lord Stewart is right." Huw was sucking on his upper teeth and staring down the road ahead, not that there was anything much to see. The riders had already gone down the other side of their hill into the next valley. "I'd say they're two miles ahead of us, but if we get any closer, they will know we are behind them and set an ambush for us instead."

Of the four young men in James's charge, Huw was the eldest at twenty-two, followed by Robbie, who'd be twenty in July; Christopher was a year younger, turning nineteen in June; and William would be nineteen a few months after Christopher. James knew Robbie best, of course, but he was growing to understand the others as well. William, the youngest, was a potent mix of Norman pride, fear, loyalty, and bravado, though admittedly with a huge heart. Given that he had Humphrey de Bohun for a father, a man who was the very definition of complicated, it was easy to understand why William had turned out as he had.

James hadn't known what to expect from Christopher. He was from Avalon, so James had initially assumed he'd be very much like David. And he was in some respects, though he'd proved to be less certain of himself, gentler, and more likely to empathize with individuals on every side of an issue. While James had been impressed with the way Christopher's easy-going manner made him universally liked, that same manner was a mask too, hiding both insecurities and a clear-eyedness that was a match to his cousin's. He wanted to do what was right. The trouble came in knowing what 'right' was.

"So what do we do?" William said.

"We keep going," Robbie said instantly. "We must determine first if Christopher is still alive, second, where he's being taken, and third, who's done the taking. And then we must rescue him."

"*We.*" Huw tsked under his breath. "The rest of you should return to Trim to tell David what has transpired. I will continue alone."

Robbie glared at Huw and swept out an arm to indicate James and William. "We aren't going anywhere. He is our friend too."

"You are heirs to lands and fortunes that nearly rival King David's own," Huw said. "Your lives are not yours to risk. Mine is another matter."

"You aren't the only one who has a loyalty to King David," Robbie said. "I owe him too."

"How has King David saved either of you?" William said. "It is I who owes him the most."

James laughed under his breath. "This isn't something we should be quibbling over. We all go together—and not for the king. This is for Christopher, who is a good man in his own right and has done nothing to deserve what has happened to him. It is no more nor less than he would do for any of us were our places exchanged."

Huw pressed his lips together, but he stopped arguing.

William bobbed his head. "It is our choice." He wasn't the boy who'd run away from David all those years ago. David had been only a prince then, and it was that adventure that had brought Gilbert de Clare into David's inner circle. Just on this journey, James had twice heard William flogging himself for his impetuousness that had ended up causing so much grief.

"I must warn you that Huw isn't entirely wrong," James said. "Although I am loath to split up, soon one of us *will* have to ride to King David to tell him not only of Christopher's abduction but of Red Comyn's arrival."

"But not yet," William said.

"Not yet," James agreed.

They rode on through the evening, maintaining the two-mile buffer between themselves and Christopher's abductors. Finally, they crossed the line in James's mental map of Ireland that told him they were now on O'Reilly land. The Anglo-Norman conquerors hadn't stretched their writ this far west in fifty years or more. There was only one real road through this section of Ireland anyway, and by now James had a pretty good idea where they were going. He had never followed this particular road before, but his brother-in-law had spies everywhere, and James had seen the maps they'd made of the terrain and the holdings of the Irish lords who ruled here.

Then they came over a rise, and he was sure. "Douse the torch."

Huw was already moving to do so because, having reached the top of the rise with James, he'd seen the danger too. In daylight, the crest of the hill would have given them an expansive view of the wide valley below. In the dark, however, the fort perched atop the hill on the far side, some three or four miles from where they stood, was lit up for all to see. The company that had captured Christopher had reached the valley floor already, perhaps hastening a bit now that they were close to home, and were clearly headed towards it.

"I suggest we watch from here to make sure they enter the fort and then continue very cautiously," Huw said, speaking slowly to match his thoughts. "They will know these lands and may have put out scouts. We don't want to be caught too."

"Do we know who rules here?" William said.

"Gilla O'Reilly," James said, dampening his urgency and his desire to race his horse down the road. "Huw is right. Gilla O'Reilly is Irish, but he isn't a fool. Another few hours in Gilla's hands will make little difference to Christopher."

After the company they'd been following entered through the fort's gatehouse, the companions watched for another quarter of an hour, and when nobody came out and the gates seemed closed for good, they began to descend the hill. The fields on either side held silent sheep and cattle, lowing occasionally, though James had never noticed that sheep cared much about anything but the grass at their feet. Regardless, the animals ignored the four strangers crossing their valley.

James begrudged every moment of the time it took to finally come within hailing distance of the fort, though of course they didn't hail it. After an excruciating two hours of careful movement, they reached the bottom of the hill on which the fort sat, and Huw found a trail that led into the woods to the left of the road.

Robbie, who'd been walking beside Huw, went with him, followed next by James and William, somewhat more gingerly, since they were leading the horses. Repeatedly, wet leaves scraped James's face, and he had to duck under a series of branches that overgrew the narrow trail. Though the rain had stopped for now, they were all still so wet that it made little difference.

Then Huw, who'd gotten some distance ahead, backtracked to James and William. "We should find a place to leave the horses."

"Through here." James had been able to make out a difference in density of the bushes to his left, and he led his horse through a gap in a nearby thicket, ending up in a small clearing that was screened from the trail. He and William tied their horses' reins to a tree branch, leaving them long so the horses could crop whatever grass they could find amidst the generations of fallen leaves that covered the ground.

Then James turned to the others. "We should stick together this time. The horses will be fine, or they won't be, but I don't want to leave anyone behind."

Nobody disagreed—as if they could, given what had happened—and the four of them crept out of the thicket and back again along the narrow trail that Huw had found. The fort ahead acted as a beacon for them—though they were careful not to look directly at the light. Even without doing so, the presence of the light on the hill served to deepen the shadows under the trees and made it nearly impossible for them to see obstacles at their feet, even as it lit up the battlements of the fort itself.

As they came closer, the fort was revealed to be larger and more imposing than James had first thought, more in the vein of a fortified manor or castle. The rise on which it was built overlooked the surrounding countryside on all sides, and it was surrounded by a wooden palisade with a ditch beneath it.

Wisely, O'Reilly had cut down all vegetation within fifty yards of the palisade—possibly to build the palisade itself—eliminating anyone's ability to sneak up on the fort. A half-dozen men patrolled the top battlement from a raised walkway behind it. The walkway wasn't covered anywhere but over the gatehouse, which was the only entrance James could see from his current position.

The entirety of the compound was built in wood. On a different day, Huw could have fired the fort with burning arrows shot from his great bow, as Cassie had done when she and Callum had rescued James from the men who'd abducted him in Scotland. It had been summer then, however, and not so wet.

"Are we sure he's in there?" Robbie put a hand over his eyes to shield them from the water coming off the leaves above their heads. William had retained the binoculars and was looking at the fort through them. They had never gotten close enough before this to pick Christopher out amidst the company.

James's own eyes narrowed as he studied the wall-walk. He would have thought that an Irish chieftain—especially one who'd just abducted the king's cousin—would have posted more watchers, but it was nearing midnight and maybe he'd fallen victim to complacency.

"I'm sure," Huw said. "If they'd killed him, they would have left his body beside the road, in which case we would have found him."

Robbie grunted his agreement but didn't apologize. Huw was the only man here not noble born, and sometimes that caused friction that manifested as an appearance of lack of respect, even though James didn't believe that was what Robbie really felt. They were all angry at Christopher's abduction, and that was creating tension and anxiety in everyone.

James gave a sharp nod. "The fact that they've bothered to keep him alive this long implies that they will continue to do so."

He thought back to his own abduction nearly five years ago at the hands of the MacDougalls. Alexander Callum, David's friend and the Earl of Shrewsbury, who was here in Ireland even now, had tracked him across Scotland and rescued him with the help of only Cassie. If Callum hadn't married her afterwards, James might have made his own play for her, because only a fool would turn his back on that kind of backbone or loyalty. James's Gilles was strong that way, and his heart warmed for her.

Thankfully, regardless of what was happening at Drumconrath or Drogheda (or Trim, for that matter), she was safe with their son at her brother's formidable castle of Carrickfergus, in the north of Ireland.

"Right. We need a plan," Robbie said. "We have to assume that they have at least forty men in there, so we can't fight our way in or out."

William rubbed his hands together. "Perhaps we might consider Christopher's Trojan Horse?"

James swallowed laughter. It was good to hear the young men considering their options. As future leaders of men, they needed to be able to think on their feet and develop a plan under duress and unexpected circumstances. "Remember, Gilla isn't some lowly raider. He's the chief of his clan."

"I agree we'll have to use subterfuge," Huw said. "Two of us should circle around to the right while the others circle to the left. We need to find a back way in."

"If there *is* a back way in. These Irish are ever at war," William said. "They won't be easy to fool."

Robbie glanced at James. "You're thinking of going in by the front door, just like you did back at Drogheda, aren't you? That would be foolish."

James scowled because, of course, that was exactly what he had been considering. "Why do you say that?"

"It would give the O'Reillys two important hostages instead of one," Robbie said.

James shook his head. "Gilla O'Reilly, if it is he who is in there and not just his kin, will not harm either the king's cousin or the Steward of Scotland. It is the same choice that Red Comyn faced, and the outcome would be the same."

"Hostages have been killed before in Ireland," Robbie said. "If you're so sure, why don't you let me go? I'm younger and less threatening."

James's scowl deepened. Robbie had called his bluff, because there was no chance that he was letting Robbie go in his stead. In truth, walking up to the front door was one of the few palatable courses of action open to them right now. He had warned them that one of them should ride to Trim, but with a tired horse, whoever he sent wouldn't arrive until morning at the earliest. And while David could marshal an army on relatively short notice, Christopher could have been moved by then—or, despite what James had just said to the others, killed.

Huw stopped the conversation with a hand on James's arm. "All the guards are gone from the palisade."

James turned to look. Where before men had been constantly moving in and out of the gatehouse tower and along the walkway, now it was deserted. The others looked too, and everyone stilled. James held his breath, straining to hear anything unusual above the dripping of water off the leaves and the wind blowing through the branches above their heads. He held up one finger and whispered, "Do you hear that?"

Underneath the natural sounds of the woods were unnatural ones, which grew more pronounced until he could distinguish individual cracks of sticks and the thud of feet on the soft ground, giving away the passage of men through the woods.

"Get down." James grasped Robbie's sleeve and pulled him behind a tree while Huw and William made themselves one with the trunk of another.

Hardly ten heartbeats later, each one pounding loudly in James's ears, they were surrounded by moving men, all heading towards the O'Reilly fort. A number of men carried long ladders, the purpose of which had to be to climb over the palisade's walls. The closest men passed no more than five feet away from where James and Robbie were crouched, but none saw them. Their attention was focused completely on the fort ahead, and the same shadows that had made it difficult for James to see well under the trees hid him now.

James and Robbie hardly dared to breathe until the oncoming army was past. Then, as one, the four companions straightened and turned to look towards the fort. The army reached the edge of the trees and stopped. For a count of thirty, nobody moved. Then the main gate on the east side of the fort swung open. That appeared to be the signal the men were waiting for because they raced forward. Roughly half made for the main gate, while those with ladders disappeared into the ditch before bracing the ladders against the outside of the palisade. Throughout it all, they maintained a strict silence, without even a curse when a man tripped on an unseen dip in the field.

"I counted sixty-two men before I gave up," William said.

"They moved fast," Robbie agreed.

"Are they Irish or Norman?" Huw said.

James shook his head. "Without hearing them speak, I couldn't tell you. Regardless, they aren't friendly, and O'Reilly can't have as many."

"Did you see how they went through the main gate?" William said. "They must have had someone on the inside to open it, as well as to take out the watchers on the walls."

"We're looking at a slaughter." Robbie moved forward to the edge of the trees, where a moment ago the attackers had been standing, and stared towards the fort.

Although no men had been on the wall-walk a moment ago, an O'Reilly was still alive, because he appeared above one of the ladders and swung an axe at the head of the lead man coming up it. Unfortunately, the defender was all alone and had no one to guard his back. Even as he brought down his axe, he was stabbed from behind by another attacker, who'd come up an adjacent ladder.

William gasped, but none of the young men looked away. No alarm had yet sounded inside the fort, implying that William was right. The O'Reillys had been betrayed by some of their own. Then, finally, a bell tolled, the sound barely distinguishable at this distance.

"What do we do?" Robbie's sword was in his hand.

James drew his own. "What we must. We go in after Christopher."

8

Drumconrath
Christopher

After eating, Christopher had been directed to a pallet laid against the back wall, about as far from the warm fire as it was possible to get and still be inside the hall. The men around Gilla stayed up around the table, talking. Actually, most of the time—at least ninety percent of the time—it was Gilla talking and everyone else listening. It was his right as the lord of the hall, and his men seemed to be used to it, waiting for a break in his monologue before speaking their minds. When they did so, Gilla listened attentively, and then launched into another long story, in Gaelic, of course.

Christopher wished he could understand what everyone was saying. He even wished, in a way, he could participate. It wasn't hard to recall the number of times he'd had conversations with medieval people before tonight. Apart from his growing friendship with William, Robbie, and Huw, he could count them on one hand. He'd naturally gravitated to the twenty-firsters, having most in common with them, or so he'd thought. But it was they who treated him like a little brother who wasn't quite grown up.

In contrast, when he talked to medieval people, the conversations hadn't been terribly dissimilar in terms of tone from his conversation with Gilla. Christopher himself had felt useless and unworthy, but the more he thought about it, the more he realized that was his fault. Nobody had treated him badly. He'd assumed that everybody was talking to him only because he was the Hero of Westminster and David's cousin. Instead, medieval people took for granted that he had something worthwhile to say and treated him with respect, talking to him, as Gilla had, as if he was a fully functional adult rather than a kid.

He leaned his aching head against the wall, wishing he could go back and revisit some of the people and places he'd seen in the last nine months. But before he could beat himself up further, he heard a noise behind the wall he was leaning against, something that didn't sound right. He'd been almost asleep, so at first he wasn't sure if he had dreamt the *thunk* and shout that had been abruptly cut off.

He turned his head and pressed his ear to the wall. The rain had stopped, but water was still *drip-drip-dripping* close by. He plugged his other ear with his finger so he could hear through the wall better, and the voices became clearer, though he couldn't make out what any of them were saying. Their words sounded urgent enough, however, that he rose to his feet.

"What are you doing?" Aine had been walking by Christopher, still awake even after the other women had gone to bed, having continued to serve wine and food to her father and his men. Christopher didn't think it was because she couldn't sleep, but because she liked being part of the action and had taken on the task of serving maid so as not to be consigned to the women's quarters.

Christopher put a finger to his lips while at the same time waving her closer with his other hand. "Listen."

Still with a carafe in one hand and a tray with a loaf of bread on it in the other, Aine pressed her ear to the wall beside Christopher. She frowned for a second, and then her eyes widened. "They're speaking English." She spun around. "Ionsaí! Ionsaí!"

Christopher had no idea what *onsee* meant, but it had the desired effect because the men at the table leapt instantly to their feet. Then he felt stupid because, if the men outside were English, they could be here for him. Still, he grabbed the knife from Aine's tray and held it in a tight grip.

Aine's father was on his feet as quickly as the others and directed his men to defensive positions at the doors. Feet pounded along the second floor walkway until Gilla waved his hand at the men who'd been running, and they slowed. Everybody listened, trying to be as quiet as possible. Waiting.

Christopher found himself holding his breath, and he forced himself to breathe deeply. The last thing he wanted to do was pass out. He had never felt this tense in his life, not even when he'd woken up a few hours ago upside down. He thought again of something David had said to him in the aftermath of Westminster: *the stakes here are always so damn high!*

Then the big doors at both ends of the hall burst open, and men surged into the room. Christopher wrapped an arm around

Aine's waist and pulled her against him, so they were both hugging the wall in the darkness underneath the loft.

Until Aine's warning shout, the O'Reillys hadn't been prepared for an attack, but it seemed that most of the men had slept in their clothes, and those who hadn't worn their boots to bed had had time to put them on. Before Christopher had gone to his pallet, he'd retrieved his armor, padding, and cloak, all of which had dried before the fire, and he'd never taken off his boots. At the time, he'd dressed again *just in case,* without a real target for his concern. Christopher knew only that if Gilla O'Reilly changed his mind about him, he didn't want to be caught without them.

More enemy soldiers swarmed into the hall. There seemed to be a hundred of them. Aine swallowed a scream as one of her father's men was killed ten feet away, and Christopher belatedly stepped in front of her so if anyone turned their way, she was protected, even hidden. The man who had died had been braced at the bottom of the flight of stairs, attempting to block the attackers from going up it. As he fell, the man who killed him leapt over the body and raced up the steps.

Christopher's hiding place in the darkness under the loft was proving to be a good one, and since he hadn't leapt to the attack along with the rest of Gilla's men, nobody had noticed him and Aine yet. Meanwhile, women and children screamed in terror from the walkway directly over Christopher's head.

From behind him, Aine moaned and said, "That's Auliffe O'Rourke." The man's first name came out *Ow-leave.*

"Which one?"

Aine drew his attention to a tall, blond man, who looked more like a Viking than a Celt. His sword was oversized too, but he was strong enough to wield it with one hand. Christopher and Aine shrank back farther into the shadows, still invisible to the attackers, but it had to be only a matter of time until they were caught. He eyed the rear doorway, ten paces to his right. The door itself was lying flat on the floor, having come off its hinges, and, at the moment, the path to it was clear. He wanted to go through it, but he was afraid to.

He looked to Gilla O'Reilly, who'd climbed onto the table in the center of the room and was fighting off all comers, though even as he skewered an O'Rourke fighter, the battle was drawing down. Most of Gilla's defenders had fallen. Another minute passed, and Gilla was alone on the table, sword held out, keeping twenty men at bay all by himself. He spun on his heel, and what he saw of the hall couldn't have been giving him any kind of hope.

One of the attackers started jeering at Gilla, and then his fellows joined the mocking, reaching in one after another to poke Gilla with their weapons, like he was a caged bear at a village fair. Christopher had seen that once and had turned away sickened. He clenched his jaw, knowing that if he didn't get Aine out of here, she would be taken prisoner, and then God knew what might happen to her. He might be a naïve twenty-firster, but these men were looking at Gilla like he was an animal, and Christopher didn't want any of them coming anywhere near this girl.

"Hold!" A man strode through the broken front doors of the house, and such was the power of his bellow that everyone did, in fact, stop moving. Christopher had never seen the man before, but again, Aine knew who he was.

"Thomas de Clare."

Christopher's eyes widened. The night had become a disaster for Gilla, but for Christopher, it was suddenly catastrophic. Thomas was Gilbert de Clare's brother and the last person in Ireland Christopher wanted to meet. "This isn't good," he said, in total understatement. "We have to get out of here."

Aine had been holding his left arm, but now she gripped it tighter. "He can't be here for you. How could he know that my father's men had taken you and brought you here?"

"I don't know, but even if this attack is for totally different reasons, I'm dead the second he finds out my name." How an alliance between the O'Rourkes and the Clares had come about, and what their plan was, Christopher couldn't begin to guess, though clearly they were willing to kill all of Gilla's men in pursuit of it.

"Come with me." Christopher began to edge along the wall towards the rear door.

Aine didn't move, and he looked back at her. She was shaking her head jerkily, saying *no*, though she didn't speak.

He could understand her not wanting to leave her father to his fate, but staying wasn't going to help. He mouthed, "We have to get out of here!" And he held out his hand to her.

She hesitated for another two seconds, still obviously reluctant, but then reached out and took his hand. Fortunately, by this time, with the fighting stopped, most of the invaders had moved into the circle around Gilla to watch the drama being played out between him and Clare. The last man standing by the back door took one more step forward, putting him a good six feet in front of the opening. Christopher's heart was in his throat as he continued along the wall, praying that his slow movements and the soldier's focus meant that he and Aine could stay out of his peripheral vision.

Meanwhile, Gilla O'Reilly, who'd faced Clare as he'd come in, spun slowly on one heel to survey his hall. For two seconds, his back was to Clare, who was still near the front door, and he was facing Christopher and Aine, who'd just reached the frame of the open rear door. For a single heartbeat, Gilla's eyes met Christopher's over the heads of Clare's men, who stood between them. He didn't nod or wink—or say a word to give Christopher away—but Christopher knew that he'd seen him, and even though Christopher was trying to shield Aine with his body, that he'd seen her too.

Gilla threw out his hands in an expansive gesture and swung back around to face Thomas de Clare. "How dare you defile the sanctity of my home?" The words thundered throughout the hall.

Even someone as inexperienced with intrigue as Christopher could tell that it was a deliberate distraction. Thus, without waiting to hear what mocking thing Gilla had to say to Thomas, he took the last step to the door, Aine in tow. He ducked around the doorframe—and ran straight into one of Clare's soldiers. They literally bounced off one another, recoiling in their surprise and uncertainty. But it was Christopher who had the advantage because he knew he had no allies outside the hall, while the soldier had to take a moment to decide if Christopher was friend or foe.

Christopher still held the knife in his hand, so he didn't think. He didn't even take the time to breathe. His left hand went to the man's shoulder to pull him closer in the same instant that he jammed the point of the knife into the man's midsection, just as Bevyn had trained him to do. The soldier wasn't wearing mail armor, and the sharp point went right through leather, fabric, and tissue.

For a second, Christopher looked straight into the soldier's eyes, but then he let go of the knife handle and stepped back. The man fell to his knees, his hands scrabbling for the hilt. As long as he lived, Christopher would never forget the stunned surprise on the man's face before he fell forwards into the muddy courtyard.

Aine grabbed Christopher's upper arm and tugged. "Come on! You've done it. We have to go before anyone realizes what's happened!"

Christopher bent to pick up the man's sword, which had fallen from his hand. "Sorry," he muttered.

Then, Aine's hand again in his, Christopher headed for the palisade. When he'd arrived at the fort earlier that evening, he hadn't gotten a good look at any part of the bailey but the front, but he'd assumed correctly that there was a back gate. That couldn't be a way out for them now, however. While he'd acquired a sword, he wasn't skilled enough in its use to defeat a soldier who was ready for him, and certainly not the one he could just make out, underneath the gatehouse.

Instead, he and Aine climbed the wooden stairs up to the wall-walk, taking the steps two at a time, with Aine hiking up her skirts so her feet could move freely. Since the fort had already been taken, nobody was on the wall-walk anymore, or at least not this part of it, and Christopher ran along the palisade, looking for a way out. They were twenty feet up in the air. Without a rope, they could kill themselves by jumping—or at the very least break an ankle. His head was pounding, and he felt like puking—whether from fear, loathing at what he'd done, or his concussion, he wasn't entirely sure.

"Christopher! Here!" Aine had been running behind him, but as she called to him, he turned back. She'd stopped and was looking at the ground on the other side.

Christopher hustled back to her and almost cheered to see the ladder propped up against the outside wall. Immediately, he boosted Aine up over the top of the palisade. It was a precarious move in a skirt, but she balanced for a second and then managed to get her feet on the second rung of the ladder.

"Stop them!"

If the cry had been in Gaelic, Christopher might not have known that the warning was about them, but since it had been in clear English, he turned to see a man hovering over the body of the soldier Christopher had killed. A second man, the one who'd shouted, stood beside him, pointing up at Christopher. Because of it, the men at the rear gatehouse were looking too, and everyone moved at once to the stair.

Aine was already halfway down the ladder. Christopher had intended to wait until she was on the ground before he started down, so his weight didn't overbalance the ladder while she was still on it, but he didn't have time for that now. He sheathed his new sword so his hands would be free, put his left hand on one of the top points of the palisade and used his arm as a lever to swing himself over the top of the wall.

Unfortunately, he mistimed the jump, so that only one foot landed on the top rung of the ladder and then instantly slid off it because it was wet. Aine gave a little shriek as he hung there for a second, one arm outstretched and his hand gripping the top point of the palisade. He had a terrified few seconds while he swung back and forth, his feet scrabbling for purchase on one of the rungs and his right arm reaching for anything at all to hold onto. Finally, he managed to grasp the right rail of the ladder with his right hand, and his right foot found one of the rungs, about six feet down from the top of the wall. Then he steadied himself and climbed down, though it turned out to be less like climbing and more like sliding as quickly as he could.

By the time he reached the bottom, his breath was coming in gasps, though he was surprised to discover that he wasn't actually trembling. It was dark on the ground outside the fort, even more as he'd ended up in a steep ditch. Regardless, he grabbed the sides of the ladder and heaved it away from the wall. It was only a temporary solution to being chased, since there were other ladders, but at least nobody would be coming down this one.

Then he looked wildly around for Aine, whom he'd lost sight of in his efforts—only to find his arm grasped by a strong hand. Christopher had sheathed his sword, so he resisted with the only weapon available to him, swinging a punch upward. But then a second man grasped his forearm halfway through the motion. "Christopher, stop! It's me! James!"

Christopher managed to pull the punch enough that it only delivered a glancing blow to Huw's jaw. "Sorry! Sorry!" He took in a deep, shuddering breath and bent forward to put his hands on his knees.

James put his hand on Christopher's back between his shoulder blades. "You're safe for the moment."

Christopher glanced upwards again. "We were seen. We need to get away from the wall."

He finally spied Aine scrambling over the rampart in front of the ditch. Christopher shrugged off James's hand and went after her, though by the time he slid down the other side of the rampart she was halfway to the woods. With her wet skirt and shorter legs, she couldn't run as fast as he could, and he caught up with her two steps into the trees.

She flung out an arm. "Get away from me!" She was gasping and sobbing at the same time.

He reached for her again, grasping both her upper arms. "It's okay! It's okay! They're my friends!"

She gaped at him, her breath still coming in gasps. "Christopher! I thought you were captured!"

"I'm sorry." He pulled her into a hug and held her until they could both breathe again.

"I've never been so scared in my life," she said. "My father—"

"I know."

At that point, James and the others ran up to them.

Huw was rubbing his jaw. "That's the thanks I get for coming to rescue you?"

Christopher put out a hand to him in another apology. He'd learned to fight since coming to the Middle Ages but, like horseback riding, it was one of the things that had come more easily, and the punch had been pretty decent. The ache of fear in Christopher's stomach eased a little, and he released Aine enough so that he could introduce her to his friends. "This is Aine, Gilla O'Reilly's daughter."

"We need to keep moving. There's nobody following yet, but that doesn't mean they won't." James set off at a brisk pace deeper into the woods.

"How did you escape?" William asked as he jogged beside Christopher and Aine.

"Luck," Christopher said. Then he canted his head, deciding he wouldn't hide the truth from his friends. "And I killed a man."

Aine bobbed her head in a nod. "To protect me."

William was silent for a second, but then he said, "Good. Maybe they'll decide you're more trouble than you're worth."

"Not if they find out who I am," Christopher said.

"Why is that?" James said from ahead of him, proving he was listening.

"Because that wasn't just an attack on the O'Reillys by a rival clan, though it was that too," Christopher said. "Their leader was Thomas de Clare."

9

South of Drumconrath
Aine

For all the brave face that she'd put on the situation up until now, Aine's teeth had started to chatter. William had offered her one of the horses to ride, but she'd declined it, thinking that she would be warmer walking. Now she wasn't so sure. Though the rain had stopped earlier that evening, the ground was still wet and the air cool. Her only saving grace was that she'd kept on her cloak after the last time she'd crossed from the kitchen to the main hall. The fabric wasn't as thick as she might normally have worn if she intended to be out walking in the wee hours of the morning, but it was better than having no cloak at all.

"You don't have to be afraid," Christopher said.

"Of course I'm afraid. Only a fool wouldn't be."

Christopher gave a little sigh. "I meant that you don't have to be afraid of me."

"Oh." She paused, realizing he was referring to her reaction to him when he'd caught up to her in the woods. "I'm not."

"You don't have to be afraid of my friends either," Christopher added. "Just because we're English doesn't mean we will hurt you."

"I know that too. The O'Rourkes are Irish and look what they did—aligning themselves with Thomas de Clare." She let out a disgusted snort.

Christopher had unsheathed his sword again, as had the other men. The care they were showing her surprised her, since concern for an Irishwoman wasn't at all what she would have expected from Saxon noblemen. In her experience, more often than not, rich Saxons cared more about wine and their own pleasures than about other people. In fact, her short acquaintance with Christopher and his friends had shown them to be quite unlike any men she'd met before, Saxon, Danish, Irish, or otherwise.

William de Bohun was the nephew of the Lord Verdun, heir to great estates himself, and here he was, slipping and sliding across the muddy fields with the heir to the Earldom of Carrick and the brother-in-law of the Earl of Ulster. In fact, the idea that five noblemen would be capable of trekking across Ireland in the middle of the night was undermining everything she thought she knew about them. Nobody had complained even once, and their primary concern, rather than their dignity, was what course of action to take next, a question that had occupied them for the entirety of the journey from the fort.

Then again, Christopher was David's cousin, and all these men served in his retinue. She shouldn't have been surprised to find that David surrounded himself with intelligent and honorable men.

Since leaving the fort, they had been heading south and somewhat west, aiming ultimately for the main road. They were afraid to get too close to any farmstead, however, in case the inhabitants weren't friendly—even to her—and such contact sent them right back into the danger they'd just fled. They'd even been afraid to light a torch and had done so only after they'd come some distance from the fort—and out of desperation, because they could see nothing without one.

James was proposing that Christopher, Aine, and Huw ride hard for Trim Castle, while he, William and Robbie, continued on foot. The others weren't in favor of that course of action, in large part because a company of six, five of whom were well-armed, was more formidable than that same company split in two.

"They wanted you," Huw was insisting to Christopher.

"Gilla's men happily abducted me, but without thought for the consequences." Christopher glanced at Aine. When she didn't comment, he added, "Clare and O'Rourke didn't even know I was there. They still might not, though killing a man on the way out wasn't exactly subtle. They haven't caught us yet, and I'm starting to hope that William is right, and they have bigger things to worry about than me."

"I'm concerned that even if they don't care specifically about you, they do want Aine," James said. "As Gilla's daughter, she could serve as leverage against him."

"But what do they want?" William glanced again at Aine, a frown on his face, which she could see by the glare of the orange torchlight. Like the others, fear for her safety seemed to be giving him more pause than fear for his own life. "Specifically, what did Thomas de Clare want?"

Aine shook her head. "The O'Rourkes want my father's lands. What Clare could be doing with O'Rourke I can't say any more than you." She didn't add that the O'Rourkes were as ruthless as their Saxon allies, and then she found her voice choking up. "My father could already be dead."

Shouts came from behind them. Instantly, everyone spun around to see who was following, and Huw doused the torch he'd been carrying. They'd run the first half-mile or so from the fort, but the pastures and fields they were crossing were so uneven and wet, their initial pace had been impossible to maintain. As it was, Aine's dress was muddy up to her knees. It had been well over an hour since they'd left the fort, but they couldn't have come more than two miles in that time.

Aine cursed unbecomingly under her breath and received a surprised look and then a grin from William. She lifted one shoulder by way of apology and said, "I've been hoping, given the time that has passed, that we were truly safe from pursuit."

William edged closer. "No apology necessary. You've been very brave."

She grimaced. "I don't want to complain but—" She broke off, lifting her head to sniff the air. "Do you smell that?"

"Smell it and see it." Huw pointed back the way they'd come. On the hill where her home had been, a fire blazed up.

Aine stared at it, the back of her hand to her mouth. Then she took an unthinking step forward, as if she could run back and try to save those who might have been left behind inside it.

William reached out a hand and tugged her back. "If we can see the fire from here, it's far too late to save anyone. You can't do anything. It's over.'"

Tears that she'd been holding back this whole time streamed down Aine's cheeks. Everything she'd ever known or cared about had been in that hall: all of her possessions, few enough as they were; her father; her friends, servants, and companions; all lost to O'Rourke's and Clare's men. She wanted to melt into a forlorn puddle on the ground.

"I'm sorry," William said.

His sympathy almost undid her entirely, but then she gritted her teeth, struggling against her grief, and she clenched her hands into fists.

"They will pay for this," William added.

"They will, if it's the last thing we do," Christopher agreed. "But not today."

Then the shouts they'd heard earlier came again, closer this time.

"They're coming this way!" James swung into the saddle of the horse he'd been leading and turned its head towards the sound.

But Christopher grasped the bridle to stop him from leaving. "What are you doing?"

"If they're following, I'm going to lead them away from you. And if they're not, I want to be able to tell David their numbers. We don't have enough information, and that could be our undoing. I've been a captive too many times to go down without a fight."

Christopher stepped back. "Okay. We'll walk as straight as we can in this direction. Find us as soon as you know anything."

"I will." James spurred his horse back the way they'd come, very quickly disappearing into the darkness.

Without needing to consult about it, the five remaining companions started off in a loping run, heading in the opposite direction.

"I should be going with him," Robbie said.

"No, you shouldn't. That would mean you both could get caught," Christopher said. "He knows what he's doing. If anything, you should be riding for Trim."

"We already determined that we shouldn't split up," William said.

"What did we just do?" Christopher came to a sudden stop. Aine was grateful for it, because her legs were shorter than everyone else's, and their brief run had her breathing hard. "I'm just saying that maybe we should do a rethink."

That wasn't a phrase Aine had ever heard before, but the others seemed to understand what Christopher was talking about and, after she considered it, so did she.

Everyone leaned against the wall they'd just reached, and now that the torch was extinguished, she realized it wasn't as dark as it had been. She looked up and saw a handful of stars blinking at her from above. Then, suddenly, the moon came out from behind a cloud and lit the night.

"I'm just trying to figure out who it makes the most sense to send," Christopher said. "Who will be in the least danger by himself?"

"You and Aine should go," William said. "We already decided that it's the two of you who are in the most danger."

"Aine is the only one of us who speaks Gaelic, and it's likely that the people in this region are more loyal to her father than to any O'Rourke. Those left behind won't do half as well without her, and I'm not leaving you to fend for yourselves in the middle of Ireland." Christopher's chin stuck out in his adamancy. "Besides, the horse will go much slower and tire more easily carrying two. Alone, one of you could be in Trim by dawn."

"Not me," Huw said. "I'm no horseman."

Aine wouldn't have minded riding to Trim. The sooner she got out of these wet clothes the better, but she could see Christopher's point. And she could admire both William's insistence that she and Christopher leave and Christopher's refusal to abandon his friends in order to get himself safe. So she turned to Robbie. "It is you who should go. You're a Scottish lord. Nobody will trouble you."

Robbie's brows knit together. "I don't want to abandon any of you either."

"We'll keep walking this way," William said. "King David can send a party out to look for us, and we'll all be warm and dry before you know it. When you get to Trim, have some mulled wine and think of us."

Christopher put a hand on Robbie's shoulder. "Don't talk to anyone who isn't David, Uncle Llywelyn, Aunt Meg, or Callum. At this point, we don't know who our allies are, not with Comyn working with Tuyt. Maybe Geoffrey de Geneville is in on it too. Even if Clare and O'Rourke have nothing to do with what's going on at Drogheda, it looks to me like Ireland is all of a sudden full of factions, and we can't trust any of them."

Robbie took in a breath. "I think you're right, Christopher, but I hate leaving you. James isn't going to like it when he comes back and discovers I'm gone."

"I'll tell him I made you go."

Even as Robbie shook his head, he pulled the horse's pack off its back and handed it to Huw. "It holds blankets and a little food. You are going to need them more than I will."

Christopher put out his forearm for Robbie to grasp. "It's the right decision. Sticking together might feel safer, but David has to know what's happened, and we are the only ones who can tell him. I'll explain that to James when he gets back."

They watched Robbie ride away, and only then did Christopher tip back his head and say, "God, I hope that was the right thing to do."

Aine was surprised that he could admit doubt, but Christopher seemed completely unembarrassed by it.

"It's what King David would have done," Huw said.

"You think so? I imagine he wouldn't have got himself captured in the first place." Christopher jerked his head to indicate that they should start walking again.

"How exactly were you captured?" William said.

Aine had been wondering the same thing, but inquiring as to how a man allowed himself to suffer such an indignity was not polite table conversation. Back at the fort, her father had told her to put Christopher at ease so he'd be more willing to answer questions later. Aine was ashamed to admit that she'd greeted this suggestion with derision, even if she'd done as her father had asked.

Christopher, however, instead of avoiding the question, actually laughed. "I was an idiot."

"My lord—" Huw wasn't happy to have Christopher deriding himself either.

Christopher motioned dismissively with one hand, implying that his mockery was of no matter, but he did stop laughing. "There's not much to tell. I was waiting with the horses for you to return. Within a few minutes of your leaving, a dozen men showed up. Even a great warrior such as I can't overcome that many men."

Aine blinked, at first thinking that it was unlike Christopher to boast about his prowess, but then as he grinned at her, she realized that he was mocking himself again. She shook her head, unable to make sense of such a thing. None of the men of her acquaintance, whether proficient with a sword or not, would ever have disparaged his abilities in battle—and he certainly would not have done so in front of other men. It made her feel a little uncomfortable.

William clapped a hand on Christopher's shoulder. "You're kidding yourself to think that any of us would have done any better."

"William's right, Christopher. You say that King David wouldn't have been captured in the first place, but you forget how he and I met," Huw said. "He *was* captured, and he got away, just like you did."

Christopher laughed again, under his breath this time, but the sound was far more genuine than before. "I suppose you're right, and from the way you tell it, Huw, that day turned out pretty well in the end. We should be so lucky."

10

South of Drumconrath
James

Immediately upon leaving Christopher and the others, James headed directly back the way they'd come, towards O'Reilly's fort, retracing their initial steps. But as the voices of the men ahead of James were revealed not to be directly following them across the pastures but angling east, James curved to the east too. It turned out that the party behind them was following the road along which James and the others had tracked Christopher from Drogheda. It was the only road in the vicinity, and short of cutting across country like Christopher and the others were doing, it was the only way back to the Pale.

Since James himself was on horseback, it took him no time at all to reach a small stand of trees on the edge of a field, within hailing distance of the road along which the company appeared to be moving. With the rain no longer falling and the moon out, he had a good view of the road back to the fort. He told himself that he was lucky they'd heard the men's voices, and even luckier that nobody in Gilla's fort had tried to trade Christopher's life for his own by revealing to Clare that Christopher had been there.

While James didn't like relying on luck, every soldier prayed for it, and the soldier who didn't have it invariably died. That was just the way the world worked. Some men might say that it wasn't luck but rather God's favor that gave a man victory. That was true too, but James had seen far too many good men die and bad men win to blame the good man for the loss instead of the bad man for betraying him. If James died today, it wasn't punishment for his sins, for all that he'd sinned plenty, but a momentary triumph for the devil riding on the shoulder of Thomas de Clare. Why God would allow the devil to win in this instance, James didn't know, but if He chose instead to make James His instrument, who was James to argue with Him?

That was what James was telling himself as he tried to pinpoint how far away the company coming towards him was and calculate how long he dared stay and wait before returning to the young people. Yesterday, he might have had more trepidation about leaving them alone, but they'd all proved themselves to be resilient and courageous, qualities James had seen glimmers of before today but not the full flowering that had occurred tonight. He was especially pleased to see the growth in Christopher. In capturing him, his abductors had found themselves with more than they bargained for—and Christopher had discovered the same truth about himself.

The thudding of many hooves on the road grew nearer. A moment later, a company of forty riders came around a bend in the road, torches shining from long poles, the ends of which were placed in rests where a pike would normally be braced prior to battle. Even though James knew the light would ruin his night vision, he drank it in, relieved to finally be able to see clearly. That the riders were carrying torches also told him what he needed to know about their task. These men weren't scouts or a party searching for Christopher and Aine. They were riding openly, uncaring of who saw them and who scurried to get out of the way. Since they'd burned Gilla's fort, they looked to be returning to wherever they'd come from.

  But then as they passed him, he realized that he wasn't entirely correct in his assumptions. A man, bareheaded and without a cloak, rode in the midst of the company. His hands were tied at his wrists, and the soldier riding in front of him held his horse's reins. James recognized the curly brown hair and beard: it was Gilla O'Reilly, Aine's father. Given the animosity between the O'Rourke and O'Reilly clans and the long history of murder and assassination between them, it was a wonder he wasn't dead. Even more curious was the fact that, while he was being removed from his own territory, he wasn't being taken west onto O'Rourke lands, but east, towards Drogheda.

  As James sat in the darkness of the trees, he considered what he should do and remembered a conversation from his visit to Westminster a few weeks after Gilbert de Clare's rebellion. Though James had come to London to pay his respects to David on behalf of King John of Scotland, he'd ended up having a private conversation with Nicholas de Carew. As David's longtime friend and advisor, Carew had played an instrumental role in David's life from the time he'd been the Prince of Wales, accompanying him to Lancaster for the fateful meeting with King Edward that had resulted in the king's death. Carew had remained loyal in the years afterwards despite the long odds against survival David had sometimes faced.

As Carew had described those terrible three days when they'd feared David dead and their own lives forfeit, James had been struck in particular by the element of not only luck but apparent chance that had marked every chapter of this story—and every story Carew told about David.

Carew had noted it too, but then he'd told James the conclusion he'd come to: when a man surrounds himself with principled people, they tended to find themselves in the right place at the right time. Even the direst circumstances could be turned around on a moment's notice. And even when they couldn't—when people died and kingdoms fell—everyone involved knew that they had done the best they could with what they had been given.

Listening to the riders mock their captive, James considered the strange set of circumstances that had put him right here, right now. On one hand, James had left his young charges alone, which perhaps he shouldn't have done. On the other hand, one of those young people was the daughter of the man who was currently riding past as a prisoner. And James was the only one who knew about it.

James himself had been a captive, and he remembered well the constant anxiety, the certainty that at any moment he was going to die, and the fear. He'd hated every moment of his helplessness, and that memory alone had the power to water his bowels and bring the taste of ash to his mouth.

Both times he'd been rescued by Callum. After that, regardless of their differences in upbringing, not only did James owe Callum his life, but he and the strange half-Scot/half-Englishman had become fast friends. As the torches faded into the distance, James found acceptance washing over him. He would ride to David to tell him what had happened, but first he could do no less for the captive Irishman than Callum had done for him.

He followed.

11

Trim Castle

13 March 1294

Meg

The great hall at Trim Castle was an enormous sixty-foot-long stand-alone building by the north gate. All the members of the Irish Parliament, which was still in its early stages compared to England's, easily fit into it. The only men allowed to be here (and it was *only* men) were the most noted noblemen in Ireland: forty people at most. The difference this week compared to previous years was that for the first time the justiciars included native Irish lords.

Needless to say, the tension level at Trim Castle was rather higher at the moment than Meg found comfortable. For that reason, she was glad that more people hadn't been invited, though Callum had wished that he could have filled the castle with David's men. It was his unease with the entire situation, in fact, which had spurred Meg and her son to find a hiding place outside the great hall. Besides, it was unseemly for the King of England and the Queen of Wales to hang around while the delegates talked, so she and David had made their way to a remote corner of the castle—in this case, the church, which was entirely empty of worshippers now that the morning mass had ended.

Like the great hall where the delegates were meeting, the church was a stand-alone building and lay on the opposite side of the keep from the great hall. While the keep had a chapel too, it was intended for the lord and his family to worship in, not for the rest of the inhabitants of the little town that was Trim Castle. As royalty, Meg and David would have been well within their rights to hang out there, but it had a fine echo that made any conversation inside the nave not quite private.

What they wanted to do was speak frankly in American about who was here and what they wanted, and the fast-paced back and forth of strangely accented English could be immensely off-putting to anyone who wasn't from Avalon, especially if they heard their own names amidst the gobbledy-gook. She and David had already discussed the aspirations of the young Edmund Butler (an Anglo-Irish lord the same age as David). A moment ago, they'd seen him stalking through the bailey with his brother, Theobold, along with two of their allies, John Fitzgerald, a cousin of the Carew clan, and Richard de Burgh, James Stewart's brother-in-law.

"We already knew the situation here wasn't easily fixable, but it's worse than I thought," Meg was saying. "Sometimes when people who have been wronged—truly wronged—subsequently achieve some level of power, they find it impossible to be forgiving towards those who wronged them. They think tolerance and acceptance should flow only towards them, and they are unable to have any thought for anyone's experience but their own."

David gave a sharp sigh. "I know it, Mom. It's like everyone here knows absolutely that they're right; they are uninterested in anyone else's point of view, no matter how reasonable; and they would rather start a war than compromise even an inch."

This resentment was a consequence of the way the conquest of Ireland had occurred over a period of years but never cohesively or as part of a grand plan. The initial invasion in the twelfth century had been led by yet another Clare (this one named Richard, known more commonly as Strongbow), who'd arrived in Ireland because Diarmait MacMurchada (anglicized to Dermot MacMurrough), the Irish King of Leinster, had been ousted by another clan and had invited Strongbow and his armies to Ireland to help him regain his throne. Dermot had promised Strongbow his daughter and his crown upon his death. Good Norman that he was, Strongbow had agreed. Dermot would have done well to have learned from Vortigern, who'd invited the Saxons into Britain in order to subdue the Picts after the Romans left. Encouraging the aspirations of foreigners across the sea was never a good idea.

Two years later, the next wave of Normans, headed by King Henry II, showed up to wrest control of the island, not only from the Irish but from Strongbow himself. Henry had convinced the pope, who was looking for a way to curb the independence of the Irish church, to support England's claim to the island.

In subsequent years, England's control had ebbed and flowed. Even with their cavalry, archers, and mail armor, none of which the Irish had much experience with before the Normans came, the newcomers had never succeeded in conquering the whole country. Large swaths remained in Irish hands, particularly (as in Wales) those lands that were less productive and would bring the conquerors less revenue.

The north was claimed by the O'Neills, who were at constant war both with the Burghs (the Earls of Ulster) and rival Irish clans. The O'Rourkes, O'Reillys, and O'Donnells held much of the middle and west, though they fought each other as much as they fought the English, and the south and far west were ruled by the O'Brien and O'Connor clans.

The Normans claimed that they'd brought order to Ireland. Before their coming, the Irish chieftains had fought among themselves like cats and dogs. While true, the same could have been said (and had been said) about the Welsh. And it wasn't as if the English weren't undermining each other at every turn, just as in the March of Wales, where families such as the Clares, Bohuns, and Mortimers had carved out mini-kingdoms for themselves and were at each other's throats as often as they fought the Welsh.

As an added complication, as in the March, after the initial conquest of Ireland, the conquerors had started to assimilate, beginning with Strongbow, who'd married Dermot MacMurrough's daughter. By now, most of the ruling families, whether originally Irish or Norman, were blended. In fact, by three hundred years from now, none of the original Anglo-Norman families would even speak French or English. They would be more Gaelic than the native Irish, and they would want to be independent of England as much as their Irish counterparts did.

Eventually, in Avalon, the Church would split into Protestant and Catholic and things would get even messier, but fortunately David didn't have to worry about that piece right now. Avalon's brutal history didn't mean that what was going on now was somehow right, but it put what David's Anglo-Norman barons were doing into context. The whole purpose of life for them was to gain land and power for themselves and their families. Just as in the Welsh March, the barons who ruled here set themselves up as kings on a par with the Irish kingdoms they conquered. David was Lord of Ireland, but the power he wielded was as flimsy as paper. It was men like Geoffrey de Geneville, Hugh O'Connor, and the Geraldine, Butler, and Burgh families who had the real power.

"What you don't know about the Middle Ages isn't worth knowing, Mom." David was perched on the edge of a table in an isolated corner of the vestry. Possibly, the priest would have looked askance at their current location, but Meg figured that between the two of them, they could brazen out any trespassing infraction.

She laughed. "I wouldn't say that. But here's a fun fact I never told you: Thomas de Clare should have been dead by now. I was really surprised to find him alive when we got here."

"How'd he get so lucky?"

"I don't know. He was supposed to have been killed by an Irish rival a few years ago. But he wasn't. Obviously."

David grinned. "A butterfly flaps its wings in Armenia."

"I think it's more that your presence in this world has proven to be a disruptive force."

"Yours too."

Meg shook her head. "I came to Llywelyn and lived here for a year, and it changed nothing except the fact of your existence."

David waggled his hand, implying *maybe*.

But Meg was pretty sure she was right. David was her son, and a large part of Meg could never be objective about him, but she'd had to learn over the ten years since she'd returned to this world to take a step back from him every now and again to see him in a more analytical light.

"I even warned Llywelyn of an ambush, but either that ambush didn't happen in Avalon, or he survived it without my help. He still went to Cilmeri. It's you and your sister who saved him. Pretty soon everything I know or you printed out from the internet is going to be useless. Too much will be different."

"See, what I'm thinking is that it was Edward who was the big cheese," David said. "It's his death that changed everything."

Squeak! The door to the chapel opened.

David and Meg frowned at each other. They'd left two men guarding the front of the church, and if one of them had entered, or admitted somebody to the church, he would have called out.

Meg half rose from her chair, thinking to see who it was, but before she moved farther than that, David put a hand on her arm and a finger to his lips, signaling quiet. Meg sat back down again, and they both listened. Whoever had come in wasn't saying anything and was barely moving too, though footfalls would be barely audible over the pounding of the rain on the roof and in the bailey, louder now since the church door was still open.

David waved a hand to her, signaling that she should move closer to him. As she approached, his arm guided her so she was pressed up against the stone wall of the vestry. A curtain separated the vestry from the chapel itself and, with faint breath, David slowly separated the edge of the curtain from the wall so he could peer through the gap. Meg found that her heart was suddenly pounding.

He looked for a few seconds at most, but apparently saw enough in that time to ease back the curtain so it was flush with the doorframe. Then he signaled to her as he might have to Callum, in that two-fingered military way of theirs, indicating that she should leave the church by the vestry door.

She wanted to ask who had come in and why David wanted her to leave silently. Ten years ago when she'd first returned to Wales after her long absence in Avalon, she probably would have—or even argued with him. She certainly would have wanted to see for herself what had caused his concern and decide if she agreed before she obeyed his command. But she'd learned something in the intervening years. Most times, her son knew what he was doing, and she could trust him. In fact, it would be stupid not to trust him. He was only twenty-five, but he'd been the king of England for almost six years now, and at nearly forty-seven-years-old herself, Meg was long past the point of underestimating the villainy that human beings could get up to.

So if her son said to go, and even if her heart was in her throat about what he knew and she didn't, she went.

The church had three entrances: the main door on the west side, through which the people David had seen had just entered the church, and two side doors. These latter two were intended for use by churchmen only. The north entrance, opposite the vestry, was reachable through the transept and was simply a smaller entrance by which the priest could come and go without opening the big double doors at the west entrance. The second side entrance, the southern one Meg was using, allowed direct access to the priest's house. Like the church, it was built close to, but not up against, the curtain wall.

Meg breathed a sigh of relief as she pushed open the door and it didn't squeak. A second later David was behind her closing it, again with a finger to his lips. Together they hustled along a short passage until they reached the main room of the house. The priest wasn't there, having been called upon to bless the conference in the great hall, so they were still alone. David bent to look out one of the two small windows that overlooked the bailey of the castle.

A half-dozen men dressed in peasants' clothes were engaged in a ferocious hand-to-hand battle with an equal number of knights.

David spun Meg around. "We have to move!" He hustled her across the room, out the back door and along another covered passage, this one leading to the priest's kitchen.

Like the house, the kitchen had multiple entrances, and the back door led to a rectangular yard. Long and narrow, it extended behind an adjacent stables and blacksmith works that had been built between the church and the barbican, located in the southeastern area of the castle. The public latrines were here too. Geoffrey de Geneville had cared for his castle, so he'd put down flagstones over portions of the bailey for easy passage from the keep to the gatehouse and the various buildings, including the great hall and the church. The rest he'd graveled, which at least minimized the mud, though after all this rain, mud was unavoidable.

At the exact moment Meg and David left the priest's house, two more of David's men emerged from the stables. They immediately started across the yard towards Meg and David, but only two strides in, five soldiers, who were not David's, rounded the north side of the house.

The nearest man waved his arm. "Go! Go! We'll hold them off!"

Bang!

The sound rocketed around the bailey, unmistakably gunfire. David grabbed Meg's hand and ran flat out with her towards the postern gatehouse, their pre-established rendezvous point should anything go awry at Trim. It would be guarded by two of David's men, who knew that they weren't to leave their post no matter what happened inside the castle, including Callum firing off a shot from his gun.

Even as she ran, and knew running was the right thing to do, every fiber of Meg's being was telling her to turn back. She wanted to grab David's shoulders and shake him, scream at him for not going to his father's aid. But she didn't. He was right not to. If Callum was firing his weapon, then whatever situation he was in had spiraled totally out of control—and yet was as under control as it could possibly be. She needed to trust Callum to protect Llywelyn as she was trusting David to protect her.

Callum fired a second time, the sound again somewhat muffled by the walls between them and where he was firing inside the great hall, but still loud enough to make Meg jump. Reflexively, she glanced back—and was extraordinarily relieved to see that the two men from the stables had been joined by four more, and they were holding their own against their attackers.

She and David reached the postern gate. Releasing her hand, with a muttered, "Wait here!" David flung open the guardroom door and leapt inside.

When no grunts or sounds of fighting came to her, Meg poked her head around the frame of the door. David stood between two dead guardsmen—she recognized them as Welshmen—who lay slumped on the ground. Both had been unceremoniously skewered through the midsection. "You didn't—"

David let out a puff of air. "They were already dead."

Meg closed the door behind her, blocking out the sound of the fighting in the bailey. "Now what?" Somewhere along the way, she had pulled her belt knife from its sheath. While she didn't have a black belt in karate—and had never been trained as a fighter—she could use the knife if she had to.

"If I wasn't worried about Dad and everyone else, I'd suggest that we climb the battlements and jump."

"But we can't."

"No."

"We need to wait for Callum and Llywelyn."

David brought up his head to look at her. "We can't."

She swallowed hard, recognizing that he was right, along with the source of his disconcerting long-eyed stare. "This isn't your fault, David."

"Isn't it?" He laughed without humor. "As I was just telling Callum yesterday, being the return of Arthur takes me only so far. This is happening because I'm here, because I pressed the issue of Ireland's governance. Maybe it's even happening because I didn't take the country over from the beginning to run it myself."

"Whatever the reason, it's done, and we have to deal with what is before us, as disastrous as that may be."

David's eyes returned to one of the dead men, and he bent to pat him down. "Do you see a key?"

She looked to the door in the curtain wall. It wasn't enough, apparently, to bar the postern gate; it had to be locked too. Callum had implemented the most up-to-date security, from a medieval perspective anyway, that he could. And the fact that he had done so was going to save them now. "Over there." She pointed to a key on a hook on the wall near the table where the guards had sat.

"Good. The fact that the door is locked indicates that whoever is taking over the castle didn't come in this way." He plucked the key from its hook and unlocked the door, which swung wide to reveal water from the moat sloshing a foot from the threshold—as well as a boat moored to an iron post just outside the door. David sighed in satisfaction. "Just as Callum promised."

12

Trim Castle
Callum

"What did I tell you? So much for compromise." Few people were as cool under pressure as Llywelyn ap Gruffydd, the King of Wales. He'd made a joke, but at the moment Callum wasn't capable of laughing.

"Stay down, and stay behind me!" They were backed into the far corner of the great hall, and Callum was protecting Llywelyn with his body. What Callum wouldn't have given to have Darren and his gun beside him, but he'd left Darren in Dublin with Rachel, who was teaching a class.

Callum had fired his first shot into the air to get everyone's attention, which it had, though not enough to halt the attack or to save the fifteen justiciars who were already dead. The assault had come so suddenly, Callum hadn't been able to do anything other than protect himself and Llywelyn.

He hadn't fallen into complacency. He hadn't assumed that all was well when it wasn't. He'd told David and Meg just this morning that he felt something was off and didn't want them anywhere near the great hall, but his unease hadn't risen to the level where he felt he could call off the conference. He hadn't gone with his gut, and men had died because of it.

Men continued to converge on him, so Callum fired a second shot, killing one of the attackers, whose identity he didn't know, with a bullet to the chest. He went down cold, the blood from the wound pooling underneath him and creeping between the floorboards of the hall.

That was finally enough to stop the men coming towards him. Medieval men didn't know enough about guns—or anything about guns, for that matter—to realize what they were facing. Rumors of the shooting by Callum in Scotland had to have spread this far by now, but likely the listeners hadn't believed the stories or hadn't yet reconciled what they'd heard with the weapon in Callum's hand.

Even now, as Callum held off three armed men standing in a semi-circle before him, he wasn't entirely sure how they'd arrived at this position. Up until a moment ago, it had been business as usual in the hall: the priest had prayed, Llywelyn had said a few words, and the pontificating had begun, with each lord, whether Irish or English, going over the same ground they'd covered yesterday. And the day before that. Callum had thought the representatives to the English Parliament tended to stand on ceremony and drone on and on about their privileges, but they had nothing on the men of Ireland.

And then, suddenly, ten of the delegates and fifteen of their men-at-arms who'd accompanied them into the hall had swung into action, knives and swords appearing as if by magic in their hands.

With brutal efficiency and a terrifying single-mindedness, they'd attacked their neighbors. The hall had been swept for weapons earlier that morning. Callum had overseen the process, but one of the agreements had been that every lord at Trim had to be involved in the security, or they weren't going to participate. Nobody trusted anyone else.

For good reason, as it turned out.

Geoffrey de Geneville lay slumped on the main table at which Llywelyn and Callum had been sitting, stabbed in the back, literally and figuratively, since many of the men who'd risen up to murder the delegates had pledged their loyalty to him. The Earl of Ulster, brother to James Stewart's wife, was dead too, along with the two Butler boys. Fighting continued throughout the hall, though it was woefully one-sided. The justiciars not in on the plan had entered the hall entirely unarmed as custom demanded during difficult peace talks.

Only five remained. They'd taken up a defensive position in a far corner, backing themselves against the wall on the opposite side of the hall from Callum and Llywelyn. Several were covered in blood. Two fended off attackers with chair legs while three more held knives taken from an attacker. Everyone else was dead or bleeding out.

"Alexander, we need to move." Llywelyn's voice was steady, and he had a hand on Callum's back as Callum had instructed, since as long as he felt Llywelyn's hand there, he could keep his eyes on the three traitors who faced him. But by calling Callum by his given name, he'd revealed his level of stress.

"Don't I know it." Callum began to edge around the wall, always keeping Llywelyn behind him and his gun pointed at his opponents. The real puzzler was the diversity of the three men: one was Irish, one English, and the third Scottish.

"Put down the weapon, whatever it be," the Irishman said in accented English. He was a MacMurrough, the clan that had been displaced as kings of Leinster a hundred years ago by the Norman conquerors his ancestor had invited in, and was brother to Niall, their clan chieftain. What he was doing standing next to Richard de Feypo, a man supposedly loyal to Geoffrey de Geneville, Callum didn't know and wouldn't try to guess until he got himself and Llywelyn out of this castle alive. Now that Callum had seen the third man—a Scot—up close, he realized that he'd met him years ago in Scotland, in the retinue of Red Comyn.

"Let us go, or I will shoot again," Callum said. "Do you really want to be killing the King of Wales?"

"Whether we want to be or not is of no consequence," Feypo said. "We are committed."

"I can see that." Callum said.

He and Llywelyn continued to move along the wall, making for a side door that would take them out of the hall and into the bailey—at which point they undoubtedly would be presented with more enemies and a worse predicament. Callum could only assume that what was taking place in the hall was happening throughout the castle. He was more glad than he could say that Cassie, his wife, had stayed home in Shrewsbury with their young son, Gareth, born in July of last year.

"Six feet to go." Llywelyn spoke low in Callum's ear.

Feypo and the others must have realized that Callum's and Llywelyn's escape was imminent because, without seeming to have exchanged any signal, they leapt forward to attack. Callum fired into the center of the Scotsman's mass and then pivoted to fire at MacMurrough at point blank range. He was swiveling back, knowing he was too late to stop Feypo but planning to try anyway, when Llywelyn swung a chair at Feypo's head. The bottom rung met Feypo's sword. While the chair splintered, the blow forced the sword from Feypo's hand, and the weapon sailed across the room.

At which point Callum shot Feypo through the temple. By now, Callum had reached the inescapable conclusion that he had to get Llywelyn out of here by whatever means necessary, and that meant using the gun. His clip held ten rounds, and he'd used five just getting them to the door. He didn't know how many more shots it would take to get them out of the castle, but he had to hope that five would be enough.

Llywelyn pulled open the side door and poked out his head. "Come on. It's clear."

Callum stooped to retrieve two swords—one from MacMurrough and the other from the Scotsman. He handed MacMurrough's to Llywelyn, who took it before crossing the threshold. Callum continued to face backwards, his eyes on the remaining enemies in the hall. He felt bad for abandoning the last victims, but two had gone down while he'd been shooting, and the remainder were outnumbered more than five to one. If Callum had been alone, he still might have helped, but he had Llywelyn to protect, and he couldn't justify risking their lives on such long odds.

Clear obviously didn't mean the same thing to Llywelyn as it did to Callum. Men were fighting everywhere, many of them dressed in peasant clothes, which meant they were men Callum himself had posted at Trim. At least he'd done that right. None of the combatants, however, were in their immediate vicinity. Callum and Llywelyn could have joined one of the groups, probably to real effect, but Callum knew his job: he had to get Llywelyn to safety.

Typically, it was pouring rain, but both men had worn their cloaks into the hall as a matter of course. The room had two fireplaces, which struggled to heat the large space on such a cold, wet day as this. Wearing the hoods of their cloaks would look normal and give them a chance to blend in with their enemies, so they pulled them over their heads.

"Meg." Though Llywelyn spoke in an even tone, Callum was fully aware of the anguish behind her name.

"She was with your son, and it would be foolish to try to search the castle for them. They'll have made it to the postern gate. They're probably in the boat already. You'll see."

Llywelyn set off at a run, staying on the eastern perimeter of the bailey and heading south, away from the gatehouse and towards the rear of the castle. The north gate would be guarded and could provide no way out for them.

Callum caught his arm and pointed ahead to where a dozen men were engaged in heavy fighting, blocking the way to postern gate. "We'll never make it."

"We must climb the battlement and jump."

Callum kept pace with Llywelyn. "Last I heard, neither of us could time travel."

"I didn't suggest that we might." Llywelyn gave a harsh laugh. "It just looks to me as if it's our only way out, and one that you and I have experienced before." He was referring to the day they'd met—if you could call Callum throwing his arms around Llywelyn's knees and falling from the balcony at Chepstow Castle *meeting*.

With his feet splashing through the puddles that had formed between the walkway's stones, Callum cursed their predicament, furious with himself on every level.

A man edged out of a doorway to their right. Callum would have run him through had he not recognized him as Magnus Godfridson, the lone Danish delegate to Parliament and the mayor of Oxmantown, the village north of Dublin to which the Danes had been exiled after the Normans took the city a hundred years ago. He had his sword out, but at the sight of Llywelyn and Callum, he immediately flipped it to catch the blade while he held the hilt out to Llywelyn. "Take me with you. We are stronger as three."

Llywelyn didn't take the sword. Nor did he break stride. "Come."

They ran down a narrow alley between the great hall and the barracks. When they reached the line of huts that abutted the curtain wall, they took a right. This alley was also cramped—so much so that Callum could have stretched out both arms and touched the wall of the barracks with his gun, which he still held in his right hand, and nicked the closest hut with the tip of his sword in his left.

He swung around to check that nobody was behind them and then faced forward again, for once grateful at the absence of walkie-talkies or mobile phones that would have allowed their attackers easy communication among themselves.

Llywelyn and Magnus had reached the last hut and stopped, crouching a little and prepared for trouble.

"I've got you," Callum said, turning backwards again to check behind them. "Keep your heads on a swivel, yeah?"

Keep your heads on a swivel wasn't a common term in the Middle Ages, but Callum used it all the time with his men, and he figured Llywelyn would know what it meant, even if Magnus did not. Still, war was in the Dane's DNA, even if he was a merchant in his day job. He went up the stairs after Llywelyn, his head moving constantly to scope out danger.

Callum had to focus hard to keep his attention on everything at once: his feet, his weapons, Llywelyn and Magnus ahead of him, and sounds from the bailey that might indicate trouble. The steps were slippery from the rain, and the last thing any of them wanted was to fall flat on his face, but this was what he'd trained for, both as a soldier and as a spy.

"Step away, son," Llywelyn said.

OUTPOST IN TIME

Callum had been going up the stairs backwards, so at first he hadn't seen the man blocking the top of the staircase, sword out and hood pulled down low over his face. At Llywelyn's words, however, the man immediately pushed back his hood to reveal the boyish face of Robbie Bruce, albeit with a grim set to his jaw.

The young man backed up and let the men come all the way up the steps to reach the cover of the roof over the battlements. Below them lay the part of the moat that, when the sluice gate was closed, made a quiet port between the Boyne River and the castle. The castle could be supplied from the river through a dock gate that came into the castle below the great hall.

"What are you doing here?" Llywelyn took a step towards the young man, his voice as menacing as Callum had ever heard it.

"I-I came to warn King David of treachery!"

Callum almost laughed. "Left it a little late, didn't you? How do we know you're not with them?"

Robbie immediately sheathed his sword and put up his hands. "I'm not! I swear it!"

"Where are Christopher and the others?" Callum said.

"I was with them earlier, but Christopher thought it important that one of us ride to Trim."

"How did you know of the treachery?" Llywelyn said.

"Not this treachery!" Robbie was wide-eyed. "Red Comyn brought a dozen ships from Scotland. We saw them yesterday at Drogheda."

Callum intervened. He'd already killed one of Comyn's men, and if Comyn was involved, Robbie was the last person of whom they should be suspicious. "We'll hear all about it later. Right now, King Llywelyn's safety is my first obligation."

He wasn't displeased to find that two men had become three and then four, but that still didn't mean they should stay and fight it out. Ieuan had handpicked David's men, with approval from Callum. Everyone was better than good, knew what he'd signed up for, and was doing his job. Callum needed to let them do it while he did his.

Robbie gave a brief shake of his head. "I don't understand what's happening."

"I can't say that we do either, son," Llywelyn said.

Shouts and the sound of running feet came to them from the other side of the barracks, and then four men appeared, moving together in double time. A moment later, four more men came out of the front door of the keep and joined them. They weren't friendlies, but they hadn't looked in Callum's direction yet either.

"Time to go," Llywelyn said.

Callum poked his head through a crenel.

"King David has jumped this far—" Robbie looked with Callum for a second, "—but it's a long way down."

"It'll be fine." Callum gritted his teeth. "It will have to be."

Then Callum's attention was caught by a rowboat just coming around the far corner of the castle to the south. Two people were inside: a woman kneeling in the prow and a man pulling hard on the oars. The woman's hood was up, but the man was bareheaded. Even from the side, Callum recognized him—and would have recognized him at twice the distance. He almost cheered. *Something* had gone right.

"That's Dafydd and Meg." Llywelyn sheathed his sword, shed his cloak, and pulled off his boots.

Callum groaned, but he followed suit, as did Robbie, his teeth chattering the moment his feet hit the cold stones of the battlement. Magnus, however, stared at them. "You cannot be serious."

By way of an answer, Llywelyn ducked out from underneath the battlement's covering and, without ceremony or hesitation, jumped.

"Lord Callum."

Callum turned to see Magnus pointing towards the keep. As long as they'd been underneath the overhanging roof, they'd been hidden from the view of the men in the bailey, but now that Llywelyn had jumped, they'd been spotted.

Callum shoved Robbie towards the nearest crenel. "Time to go!"

Robbie didn't wait to be told twice. Overcoming his inhibitions in two seconds, he scrambled into Llywelyn's crenel and leapt from the gap.

Robbie's and Llywelyn's heads both bobbed back up to the surface, and they began to swim hard towards the boat. It had been smart to remove their cloaks and boots, though they might regret their absence when they hit shore. But with the distance they had to swim, divesting themselves of the weight could mean the difference between drowning and not.

Callum glanced at Magnus. "Take your chances with this or with them." He climbed into the crenel.

Magnus cursed and tugged off his boots. "You people are mad."

Callum grinned as the Dane scrambled into the adjacent crenel. "Make sure you get enough distance from the castle wall so you don't kill yourself."

Magnus had a wide-eyed look to him that matched Robbie's of earlier, but he met Callum's gaze and nodded. Callum himself took heart that the others had done it. Even now, he could see David easing back on the oars, having seen Llywelyn and Robbie leap from the battlement and start to swim towards him.

Callum drew in a deep breath and jumped.

13

South of Drumconrath

Aine

Aine woke to find blessed daylight filling the shelter, so much so that it had to be mid-morning already. Huw and William were still asleep, but Christopher stood near one of the posts that supported the roof, his attention on the fields and pastures before him. Though the rain had stopped by the time Christopher had arrived at her father's fort last night, it appeared to have returned. A rainy mist hovered close to the ground, shrouding the trees and valleys. That was good news, in a way, since that meant it also shrouded them.

Although the night had been one of the most miserable of her life, Aine had worked hard to put a brave face on it. They'd walked another hour after Robbie had left, and then the men had decided that they needed to find shelter. While she hadn't wanted to be the reason they stopped, she'd been overtly shivering.

Sleeping in a shepherd's two-walled shelter had been a new experience for her. She suspected that it had been new to the men too, though none had complained about it. With the moon rising, it hadn't been too dark to see without a torch, but somehow lighting a fire hadn't felt like too great risk. Dry kindling had been stacked against one of the walls—a gift from God, or so it seemed—and they had used it.

All of them had been forced to forgo modesty in stripping off their outer clothing and hanging their garments over makeshift racks that the men had constructed out of fallen branches scavenged from a nearby stand of trees. The clothes-covered racks had the additional benefit of blocking the light of the fire from the view of anyone passing by, though the draped clothing also blocked much of the breeze from getting near the fire, and the little shelter had soon become heavy with smoke. The four of them had slept close together, wrapped in the two blankets that had come from the saddle bag.

Now fully awake, Aine dressed quickly. Even though the hem of her skirt was hopelessly stiff with dried mud, she was more thankful than she could say to be warm and dry. She glanced to where their companions still lay asleep on the floor, acknowledging what she owed to each of them. Then she went to stand beside Christopher. "Did you sleep?"

"William, Huw, and I took turns watching and keeping the fire stoked." He turned his head to look down at her. "Are your clothes dry?"

"Mostly." She pulled the cloak closer around her shoulders, knowing the men must have rotated the clothing on the racks to have dried them so evenly, but found the words to thank Christopher for his thoughtfulness sticking in her throat. "James never came back?"

"I didn't expect him to. He had no real way to find us. I knew it when he left."

Christopher's straightforward statement nonplussed her. "Why didn't you say something?"

"I thought—" He stopped for a moment before trying again. "I wasn't hiding it or protecting you from the truth. I thought you all realized it too."

"It looked to me as if James intended to return."

"But he hasn't." Again, the matter-of-fact tone of a man who had seen the truth and accepted it without complaint. "Do you know where we are?"

"South of Drumconrath," she said, and then when he looked at her with narrowed eyes, she added hurriedly, knowing she'd come off as dismissive when she'd meant merely to jest, "I don't know. I haven't explored this part of Ireland like my brother has."

Aine was sorry about that now, but she'd never run with the boys or wanted to. Some of her cousins and companions had been given free reign as girls, but Aine hadn't ever joined them, not liking twigs in her hair or her dress dirty. When she was six or seven years old, she'd been given her first pair of boots, and every time she'd gone outside, she'd made sure to wipe off any stray blade of grass or dust that marred them. She'd loved those boots.

For most of her life, she'd lived at her family's seat at Cloughoughter, some distance to the northwest and farther into purely Irish territory. Her family had wrested the castle from the O'Rourkes, who'd been the original builders. In light of that history,

Auliffe O'Rourke's action last night was less of a surprise than it might otherwise have been, and fully explained why Cloughoughter Castle had been built on an island in the middle of a lake.

In fact, given the constant enmity between the two families, she wondered that her father hadn't been more prepared for an attack. The O'Rourkes' strength had been on the wane since their loss of Cloughoughter, but that should have been all the more reason to remain wary. It was always the cornered dog that was the most dangerous. She could excuse his lapse only in that, of late, he'd focused on his Saxon enemies, not his Irish ones, and it might never have occurred to him that the O'Rourkes would ally themselves with the Clares to defeat him.

"I was hoping you knew the country better than I did." Christopher sounded, of all things, *sad*.

He was a good ten inches taller than she was, so she had to lift her chin to look into his face. "What's wrong?"

"Besides everything, you mean?" All of a sudden Christopher's shoulders shook with silent laughter, and he put the back of his hand to his mouth to contain it and not wake his friends. He chuckled to himself while she stood awkwardly beside him, made uncomfortable by his strange amusement and unable to join in because she had no idea what he found so funny.

After another few moments, he put out a hand to her. "I'm sorry. I'm being rude." Then he gestured towards the hills and valleys before him. "Ireland is beautiful. I didn't expect it."

"And you find that amusing?" She shook her head. "A moment ago you were sad."

Now he took in a breath. "Yes. I am sad, and that's why I laughed. I do that sometimes when things are awful. I wasn't laughing at you or at Ireland, but at the situation we're in. Killing over something so beautiful makes me sad, and if we can't stop the killing here, it will go on for a thousand years."

"I—" She paused, realizing that she'd been about to say the wrong thing. He wasn't really talking about the war. He was talking about himself. "If you're regretting the life of that man you stabbed at the fort, you had no choice but to do as you did. You know that."

"There's always a choice. In that case, the choice was to kill him or to be captured or killed myself. I chose to kill."

"To save my life too."

He took in another deep breath. "Yes. I don't regret the choice. I do regret the need to choose." He turned fully to her now, no longer looking at the view. "I dream often about Westminster, about crossing here from Avalon and killing Gilbert de Clare. They aren't good dreams. And now I have another death to dream about."

The conversation had veered into personal matters and exposed Christopher's vulnerability in a way that she found disconcerting. But she tried to answer as best she could.

"Most men dream as you do," she said gently. All of a sudden, he seemed very young not to have known this already. "It's why they drink themselves into a stupor every night. War has always been a part of my life. I was a little girl the first time my father came into the hall and beckoned to me that I should help him remove his armor. I could hardly lift his vest, and it was made of leather, not mail."

"As you can probably tell, I didn't grow up with war." Christopher touched the red dragon on his chest, David's personal crest. It was another indication of how much higher Christopher's station was than hers. Perhaps in the king's household, these thoughts were discussed all the time. David's intelligence and wisdom were well-known, and while she had joined her countrymen in their admiration of him, before meeting Christopher, she hadn't had a context for his life.

Having grown up among men for whom killing was as natural as breathing, she couldn't imagine what it might be like to live with men who both knew how to kill and yet could talk about it the way Christopher did. She had never met anyone who allowed a stranger such as she to see what was in his heart. Among the O'Reillys, men were strong at all times, or they were nothing. The only exception would be when they'd drunk too much or allowed themselves to be moved by a ballad sung in the hall of an evening. In the latter instance, they were usually drunk too.

And, given Christopher's actions today, she didn't entirely believe that he had as little experience as he claimed. "Is that because there is no war in Avalon?"

Christopher looked at her sideways. "How do you know about Avalon?"

"We all know." Her brow furrowed in puzzlement. "How could we not know?"

He raised his hands and dropped them in a gesture of surrender, before answering her first question rather than her second. "I've always been David's cousin, but I wasn't raised as royalty. For a long while, my mother pretended that David wasn't a king at all, but I spent my childhood dreaming of coming here to fight alongside him."

"And now that you stand at David's side, is it as you dreamed?"

Christopher guffawed. "No." Then he tipped his head back and forth, amending his initial denial. "Yes and no. I have learned more about life and about myself than I would have thought possible. But from the first instant I got here, I've been in way over my head."

Aine hadn't ever heard that turn of phrase before, but she thought she understood what he was saying. "You feel like you're drowning?"

"Every day." He was totally sincere.

"I think you shouldn't say such things about yourself because they aren't true. I'm alive and in one piece because of you. You did kill a man, but you *did* save me."

"That is the one part about all this that I don't regret, but I'm pretty sure you would have gotten yourself out just fine without me."

Aine looked away. While she was grateful for his actions and found Christopher's honor compelling, she found his frankness off-putting. He'd told her more about himself in the few hours she'd known him than most men might say in a lifetime. She wasn't used to knowing so much about what went on inside a man's head—and she wasn't sure she liked knowing.

Christopher cleared his throat, drawing her attention back to him. "I didn't tell you that your father saw us right before we left the hall."

"What—what do you mean?"

"Over the heads of the men between us, just for a second, we met each other's eyes. It wasn't like he nodded, but I got the message that he was counting on me to get you out. So I did."

For the first time since they'd escaped from the fort, Aine smiled. Her father was known as a hard man, but she knew that he loved her, and when asked, he'd been known to say that she was his most treasured possession. If he'd died at Clare's hand last night, he'd gone to his grave knowing that she lived.

"Do you miss it?"

"Miss what?" Christopher said.

"Avalon."

"I do." Christopher's answer came quickly, but then as he looked at her, the lines around his mouth and eyes smoothed, and he appeared less stretched and thin with tension. "But I'm not ready to go back. There's still too much to learn here."

"I can teach you Gaelic if you like."

He smiled that sweet smile of his that she'd seen only a few times. "I didn't quite mean that, but I'd be happy to learn."

Then Christopher seemed to shake himself, and his tone became much more straightforward. "We should get moving." He strode to where William and Huw were sleeping and poked at Huw with the toe of his boot. "Wake up." When Huw didn't stir, he bent to shake first him and then William. "Come on. It's time to go."

"What? What?" Huw sat up with a start. "Are we in danger?"

"Not seemingly at the moment," Christopher said.

"Has James returned?" Huw ran his hand through his hair to tame it, his expression serious. Now that she had a chance to look at him by the light of day, he was older than Christopher, into his twenties by the look of his morning beard.

"He has not," Christopher said shortly.

William rose from the blankets fully dressed, which made sense if he'd taken his turn watching in the night. All he had to do was pull on his boots, which had dried, like their cloaks, before the fire. He looked at Aine intently. "Can you get us to Trim? Or at least headed in the right direction?"

"I will try."

"Some would say that there is no *try*." Christopher picked up the pack and swung it over his shoulder. "But I think that's all we have any right to ask."

14

Trim Castle

David

"Get in! Get in!" David reached down a hand to his father while his mom grasped the back of Dad's tunic and Callum pushed up from below. They hauled him in first and then Robbie Bruce, though what he was doing by himself at Trim Castle David didn't know and couldn't guess. They fell in turn into the bottom of the boat.

The white rowboat was approximately ten feet long and five feet wide, one of those flat-bottomed boats found everywhere. The iron fittings for the oars were well worn from years of use, but Geoffrey de Geneville had taken care of his domain, and the overlapping strakes that formed the hull didn't leak. The water that had accumulated in the bottom of the boat was coming entirely from the rain, which continued to fall, and from Robbie's and Dad's dripping wet clothes.

The Dane, Magnus, clambered in next, followed by Callum. He hardly needed any assistance, which prompted a sour look and comment from Dad. "You would show me up."

"It's because I practice climbing into boats all the time." Callum pushed back his hair and huffed a breath as he sat beside David on the seat. He picked up one of the oars, as if rowing a boat was something he did every day too, and set to work.

David laughed at their exchange, more relieved than he knew how to express that his father and Callum had gotten out of the castle in one piece. As far as he could tell, neither was wounded either. And whatever their experience had been, it seemed to have solidified the relationship between them. Not that they hadn't been on good terms before, but Callum was David's friend and companion and spoke virtually no Welsh. His initial experience in this world had also come in the process of trying to capture David's mother and father—not perhaps the greatest start to, or foundation for, a friendship.

"What about the rest of our men?" David looked towards the walls. He saw a few heads, but nobody seemed to be following. Nor had anyone launched a boat after them.

"They're fighting. We had to leave them to it."

His father leaned forward and put a hand on David's shoulder. "They weren't outnumbered."

David pulled on his oar, feeling cowardly for fleeing. "How did this happen?"

"A portion of the delegates and their retainers ambushed us." Callum gave a summary of what had gone on in the great hall. "I used five bullets. I have five left." He briefly set down the oar to check the gun and its clip. Long gone were the days when guns and ammunition weren't waterproof—as Callum had proved years ago when he'd fallen into the Thames following David's parents.

"You were right not to shoot more than you had to," David said.

Dad nodded. "You should know that the insurrection looks to be an alliance of various Irish and Norman forces—and Scottish too, though what role they could be playing in this I can't say."

"A lot of things had to go right for them to have achieved so much." Callum nudged David with his elbow, and they turned the boat towards the river, which fed the moat. Because of the near constant rain, both the moat and the adjacent river were full. Geoffrey had taken advantage of the high water to open the sluice gates that controlled the water level in the moat in order to flush out the castle's waste, which (as was the case for most castles) was disposed of in the moat. "This is my fault. After France, there's no excuse for allowing this to happen."

"You can't protect yourself completely from allies," David said. "I trusted Clare implicitly. This is different."

"This is a dozen lords conspiring together," Dad said. "You couldn't know."

"We shouldn't have come, not without a better spy network." Callum shook his head, even as he pulled on the oar in unison beside David.

David tried again. "You brought your gun to the hall, and it was your caution that had Mom and me hiding in the church. It was your foresight that set up the postern gate as a rally point and means of escape."

They coasted the boat through the open sluice gate and into the main channel of the river. Following the current, they set off downstream, towards Drogheda.

Callum spoke again. "I don't know enough about the players to tease out the specifics, and I don't know who is the driving force behind the attack, but it wasn't the Burghs, Butlers, or Fitzgeralds."

"What about Theobald de Verdun, William de Bohun's uncle?" David said.

Callum gave him a rueful look. "He was targeted in the first wave and fell early on."

"Geoffrey de Geneville is dead too," Dad said. "This wasn't his doing."

"Part of me is relieved to hear that, but—" David shook his head. "I liked him." The adrenaline that had gotten him this far was starting to ease off, leaving him exhausted. Fortunately, they weren't pulling against the current, so he didn't have to do much to keep the boat going in the right direction.

He glanced behind him at his mother, who was sitting beside his father in the bow. Her face was pale, and she was looking weepy. He glanced away, knowing he didn't have time for emotion, but it was right below the surface for him too. He faced the rear to look at Magnus. As tall as David, as a Dane should be, he was twice as wide as Robbie, who was shivering next to him in the stern of the boat. "How did you escape?"

"I was in the loo." Then he gave David a wolfish grin. "Nobody but you and your father were interested in hearing what I had to say anyway, so I was taking my time."

"I guess it was your lucky day," Callum said.

"Red Comyn is involved," Robbie blurted out. "Yesterday evening, we watched a dozen ships flying his colors sail up the Boyne River to Drogheda. He was met by John de Tuyt. James and I rode down to the dock and spoke to them. Comyn claimed to be inspecting his wife's lands here in Ireland."

David stared at Robbie. "Why am I hearing of this only now?"

Robbie took in a breath. "Because when we got back to where we'd left Christopher guarding the horses, he had disappeared—along with the horses. He'd been abducted by Gilla O'Reilly's men. We had to go after him." His look was pleading, begging David to understand. "He got away. Last I saw he was okay."

Robbie, like many young people in Britain, had adopted *okay* as the catch-all word it had become in Avalon. Its use had started ten years ago with the arrival of David and Anna, but by now it was everywhere, though David was pretty sure Robbie's adoption of it was Christopher's fault.

David would have teased Robbie to put him at his ease, since the story was so preposterous that David couldn't be angry, but Robbie was too distraught. As the young man had told his story, David had stopped rowing, and with only Callum's oar in the water, the boat started to go off course. Callum nudged him, and David blinked and began again to row.

"So where is Christopher now? Tell me you know," David said.

"I don't." But before David could chastise him, Robbie hurried to add, "Or not exactly. He escaped all on his own after Thomas de Clare and one of the O'Rourke lords attacked O'Reilly's fort at Drumconrath."

Robbie poured out the story, though his voice trailed off at the end where James had ridden off in one direction and Robbie in another.

"How could you?" Mom glared at Robbie. She'd been forgiving of Callum, and accepting as their fate the overtaking of Trim. But this was different. In her eyes, no matter how many times David or Christopher himself told her otherwise, Christopher was her responsibility, in large part because her sister would think he was. To have lost him in the middle of Ireland was a nightmare to her. Not long after he'd arrived in this world, she and Christopher had gone at it, in fact, about David's plan to teach him to be a medieval nobleman. *Swords were for killing*, she'd said.

Nobody had ever pretended otherwise, and David understood her concerns, as did Christopher, at least theoretically. But arriving as he had, killing Gilbert de Clare and being heralded as the Hero of Westminster, left them with few options as to what profession he could pursue. And the truth was, Christopher had wanted to fight at David's side ever since David had shown up on his doorstep in Pennsylvania when Christopher had been a little boy. Mom had no business denying him the right to become a man on his own terms—

which in this world happened to mean turning himself into a knight, just as David had.

"So you don't actually know where Huw, Christopher, and William—or James for that matter—have got to?" Callum said.

"No, sir. Christopher thought it was more important that you know about Comyn's arrival and the attack on Gilla O'Reilly." Robbie gestured behind him to where Trim Castle was receding into the distance. "He was right."

"Why did Gilla want Christopher?" Mom asked.

"I'm not sure that he did," Robbie said. "He wasn't with his men when they came upon Christopher and abducted him. It was kind of a spur of the moment thing."

David snorted laughter. All of Christopher's friends were starting to sound like him.

"I *can* tell you," Robbie continued, "that neither Christopher nor Aine—Gilla's daughter, who escaped with Christopher—thought Clare knew he was there. If he had, he would have demanded him from Gilla first thing. Instead he killed most of Gilla's men and was gloating about it." Robbie gave an uncontrollable shiver, and his teeth chattered.

They were all cold and wet, and Robbie's blue lips were a reminder that they couldn't stay out on the water much longer. They needed shelter, new clothing, horses, and a plan—none of which looked to be immediately forthcoming. They'd already passed an Augustinian friary, the cathedral of St. Peter and St. Paul, and a leper hospital, but all were within a stone's throw of Trim Castle, and David hadn't thought any of them could be a safe place to find refuge.

He pulled on his oar. "So ... you ride to Trim to warn me, only to find that Trim is under attack too. You're lucky you didn't end up dead. How'd you escape?"

"My horse went lame a few miles out of Trim, so the going became even slower. I'd just arrived and was seeing to my horse when I heard shouts and people running. Because of what happened last night to Gilla O'Reilly, I was warier than I might otherwise have been. Once three men outside the stables turned on their companions right in front of me and killed them, I hid myself." Robbie shook his head. "It all happened so fast!"

"The attack was long planned and almost perfectly executed," Callum said.

"Almost." David looked at Callum. "It's a good thing that you sent us away, Callum. They were coming for us too."

"Why wouldn't they kill you first, my lord?" Robbie said.

"They tried," David said. "They were slow about it."

"I know why," Mom said, "though you're not going to like it."

"Just tell me," David said, though her reluctance told him he already knew.

"Because you're the return of Arthur, even to the Irish."

"Bad luck to kill the return of Arthur," Callum said through teeth gritted against chattering. "Nobody wanted to do it."

"Well, if I had to pick a moment to be the return of Arthur, then today is as good a day as any," David said.

Mom made a *huh* sound, and when she spoke next her voice was thoughtful. "In a single hour, a significant portion of the nobility of Ireland, both Irish and English, were murdered. Have you noticed that the men who died were of the most powerful class, while the ones doing the killing were the next rung down on the ladder?"

David hadn't thought about it like that before, and maybe nobody else had either since everyone remained silent as David and Callum maneuvered the boat around a half-submerged tree that had fallen into the river.

"I think you might be right, *cariad*," Dad said.

"We need to regroup," David said. "We know much of the *who* now, but hardly any of the *why*, and we're not going to find answers out here on the water."

"Where can we go? I don't know this country well at all." Mom looked at Magnus. "Do you?"

"Well enough, but whom can we trust?" Magnus said.

"I had a hope when we first found the boat that we could end up at Drogheda Castle, which is downstream, but Robbie's news makes that impossible," David said.

Mom leaned forward to speak to Robbie. "Do you have any sense as to what Comyn was really doing?"

"At the time, just talking."

Callum growled under his breath. "A man doesn't bring a dozen ships to Ireland to just *talk*. Each ship could have been carrying fifty men and horses."

David nodded. "That means five or six hundred men."

"That's what we concluded," Robbie said. "He didn't get those men just from his own lands either. He has to have been sent by King John."

"I shot one of Red's men in the great hall," Callum said. "What are the chances that Aymer de Valence isn't far behind?"

"High." Dad and Mom said together.

David glanced behind him to his parents. Dad needed to get warm and dry sooner rather than later. His mom hadn't had to swim, but his father had, and both of them were looking as blue around the lips as Robbie. David's stomach clenched at how close they had all come to dying today. This was so much worse than David's sojourn into France last year. Then, he'd had only himself and King Philip to worry about—and he hadn't cared all that much about Philip as a person.

"This isn't all on you." Callum elbowed David—reading his mind, as he so often could. "We'll get ourselves safe, we'll get Christopher back, and we'll figure this mess out, all of us together."

David nodded. Callum was right, and he would be smart to remember it. "So ... do we know where we might find the nearest Templar commanderie?"

15

The Boyne River

Meg

Unfortunately, the Templars could not be the answer this time. Ireland was about as far from the Holy Land as you could get and still be part of the known world, so while there were Templars here, their centers were exclusively in English territory, which wasn't any safer for Meg's family today than Irish-controlled lands. David had archers in Dublin and ships in the harbor, but they were twenty-five miles away. Nobody was going to be able to walk that distance without food and dry clothes.

"How about just a regular abbey?" Llywelyn gestured ahead to the bell tower of a church, poking up above the trees that lined the Boyne River.

The tower was made of gray stone, and until Llywelyn pointed it out, it had blended in with the gray sky, water, clouds, and air around them. Ireland was green, admittedly, but in order to get that green, it had to rain a lot. Even after living for so many years in rain-soaked country, first in Oregon and then in Wales, Meg had rarely felt so waterlogged. Three days in Ireland, and she was convinced she was growing mold between her toes, the fear of which this trip down the river had done nothing to assuage.

"That's Bective Abbey," Meg said.

David twisted in his seat to look at her. "Please tell me it's Cistercian."

"Oh yes. One of the big ones. They're rich, and though it was founded by an O'Rourke before the conquest, it's English now."

"I don't know if that's good or bad," Callum said.

"That it's Cistercian gives me hope," Llywelyn said.

He and David had a particular fondness for Cistercian abbeys because those in Wales had refused to fall in line when the Pope had excommunicated Llywelyn during the wars with England. Whether that independence of thought would translate to shelter for them in Ireland, however, remained to be seen.

"Ultimately I don't think it matters," Meg said. "This is Geoffrey's land, or was. Surely whoever is behind this coup wouldn't waste men garrisoning an abbey—or spend much effort trying to convince the monks there to be disloyal to Geoffrey in advance of the rebellion."

David glanced at Callum, who nodded. "I agree that it's worth the risk."

"Okay." David began to steer the boat more towards the left bank of the river.

The Boyne River wasn't dammed, so from Trim Castle, it wended its way sinuously until it reached the town of Navan, at which point it began heading more directly east to the Irish Sea. They were south of Navan, so the left bank was the western one, putting them *beyond the Pale*, as the English in Ireland said. Meg loved that people in the United States used this phrase all the time without a clue as to its origin, even if they knew the meaning: *here be dragons*. Thus, the abbey had been built beyond the Pale. As she'd told the others, its origins were Irish, not Norman.

"This could get interesting," she said under her breath for only her husband's ears. Still, Meg was glad that they were going to ask for sanctuary, because she was colder than she'd ever been in her life—and she hadn't spent any time in the river. She hated to think how everyone else was feeling. She'd been holding Llywelyn's hand in both of hers, and it was cold too, though perhaps slightly warmer than her own.

Llywelyn leaned in to speak to her, also in an undertone. "Are you all right?"

"I was going to ask the same thing of you."

Since his brush with death a few years ago before David had been crowned King of England, Llywelyn had worked determinedly to maintain his health and fitness and had the body of a man at least twenty years younger. It helped that the men in his family tended to be long-lived, provided they weren't killed in battle or, in the case of Llywelyn's father, by falling from a window in the Tower of London while trying to escape. Which, now that Meg thought about it, hit a bit too close to home today of all days.

The boat nudged against the bank, and David and Callum eased back on the oars.

Llywelyn was in the bow, so he hopped out first, and then he helped Meg over the rail. Callum and Magnus, both wet from head to foot, sloshed through the water on their own and helped drag the boat farther up the bank so it wouldn't float away.

While he waited for the others to get out, David stood on the rowing seat with his hands cupped around his eyes to protect them from the rain.

Meg looked with him. "See anything?"

He dropped his hands. "It looks quiet to me." He clambered out of the boat last, following Robbie, whom he allowed to go ahead of him. The young Scotsman seemed hardly able to move for the stiffness in his limbs, and Meg grabbed his hand to steady him as he staggered up the bank.

Meg waited for David before following the others towards the abbey. "The monks shouldn't have any idea what has happened at Trim yet. It's wet. They'll be indoors where all sensible people should be on a cold March day."

"You're a hopeless optimist, Mother," David said.

She shot him a grin. He only called her *mother* when he was teasing her, and the fact that he was capable of it after the morning they'd had gave her hope. God forbid they ever got used to the death, chaos, and carnage that was part of life here, but that didn't mean they couldn't meet what came at them head on with humor, macabre or otherwise.

She set off resolutely after the others, down a narrow path that followed a stone wall. The closer they got to the abbey, the quicker everyone walked, despite (or maybe because of) their bare feet. She was pleased to see that the abbey looked more than prosperous. All the buildings were built in stone, with glass in the windows of the church itself.

Within a few minutes, they arrived at the gate and stood under the shelter of the gatehouse eaves. Unlike a castle door, the entryway into the abbey wasn't much—just a wooden door with a smaller inset wicket gate. It didn't have a guard tower either.

Magnus pursed his lips as he inspected it. "This place isn't defensible."

"It's an abbey." David reached up to ring the bell, which jangled on the other side of the wall. "Unless a compound belongs to Templars, it rarely—not to say never—is."

Magnus still didn't look happy, the irony being, of course, that Magnus's Viking ancestors had sacked hundreds of monasteries over the centuries precisely because they weren't defensible. Meg laughed—at that thought and in her relief at the prospect of finally being warm and dry. "I've never seen a more bedraggled group."

"We were pretty worse for wear when we arrived in Windsor from Avalon," Llywelyn pointed out. "We were wet then too."

Llywelyn and Meg grinned at each other and turned to face the door in time to see its little window open. Again, it wasn't at all a defensive construction. More than anything, the purpose of the wall appeared to be to keep out the riffraff.

Cistercians liked their privacy, and their purpose was prayer, not healing the sick or succoring the poor. In fact, many Cistercian abbeys had become extremely rich due to owning large tracts of cultivated land and pasture for sheep and cattle. It wasn't any wonder that when Henry VIII dissolved the monasteries two hundred years from now (in Avalon) and confiscated the Church's wealth, there'd been something gleeful in his actions.

The monk who answered the bell was a thin man in his middle-thirties with bulbous brown eyes. As he looked them over, David pushed back his hood and opened his cloak to reveal his sword, a match to the ones the other men wore. Though their bare feet seemed to give the monk pause, he hastily rearranged his expression from his initial suspicion and skepticism to obsequiousness. The Church tried to stay above the petty politics of the region, but wealth and authority were to be respected. "My lords! How may I help you?"

"As you can see, we are in need of shelter," David said, "and we need to speak to your abbot on a matter of great urgency."

"Of course. Of course. May I ask your names?"

They all looked at each other, and Meg almost laughed again because they hadn't discussed a cover story, if that was, in fact, something they needed. Despite being rulers of England and Wales, not one of them knew how to lie properly, other than perhaps Callum, who'd been a spy. As the monk waited for a reply, Meg could see David dithering. She knew that he was worried that this was France all over again, which it could easily be.

Then Llywelyn stepped up to the plate. "I am Llywelyn, the King of Wales." He introduced everyone else, saving David for last with just the words, "This is my son. I'm hoping that this is enough for you to not keep us waiting on your doorstep." He had left off David's name and title with the understanding that anyone in the known world—even an isolated monk in a Cistercian abbey in Ireland—should know that Llywelyn's son was the King of England.

As Meg would have hoped, the monk's jaw dropped. Outside of the justiciars who'd gathered in the great hall at Trim, it was hard to imagine six more important people in Ireland—especially if one took into account that in Avalon, the grown up Robbie Bruce became *the* Bruce, the King of Scotland.

"My lords." The monk recovered himself and swung the door wide. "I apologize for the delay. Please follow me."

He gathered his voluminous undyed robes, holding the hem well above the wet of the courtyard, and hastened towards the guesthouse. It was a substantial building located next to the stables and, as was usually the case with abbey guesthouses, separated a bit from the rest of the monastery buildings. A stone foundation ran all the way around the bottom of the building, above which were two stories built in wood. Even better for their purposes, a chimney poked up above the roof at the back, giving Meg hope that warmth awaited them.

Once through the guesthouse door, the monk beckoned them inside with the comment, "Give me a moment, and I will tell the abbot that you are here."

Callum had been the last to pass through the gate and, once inside the courtyard, he held back, his eyes searching the area—inside and out of the monastery—for signs of pursuit.

"See anyone?" Meg said, holding the door open for him.

The others were already standing before the fire, and she could see the steam coming off their clothes. The monk took a stack of blankets from a cupboard and gave one to each of them. Meg accepted hers gratefully.

Callum shook his head, but he still looked worried. "They saw us jump. They know that they don't have you and David either. Why haven't they followed us?"

"I imagine they have bigger things to worry about right now," she said.

"Maybe." Still in the courtyard, Callum faced away from her, looking northeast. Then he motioned with one hand, saying *come here.*

David noticed. He dropped his blanket onto a nearby chair, passed Meg in the doorway, and returned to the courtyard. Once outside, David looked to where Callum pointed. "Boats, Mom." He took off at a run towards the abbey's perimeter wall.

Meg had remained in the doorway, so the angle was wrong for her to see what they were looking at. She looked longingly at the fire, but she was the least wet and, unlike Callum, wearing boots. With a sigh, she went after them.

"Whose boats?" Llywelyn called after her. "Comyn's?"

"I need to see this." Magnus left his post by the fire and followed.

By now, David and Callum were standing on the chest-high perimeter wall, which, like the gatehouse, wasn't built for defensive purposes but to keep out stray animals. The wall even had a stile built into it to allow someone to climb over it rather than be forced to go around by the gatehouse.

Meg supposed she couldn't really get any wetter and accepted David's hand to climb up next to him. Soon, the six of them were standing on the wall, looking towards the river.

"They fly no flag," David said.

"Those are Drogheda's river boats," Robbie said.

"You're sure?" David said.

"Yes. We saw them yesterday when we crossed the bridge to speak to Red Comyn."

"Dear God," Meg said.

Llywelyn grunted his dismay. "They're headed to Trim."

Magnus turned to David, his fist to his heart. "Tell me what to do, my lord, and I will do it."

"Thank you, Magnus." David ran a hand through his wet hair. "We can't do anything about those boats right now, but believe me when I tell you that we will."

16

Drogheda
James

For hours, James had been cursing himself for the idiot that he was. If he'd figured out at the start that Gilla O'Reilly was being taken right back to Drogheda Castle, he could have caught up with Christopher and the others before too much time had passed and they were irretrievably separated. But he'd left it too late, and now James was right back where he'd started the day before, staring down at the town of Drogheda. Worse, while most of Comyn ships remained at dock, a quick count revealed that there were fewer than before, and all of Drogheda's river boats were missing.

As James crouched in the trees not far from where he and his charges had observed the ships' arrival yesterday, he had to accept the fact that not only had Clare and O'Rourke allied to take down Gilla but they were also allied with Comyn and Tuyt. *Disconcerted* didn't even begin to describe how James felt.

Gilla O'Reilly had disappeared inside the castle a quarter of an hour before, but James watched the front gate for a little while longer, just to see if anything else was going to happen. He didn't even know if Comyn and Tuyt were still here, though it seemed unlikely given the absence of the boats. Neither O'Rourke nor Clare had been among the riders either, which meant that all four leaders were roaming the countryside, together or separately, and James had no idea where they'd got to.

He had learned over the years to put aside what he couldn't control, and the whereabouts of the ringleaders was one of those things. His immediate concern instead was the missing flat-bottomed boats. With them, the Boyne River was navigable to the bridge at Trim Castle, twenty-five miles upriver. James could only think that they intended to besiege it, else yesterday Comyn would have simply said that he was part of a new Scot delegation to the Irish Parliament. He didn't need five hundred men for that, of course, but it would have been a plausible answer. And yet, it wasn't the one he'd given James.

Sadly, James had to admit that rescuing Gilla O'Reilly all by himself was an impossible task—a death sentence in fact. Christopher's strategy of the Trojan Horse passed through his head, but the only gift that Comyn and the others would accept would be James himself—and that wasn't one he was willing to give, not if there was even a chance he would find himself in a cell next to Gilla O'Reilly.

For the first time since he'd lost Christopher, a smile came to James's face at the thought of the proud Irishman behind a barred door. It wasn't that James enjoyed the idea of caging Aine's father, but rather that James had heard the man speak. He was quick of mind. Even more, he was quick of tongue and had an ability to talk incessantly. His captors might well be regretting his presence already.

With that thought, James made up his mind. He mounted his long-suffering horse and turned its head inland, as he should have hours ago. He didn't know where Robbie and the others were now, but last he'd seen they were making for Trim. They were on foot, however, and he'd delayed too long informing David that his cousin was astray in Ireland, never mind the insurrection that had sprung up unexpectedly in his domain.

He trotted through the morning mist and rain that seemed endemic to Ireland, his thoughts as gloomy as the weather. While David rightfully would never trust him again, he might even think that James was secretly working with the rebels and had abandoned Christopher on purpose. James's brother-in-law was the Earl of Ulster, after all. Who was to say that he and James weren't in league with Comyn and Tuyt, if not with O'Rourke and Clare?

Worry occupied James for three-quarters of the journey to Trim. At the approach to Navan, he considered leaving the main road, uncomfortable with riding under the eyes of the castle there. If Tuyt could betray Geoffrey de Geneville, anyone could, including the Angulo family, who controlled Navan Castle. Like Tuyt's ancestor, the Angulos had come with Strongbow at the first conquest of Ireland. But as was the case with all these lords, they held their estates at the behest of David, who remained the Lord of Ireland.

On one hand, the uncertainty of their allegiance meant that James didn't dare risk enlisting their help. On the other hand, he decided that they wouldn't view a lone rider on the road as a threat, and he rode through the town as if the devil himself was at his heels. Which wasn't, in some sense, far off.

James could have crossed the Boyne before the bridge at Trim. Good fords existed along the river, usually wide places where the water spread out enough to allow a not too wet crossing. But James was hesitant to trust any Norman lord, not just the Angulo family, and he had to assume that every ford would be guarded. At the same time, rather than riding straight across country from Navan to Trim, he opted to take the longer route that brought him closer to the river. He wanted to be able to provide useful information to David to make up for all the bad news he was also bringing. In this case, he could give him an accurate picture of how far the river boats had traveled.

Finally, just short of Trim, the host of flat-bottomed boats hove into view in the distance. He peered ahead, cursing his distance vision, which wasn't what it used to be. It had been difficult going for James to ride into the wind for the last twenty miles, and it must have been far more heavy work rowing up the Boyne in this weather. Comyn's men had nearly done it, however, passing Bective Abbey, which lay to James's left, within moments of he himself reaching it. Both they and James had five miles to go.

But rather than push his exhausted horse on to Trim and beat the boats there, James slowed. Despite having come this far, any further effort would be wasted because the men on the walls of Trim Castle would see the boats coming towards them long before James himself could reach the castle. David might want to know what had happened to Christopher, but in the face of such an imminent threat, there would be little he could do about it. At this point, it would be far better for James to turn north and see if he could find his young friends himself.

In addition, James found it unlikely that Comyn would have committed his army to battle in Ireland without commensurate support from allies other than Tuyt. In fact, the more James thought about it, the more likely it seemed to him that Trim might already be under siege. Even more than at Drogheda, James didn't want to find himself caught while Christopher and the others were still lost.

Knowing he had to rest his horse, regardless of his urgency, and in the hope of at least learning something of the boats and the number of men and horses they carried, James turned onto a path to the river. But as he neared the entrance to the abbey, he reined in at one of the strangest sights he'd ever seen: five men and one woman were standing on the eastern wall that protected the abbey, staring at the boats as they rowed by.

Then, as he watched, one of the men put a hand on the shoulder of another, in a gesture that James would have recognized a mile away. Callum was on that wall, standing next to King David. Then one of the other men pushed back his hood and turned to speak to Callum. It was King Llywelyn. At long last, God had brought James to the right place at the right time.

"Yah!" James whooped and spurred his horse towards the entrance to the abbey. His call, and the sound of the horse's hooves, traveled the distance between him and the people on the wall, who turned to look.

James continued riding, but by the time he reached the gatehouse, he had sobered considerably. He had been fearful of telling David that he'd lost his cousin, but for David and Callum—along with the king and queen of Wales—to be standing on the wall at Bective Abbey with no guards or anyone to support them but two retainers, whose faces James hadn't yet made out, things were far worse than he had feared.

Leaving his companions to make their own way down from the wall, David leapt agilely to the ground and loped to the gate, opening it just as James reined in. The monastery's gatekeeper had been caught on the hop and was only now huffing towards them through the rain from one of the buildings surrounding the courtyard.

Thus, the two men had a moment alone together in the shelter of the gatehouse. Both spoke at the same time. "What are you doing here?"

David gestured with one hand, to suggest that James go first, but James bowed and said, "Please, my lord. What brings you to Bective Abbey?"

"Trim Castle has been taken. Twenty lords were murdered where they sat in council."

James was aghast. "By whom?"

David made a frustrated sound in the back of his throat. "An alliance of Irish, English, and Scots. Now your news. Have you seen Christopher?"

"Not since last night." James hesitated. "How did you know we were separated?"

Before David could answer, the rest of the party—including Robbie Bruce, of all people—joined their circle. James and Robbie stared at each other for a moment, equally horrified that the other was there.

"You—" James began.

"Christopher decided—" Robbie started to say.

David waved a hand. "Robbie has told us everything that happened up until he left the others in the middle of a field southwest of Drumconrath."

James was still in shock. "You left them too?"

Robbie grimaced. "We decided that King David needed to know what had transpired, so I left the others to ride to Trim. It just so happened that the insurrection there began right after I arrived. I escaped the castle with Lord Callum and King Llywelyn."

James gave him a baleful look, hardly able to argue since he himself had left Christopher for what at the time had seemed to be a very good reason. And then he related what he'd done, which was far less—merely trailing Gilla O'Reilly's captors to Drogheda.

Once James finished, David again ran a hand through his wet hair, pushing it off his forehead. "Good news and bad news."

The others looked at him questioningly. "I'm having trouble seeing the good news aspect of our situation, my lord," Callum said.

David lifted one shoulder. "It was one thing for this—" he waved a hand, "—gang? cabal?—to assassinate the most powerful lords in Ireland in one go. Okay, that's bad. But the fact that they're going in the other direction is a little bit crazy. And good news for us."

"I'm sorry, my lord," James said. "What do you mean by going in the other direction?"

"It's something we talked about earlier." Meg put a hand on David's arm, letting him know that she wanted to answer. "What David means is that the likes of Feypo, Clare, and O'Rourke are second tier barons compared to those they killed. While it's bad that they've created an unprecedented alliance in order to take over Trim, for them to turn around and take down Gilla O'Reilly, a relatively minor lord who might have been on their side if they'd made overtures to him, indicates that their alliance isn't coherent and might even be transitory."

"These are men who've never seen the benefit of allying at this level before," David said. "What would it take for them to turn on one another? What can I offer some of them to save their own skin?"

"You would bargain with rebels?" James stared at David. It wasn't that such a move couldn't be wise, but that he never would have thought such a proposal could come from David's lips.

David scoffed. "To avoid civil war? I would."

Llywelyn spoke for the first time, his expression thoughtful. "Years ago, I allied with Simon de Montfort and Gilbert de Clare. We were three disparate men with the temporary yet concurrent interest of removing Henry III from power. Later, others accused me of disloyalty to Montfort in that last battle, but I merely saved my men to fight another day after the cause was lost. Gilbert de Clare had already turned his coat and sold us out to Henry and Edward when they made him a better offer."

David looked at James. "I'm sure I will find the process as distasteful as Edward must have when he returned Gilbert de Clare to his fold."

"First we have to figure out who else is in the alliance," Meg said. "They took Trim, but they missed you, David, and lost men, whose heirs might not be as supportive of their endeavor as the men who died."

Llywelyn canted his head towards his son. "There lies opportunity."

David's hands clenched into fists as he looked at his father. "We will *not* allow Ireland to be taken over by men who gained their position by murdering their predecessors."

Everyone else was silent for a few heartbeats, and it was Robbie Bruce who put into words what all of them were thinking. "So what's our better offer? And how exactly do you propose we stop them?"

17

Beyond the Pale
Christopher

They came out onto a road near a real town, and all together breathed a huge sigh of relief to have finally reached some place familiar.

"Kells," Aine said.

For the last few miles, they had steered towards the ninety-foot watchtower that was part of the abbey here, where the Book of Kells (even Christopher had heard of it) was kept.

"We need to avoid the castle," Christopher said. "Aine's father told me that its castellan, Walter Cusack, is in league with Tuyt and Comyn." Then he realized how that sounded, and he started to laugh.

The others looked at him warily, and he was sorry he couldn't share the joke with them because they wouldn't know anything about ancient Egypt. He'd tell David, though, when he next saw him: Tuyt and Comyn. *Tutankhamun*.

Even better, Kells had an inn, sitting about twenty yards away, the first building any visitor encountered when entering the town from this direction. Christopher wouldn't have known it was anything other than a slightly larger than normal house if it weren't for the sign hanging in front, a picture of a white horse. Probably the proprietor couldn't read anyway, the same as all of his clientele, so there wasn't any point in bothering with lettering. Christopher *was* glad it wasn't a black boar, since that had been the inn that they'd had such bad luck with in Caernarfon.

It was the middle of the day, and it was still raining, but even so, there was movement in the streets. As in England and Wales, if people didn't do stuff in Ireland because it was raining, they never did anything at all.

William's stomach growled. "We have money. We can buy food."

Christopher turned to his friend, intending to grin at him, but his pinched look was one that Christopher had never seen before on William's face. He didn't ask what was wrong. He knew. They all knew, and though he was worried too, Christopher put out a reassuring hand. "Give me a second."

"What are we waiting for?" Huw said.

"For me to decide that it's safe," Christopher said. "I don't want to escape Drumconrath only to find ourselves captured by somebody else. We know we can't trust Cusack. Tuyt and Comyn are in cahoots. So are Clare and O'Rourke. Who else might be? And who else might be unhappy about the four of us wandering around the countryside together?"

It was a long speech for Christopher, but he'd spoken fairly authoritatively and managed not to laugh about the names. Since all four of them, even soaking wet, would be known as lords or at least wellborn, by entering the inn they would immediately call attention to themselves. They would get food and warmth if they asked, but Christopher had been abducted less than twenty-four hours ago. If Gilla O'Reilly had thought he was a prize, it was in Christopher's head that other people might think so too.

The worst treachery Christopher had experienced before Gwenllian and Arthur had arrived in Avalon was at the hands of bullies at school. Usually what those bullies had in store for Christopher was a bit less life-threatening, and at least then he'd known what he was facing and could make plans to avoid the boys he feared. Here, it was hard to fight when you didn't know who your enemies were.

He hadn't known it at the time, but life back at his parents' house hadn't been nearly as complicated as he'd thought. Mostly, he tried not to think about his family and Avalon. He had to assume that everyone was okay and that they'd survived their run-in with the FBI and whoever else had been chasing Gwenllian and Arthur. He hoped they weren't worrying about him all the time, though that was a faint hope in his mom's case. Mothers worried. It was pretty much their job.

Huw's hand came down on his shoulder. "Maybe we shouldn't stop. We could head straight for Trim."

Christopher chewed on his lip but ultimately shook his head. "I think the opportunity to eat and get warm is worth the risk. We have a long way to go yet. It would be even better if we could buy horses because then we could travel faster."

"What about James and Robbie?" William asked.

Again, Christopher tried to be both reassuring and realistic. "It isn't like we can wait somewhere for them, since they don't know where we are. Maybe we should have stuck together. Part of me wishes we had, but I don't really regret letting Robbie go. I honestly think he made it to Trim, which means that David knows what's happened. It makes the fact that we're cold and wet right now a lot less of a big deal."

He didn't wait for his friends to admit that he was right, just took in a breath and set off across the road towards the entrance to the inn. He could picture the fire burning brightly in the hearth, and his hands were warmer just at the thought. Unfortunately, anticipation made the disappointment that much worse when he pulled open the front door and discovered that not only was the common room entirely empty, but the stack of dried peat in the fireplace wasn't lit.

At the sight of the cold grate, Aine sighed. She didn't complain, however. Instead, she put her hands to her mouth and blew on them to warm them.

Christopher made a rueful face. "Not exactly the comforts of home."

"I'll see to it." Huw, always the handyman, pulled out his firestarter kit and bent to the hearth.

Meanwhile, William rapped on the bar. As a nobleman, he wore his entitlement like a second layer of skin and expected to be treated well at all times. Christopher looked around the room interestedly. He'd spent a not insignificant amount of time in taverns since his arrival in the Middle Ages, and while this one was on the poorer end of the spectrum, it was nowhere near a hovel. In fact, the wooden floor had recently been swept clean, the tables were scrubbed smooth and spotless, and there wasn't a cobweb in sight. Christopher had a flash of hope that the food, if someone could be convinced to wait on them, might actually be good.

Finally, in response to William's *halloo* into the recesses of the inn, a man in his forties, short and dark and wiping his hands on a cloth, appeared through a door somewhere in the back. The smell of fresh baked bread wafted to them from beyond the hallway, and Christopher's stomach growled as William's had earlier. The man approached the bar casually at first, but then his eyes traveled to each of them, and between one second and the next, he changed from a busy man who didn't know if he wanted to bother answering the door to plucking at his forelock and bowing.

Christopher generally hated being treated like a lord, since pretty much one hundred percent of the time it made him feel like a fraud, but he decided he would accept it from the innkeeper if it got them food.

"May I help you, lords?" He bobbed his head to Aine. "My lady?" He spoke in English.

"We'd like food and a fire." William gestured to Aine. "The lady is soaked through."

"Of course, my lord. At once." He took a step back down the corridor and gave a piercing whistle that split Christopher's eardrums.

Aine met Christopher's eyes, laughter on her lips. Christopher shrugged, glad to see her smiling, which hadn't happened often enough so far. The man's whistle appeared to have the desired effect too because, a moment later, a young man Christopher's age with red hair like his, except curly, appeared through the back entrance. The innkeeper and the young man conferred briefly, and the red-haired man went back outside.

Then the innkeeper gestured that Christopher and his friends should sit at one of the tables. "I apologize for the accommodations, lords, but we are a humble establishment. I am ashamed to say, we have no parlor here."

Christopher lifted a hand. "It's fine."

Huw had gotten the fire going by now. Without needing to discuss it, they chose the table nearest to it. Before sitting, Christopher went to the hearth, hands out, and the warmth was just as he'd hoped it would be. He wished that his parents could see him now. His father had always felt that it was important for Christopher and his sister to experience some physical hardships in life. That's why he'd liked Christopher working on his friend Jon's farm. Christopher figured that trekking half the night and sleeping outside in a stable qualified too.

William pulled out a bench for Aine and him to sit on, but Huw went to the lone window and looked out. After a few seconds, he turned back to the others. "I'll do a circuit, shall I?"

Christopher hoped Huw wasn't offering to inspect the perimeter because he didn't feel like it was his place to sit with them. The fact was, Huw's idea was a good one. "Don't be gone long, okay? And maybe you can see what they have for horses in the back."

"I'm no judge of horseflesh," Huw said, "but I can find out if they have any to sell."

Once Huw left, William leaned forward. "You're the king's cousin. You could just take them, you know."

Christopher glowered at his friend, surprised that William would suggest it. Christopher's parents had always been ones for obeying the rules, and he had a natural tendency to do so. One of the things he'd learned fairly quickly about the Middle Ages, however, was that for him, there was no rule he couldn't break. As the king's cousin, he got what he wanted, and one of the first things David had hammered into him about his life here was that he shouldn't be taking advantage of those beneath him. They would offer, and sometimes he just shouldn't take.

He hadn't needed a lecture—especially not the incredibly embarrassing one Aunt Meg had given him about girls. It didn't take a genius to figure out that pretty much every girl in England thought Christopher was the next best thing to sliced bread, and if he wasn't careful, he'd find himself tied to someone he didn't want to be tied to.

Christopher was sure that Aunt Meg would put Aine in the same category as every other girl Christopher had met so far. She said he'd saved her life, which meant that if he tried to get closer to her, and she let him, it would be because she was grateful, and he'd be taking advantage.

Not that he would. And really, not that he wanted to. He liked her well enough, but he couldn't say he understood her. And seriously, she looked way too much like his little sister to think about kissing her.

William saw Christopher's appalled look, and his expression turned sheepish with a headshake and a half-shrug. "I don't like the look of this place. It's as if they already know who we are." His mouth dropped open, and he started to push to his feet. "The innkeeper could have already sent word to the castle that we're here!"

Christopher put out a calming hand and got his friend to sit back down. "Nobody has any way of knowing who we are unless we tell them. Even if every person in this village is in on some plot with Cusack, we didn't know we would be here before ten minutes ago. Nobody who is anybody knows where we are, much less whose lands we're on. And how likely is it that anyone in this inn has seen us before? Even if they know we're noblemen from England, we're totally anonymous. Relax. It's going to be okay."

Christopher didn't actually know that for himself, but he'd learned by now that people thought less clearly when they were panicked and worried—and hungry. William subsided on his bench and even took in a deep breath. "You're right. You're right. I'm getting muddled in my thinking."

"You're just worried. I am too, but worrying isn't going to help. We need a plan, but we need food first."

Aine was looking around. "I agree with William that we would be better off among my people. I can't help you at all here."

William shook his head again. "That wasn't what I meant. We should have headed east, to my aunt's castle of Roche. It would be a safe haven for us."

Christopher didn't actually laugh at how ridiculous the idea was, but it was a close thing. "At Kells, we're ten miles from Trim. You're talking about walking thirty in the opposite direction."

"It was only fifteen miles away when we were in Drumconrath." William had a stubborn set to his chin.

"I'm sure we would have been safe there, William, but how could any castle be safer than Trim? That's where David is. All we have to do is get there." Christopher knew he was repeating himself, but William hadn't listened the first time, and he wasn't listening now.

Neither was Aine. She hadn't been ignoring their conversation, but she'd been staring into the distance, and her expression had turned thoughtful. She tugged on her braid, which was no longer pinned to the back of her head in a bun but lay over her left shoulder. "It's easy to understand why the O'Rourkes would want to attack my father—but why would Thomas de Clare help them?"

"For the same reason anyone allies with anyone else. It isn't out of the goodness of his heart. It would be because he was getting something out of it," William said.

"That's what I was thinking," Aine said. "Years ago, Thomas de Clare was given the kingdom of Thomond by your King Edward, but he has spent every moment since then attempting actually to win it from the O'Briens, who control it. The reason I can see Clare helping O'Rourke defeat my father is if it was in exchange for the O'Rourkes' help in defeating the O'Briens."

"One down, one to go," William said.

"I think we have to conclude that this plot could encompass all Ireland," Aine said.

William frowned. "In that, I think you're jumping to conclusions."

Aine's chin developed a determined set to it. Between her and William, it was hard to think who was more stubborn.

"I should go to Galway and warn the O'Briens," Aine said.

"By yourself?" William was appalled. "That's a hundred miles from here. Clare's probably heading there now. It's too late."

"Besides, we already lost Robbie and James. We're not separating again," Christopher said. "David is the smartest person I know. If Robbie reached him last night and laid out what we know to him, then he's probably figured all this out already. Going to Trim still makes the most sense."

"If only we could." Huw had returned, coming down the corridor from the rear, through which no food or drink had yet come, Christopher was sorry to see. "You're right that we need to go, but it can't be to Trim."

"Why not?" Christopher had never sat down, and the others were on their feet in an instant. "What's happened?"

Huw motioned with his arm. "Come with me. You can talk to him yourself."

The other three followed Huw out the back door of the inn to a wide yard which held the stables, the kitchen, and various huts the purpose of which Christopher didn't know. The yard itself was mucky from the rain but, as at Trim, the innkeeper had laid stepping stones that crisscrossed the yard so they weren't sinking six inches deep in mud as they walked from the main building to the stables.

Once there, they found a man brushing down a horse. He was slight, like a jockey, with leathery brown skin and close-cropped brown hair. Christopher couldn't have said how old he was.

"Tell them what you told me," Huw said.

The man put down his brush. "Lord Cusack has had word from Trim, brought by one of Richard de Feypo's men. Most of the justiciars are dead." The man spoke matter-of-factly, without any emotion at all.

Christopher stared at him, unable even to begin to process what the man had just said.

Aine, on the other hand, gripped one of the posts holding up the roof. "K-K-King David?"

"He and King Llywelyn escaped." The man started brushing the horse again. "But Lord Cusack doesn't want you to know that. He's putting out that David is dead and the castle held by the rebels who did the killing, though that isn't true either. I myself brushed down the messenger's horse and heard it firsthand from him, who must have thought I was loyal to Cusack." He shook his head. "I just help out in his stables from time to time. He told me that the garrison defeated the rebels, and the castle remains in royal hands."

William heaved a sigh. "Then we can be safe there."

The man shook his head. "Red Comyn and John de Tuyt have brought an army up from Drogheda to besiege it. Cusack is gathering men to support Comyn and Tuyt, not the castle."

"I don't understand any of this," Aine said.

William put out a hand to her, speaking more gently, Christopher thought, than he might if he had been contradicting *him*. "It's obvious. Cusack is part of the conspiracy. He's telling everyone David is dead to spread confusion. Who's going to know what is and isn't true?"

Huw nodded. "Look what happened last year when Clare told everyone King David was dead."

"Wait a second!" Christopher found himself growing angry, which was better by far than being afraid. "Cusack is going to besiege Trim with Comyn, but he's calling the men who hold it rebels?"

"Yes, my lord," the stableman said.

"What else did he say? Who is dead for sure?" Christopher said.

"Geoffrey de Geneville, for one. Butler, Fitzgerald, and Burgh for three more."

"What about Turlough O'Brien?" Aine said.

The man shook his head. "Gone."

Aine's face fell. "I was thinking we might go to him for help."

The ringing in Christopher's ears that had come on when the man had first started speaking had stopped. Truth be told, as long as David was alive, good things would continue to happen. Maybe that was totally illogical and based on nothing but air, but he believed it anyway.

Some of the color had returned to William's face too, and his chin firmed. "Now I'm sure that we need to go to Castle Roche. We should have gone there in the first place."

Christopher had the feeling that he was never going to live down the decision to come to Trim. But he knew too that it had been the only decision he could make when he made it.

"Did the messenger say who was behind the taking of the castle?" Aine said.

"No."

"Not Comyn and Tuyt, clearly," William said, "though sailing all that way upriver from Drogheda overnight is quick work."

"Feypo might be one, if it's his messenger who rode to Cusack," Christopher said, "and that means the conspiracy goes far beyond even the five lords we know of right now."

"I don't know if Feypo was involved, seeing as how he's dead too," the man said, as if it was simply a by-the-way.

William had gone pale again. "My uncle was at Trim. He could be dead or—" he put both hands to the top of his head, "in on it!"

The possibility had occurred to Christopher about two seconds earlier, but he hadn't suggested it because it would have seemed like he was still back on the question of whether or not they should have gone to Castle Roche. He didn't say anything now either because it would have come out too much like *I told you so*. "The only thing that matters right now is that Cusack is allied with Red Comyn, and since we are most definitely not allied with *that* crowd, we really don't want to be here another second."

"Who's your uncle, my lord?" the man said to William.

"Verdun."

The man made a rueful face. "He's another who's dead."

William looked like he was going to puke. They didn't have time for that, so Christopher gripped William's shoulder. "We need to find some place safe to regroup."

"Can we trust anyone?" Huw said.

"Only someone who would never ally with any of these men," Aine said, her eyes on William. She moved closer to him, implying comfort, though she didn't touch him. "I'm thinking of a clan nobody has mentioned so far. They didn't come to Trim, but they haven't allied with any of the Irish in recent campaigns against the Saxons either."

"Who?" Christopher said. "Don't keep us waiting."

"Hugh O'Connor, King of Connaught," William answered tonelessly. He'd turned away to stare out at the yard.

"*Aodh*, we call him." She pronounced his name *Ay*. Aine gave a mocking laugh. "He has pretentions to the High Kingship and has been known to ally with the Burghs on the rare occasion when he allies with anyone."

"How far would we have to go to get there?" Christopher said.

"Last year he took Roscommon Castle from the Saxons, and he has made it his seat," she said. "Fifty miles."

18

Bective Abbey
David

It was a standing joke among David's companions that he loved maps. He collected them, good and bad, accurate and hopelessly wrong. They covered the walls of any castle where he spent any time. Upon entering the office of the abbot of Bective Abbey, David was therefore pleased to discover that the abbot appeared to feel the same way. Maps didn't adorn the walls, but Abbot John had an entire table devoted to map after map—not only of Ireland but of the known world.

With a flourish, John spread the map he'd chosen in front of him on his desk and held down the corners with a diverse series of paperweights. "If the Irish are rising, we might look to retreating into the Pale."

"That's just it, Father," David said, "it isn't only the Irish rising. It's an alliance of Irish and English—and Scottish, for that matter."

Abbot John froze in the act of adjusting his ink jar on one corner of the map and stared at David, seemingly not having understood the full scope of the plot until that moment. "How—how is that possible?"

"That's what we all want to know," Callum said. "We don't know how. Only that it's happening."

"But-but-but—" Father John was literally stuttering in front of them. He was of middle age, as was usual for a monk who'd reached his station, a little on the plump side, perhaps as came naturally to someone who ate plenty of good food and didn't exercise enough. "Is anyone trustworthy?"

"We can begin with Gilla O'Reilly," James said, "and anyone else who had a family member die today."

"The Butlers, the Burghs, the Fitzgeralds, and the Verduns, to name a few," Llywelyn said.

"They're *all* dead?" Abbot John said.

"Callum and I saw them fall," Llywelyn confirmed.

"What about among the Irish?" Abbot John said. "You said Irish were slain too."

"Turlough O'Brien is dead, along with the chief of the O'Neill clan," Llywelyn said.

"The O'Neills are at odds with the Burghs," Abbot John said. "Why would they both be dead?"

"The one who killed him was a cousin, who is presumably hoping to take his place," Callum said matter-of-factly. "As we said, it isn't just war between English and Irish this time. It's carnage among the clans."

Abbot John tipped back his head to stare up at the ceiling as he tried to encompass the magnitude of the plot. Then he brought his head down to look at David. "You must work quickly to confirm the heirs in their holdings, my lord. This is a disaster for the families. First born sons aside, not everyone has a viable heir, and among the Irish, many of those seats will be challenged by brothers and cousins, since sons don't necessarily directly inherit."

David bobbed his head in a nod, having figured that out for himself already. "For now, we will work with whoever is willing to work with us and worry about the consequences later."

Callum put heavy hands on the table and leaned on them to look at the map the abbot had brought out. "What can you tell me about the lands around here and likely supporters of either side?"

Abbot John was still shaking his head at what they'd told him, but he knew his maps. With sweeps of his pen, he'd carefully written in the name of each landowner, with a general sketch of his holdings. Magnus approached as well, and the three of them put their heads together, picking over the political alliances of the various lords.

Leaving the immediate logistics to them, David went to the window to look out. Rain fell against the glass, the installation of which was a sure sign of the abbey's wealth. All of them were completely renewed in clean, dry clothing from head to foot, including sturdy boots, though David himself still wore his own, since he hadn't been one of those to jump. Other monasteries went in more for sandals, but these monks had shown themselves to be practical.

"What are you thinking?" Dad stepped beside him.

Now that they were working on a plan, the realization was growing in David that he would have to lead men into battle—today, tomorrow, soon, anyway—and he needed to be prepared for it. But instead of the necessary resolve, he felt resignation and a kind of seeping sadness that it had come to this, despite every strategy he'd come up with to avert war. He'd avoided the problem; he'd been hands off; he'd given as much power to the people as he could. And all it had done was show the barons here that he was weak.

David didn't want to talk about his despair, so he deflected to analysis. "What went down at Trim this morning was not without precedent, either in history or in fiction."

"Like in the *Mabinogion*," Dad said, referring to a compilation of Welsh legends. "And if Ieuan were here, he would remind us of William de Braose and the Abergavenny Christmas massacre."

"I know he would, but that's no comfort since Braose won. What we have to figure out is how *we* win."

"I have an idea, but it would require you to accept more power here, at least for a time. I know you've been reluctant to take on that role." David's father rubbed his chin. "I would, in fact, have you crowned High King."

David didn't say anything for a moment. It wasn't as if he hadn't known this was coming. Years ago, it had been his father who had pushed David to throw his hat into the ring to become King of England. His father hadn't been wrong about the merits of the idea, even if in the end David had taken up the crown because he'd been asked to do so by the people themselves, as well as the English barons. Because of that history, and the way the idea seemed to have inevitability around it, he didn't immediately dismiss his father's suggestion as his gut wanted him to.

"I can see why you would see my reluctance as a mistake," David said, choosing his words carefully. "Callum said as much yesterday. If I'd stepped up, maybe Ireland could have been farther along towards peace by now."

"I wouldn't go that far," Dad said. "I didn't mean to imply that you should have put in a bid for the throne before now. Only that now does seem to be the time."

"You're telling me to fish or cut bait?" David waved a hand, not so much dismissively as in acknowledgement of that truth. "You're right that I'm here now, but I have no army, and without one, any idea of becoming High King is moot."

"So we need to come up with an army." His father lifted his chin to point to where Callum was talking to the others. "Delineating our allies is a good start."

David laughed. "Yeah. If we have any."

"You know already that you don't need any barons on your side to win, right? You have the people."

"The barons have all the power in Ireland."

His father scoffed. "What have you taught me? Those who govern do so because the governed allow it. If the people rise up, they outnumber those who rule them by a thousand to one. Those people are your people."

"You want me to lead farmers into battle?" David would never mock his father, but he was incredulous.

"This is Ireland, Dafydd. Every man in Ireland knows how to fight."

"Like the minutemen. Hmm." David pursed his lips.

"Minutemen?"

David lifted a hand. "Back in Avalon, during the Revolutionary War, the men in Massachusetts, though farmers and merchants, formed themselves into military units. They were called minutemen because they were supposed to be ready in a minute. They trained and drilled, and when the English soldiers came, they all fought. Thousands of them." He tipped his head. "They won too."

"Much like every Welsh farmer knows how to use a bow or a spear."

"Exactly. We learned because we had to. Honestly, I need to do better in England. It's been so long since we were invaded, not enough people are taking training seriously anymore." He took in a breath, searching for the elusive resolve, and swung back around to the table. "Right. We need a list of our known allies, their lands, and their forces. We'll start with them."

Abbot John gestured to his map. "I was just saying that the list of men who fell is our starting point, even among the Irish, though that isn't something I would have thought I'd ever suggest."

Mom canted her head. "Do you have any Irish monks here?"

The abbot suddenly looked far more cheerful. "Though we were founded by an Irish lord, before I became abbot five years ago,

Irish novitiates were discouraged. I changed that policy. We've grown from having a handful of Irish monks, mostly elderly, to nearly one-third Irish."

"What made you change the policy?" David said.

Now Abbot John appeared almost abashed. "I dreamt that I should." He spread his hands wide. "We are all God's children, are we not?"

Dad's eyes gleamed, and David bent his head in a sign of respect. "I have always thought so." He clapped his hands together. "As it is, I'm glad you did, because we are going to need every one of your monks who can travel."

"But—" Abbot John stared at him. "Many have never left the monastery!"

"I know, and I leave it up to you whom you choose, but Ireland needs every man you can send."

"Send where?"

"You intend to raise the countryside?" Callum stepped closer. "You have to be sure this is what you want, and that you have the stomach to follow through. There's no going back after this."

The two men stood only a foot apart. Callum hadn't spoken angrily, just intensely and, as always, David respected him for it.

"I have been thinking about what you said to me back at Trim." He lifted one shoulder. "Whether or not I'm completely comfortable with the power, I do know that I must stop what is happening here. If taking hold of the reins of Ireland is the only way to do that, then that is what I will do. Afterwards maybe we can find a solution like the one you found for Scotland. Power can be given up, but first it must be taken up."

"Yes, my lord." Callum bowed. When he straightened, his look encompassed everyone. "So, we send out the monks—and ourselves, I presume. Where should I tell everyone to meet you?"

David hesitated, and then his mother touched his arm. "Do you remember what you've read about Alfred the Great?" Then she went on without waiting for him to tell her that he apparently didn't remember enough. "The Danes had sacked Winchester, and he'd lost everything, his crown included. Rather than fleeing to France, he regrouped and called for his people to meet him at Egbert's Stone, named for St. Egbert, an Anglo-Saxon monk from Northumbria. It means little to us, but it meant everything to them."

"So what would you suggest?" David said.

"You're claiming the High Kingship, right? Then everyone should come to Tara. That's hardly three miles from here."

David looked at the others. "Is five days from now enough time?"

Dad snorted. "We need men now. Even a one-day delay will give these rebels time to consolidate some of their holdings."

"Our allies must be discreet too," Mom said. "We can't let our enemies know we are regrouping before we're ready."

"Tara is within the Pale, sire," Abbot John said, using David's title for the first time. "Some of the Irish armies will be reluctant to cross the Boyne River."

"The fact that I'm inviting them to do so, fully armed, will send exactly the right message. I'm telling them that I see no difference between Gaelic Ireland and English Ireland. All are welcome, and as High King, that is how I will rule." The words rang out throughout the room before David realized he'd raised his voice.

Dad nodded. "That is the message we will carry to every corner of Ireland." He looked at Abbot John. "Gather your brothers. We must all leave within the hour."

19

Kells

Christopher

"Give me a good road and a car, and I could be there by noon," Christopher said under his breath.

Sadly, neither car nor road were to be found and, as horseflesh went (in the techno-speak of the Middle Ages), the horses they'd bought at the tavern were nothing to write home about. They'd needed four and could buy only two, and though the horses were large, docile, and used to being ridden, they weren't going to win any races. Perhaps that was just as well, since they were both going to have to carry two.

At first they didn't ride them at all because riding horses was a good way to draw attention to themselves, especially for strangers in a village, even a community that sat at a major crossroads like Kells did. They'd come into the town on foot and hardly encountered anyone initially, so Christopher hoped that their anonymity could continue long enough for them to get out of the village unseen and unscathed.

Though the innkeeper had been pleased to take their silver for horses, food, and dry clothes, he'd only reluctantly loaned them one of his stable boys to show them a back route out of the village. The stable boy, though English, wasn't the man who'd told them about Trim, and he spoke a version of the language that was so accented that half the time Christopher had no clue as to what he was saying. The boy did seem to know where he was going, however, in that he was leading them through a small wood that grew close to the edge of the village and seemed to be taking them to a path that led to the main road west out of Kells. Christopher could see the road through the gap in the trees up ahead.

Typically Aine, who was walking just in front of Christopher, had overheard his wistful comment. She slowed to let him come abreast. "What do you mean by that?"

He shook his head. "It isn't important."

"It was important enough for you to say it," she said.

He let out a breath, knowing he shouldn't have said anything at all. "I was thinking of home."

"You're speaking of Avalon," she said with assurance in her voice, "not England."

"Yes. I don't know if you've heard about the vehicles we have there, but they're like carriages, and they run on burning naphtha, without the need for a horse to pull them."

Aine pursed her lips for a second. "That sounds like a singularly unpleasant experience."

He laughed. "That would have more to do with the fact that I explained it badly than because it is. The difference is that inside the vehicle, you're protected from the weather, and most roads are so smooth, you're hardly jarred at all. Someday, if I get the chance, I'll show you my car, which is back in England. There's no real place to drive it, because the roads aren't smooth enough, but maybe you would change your mind about how unpleasant it is." *Man, he'd loved that car.*

They were interrupted by the sound of hooves on the road ahead. Christopher could see more questions on the tip of Aine's tongue, but she didn't ask them, and he put out a hand to the others, in case they hadn't heard the sound over the noise of the rain on the leaves and the wind in the trees. The stable boy, who was several paces ahead of the group, looked back questioningly.

Christopher led his horse behind a large bush and motioned that William should do the same, so the animals were screened from the road.

"Do you think we've got trouble?" Huw spoke low in Christopher's ear.

"I don't know." He handed the reins to Aine and hustled forward towards the road. As David said fairly often, knowing was better than not knowing pretty much a hundred percent of the time.

He reached a stone wall, overgrown with vines, and crouched behind it with the stable boy, who'd gotten there just ahead of him. They were under a large oak tree, exactly like those at home, which sheltered them from the rain.

He pushed back his hood so he could hear better. "It sounds like a lot of horses."

"Yes," the stable boy said, the one word Christopher could understand, as it seemed to be the same in any version of English.

The drumming on the road grew louder, and Christopher rose from his crouch to look over the wall in time to see what was coming. He was standing on a natural rise, so he found himself looking down on a formidable company, with both cavalry and footmen. They were heading into Kells from the west, the road Christopher had hoped to travel on going the other way, towards Roscommon. Banners bobbed above the men's heads, but Christopher didn't recognize the crest on any of them.

Having abandoned the horse to William, Aine appeared beside Christopher and looked over his shoulder at the riders. At the sight of them, she gasped and recoiled. "It's my brother, Matha."

Christopher's heart sank. "He shouldn't be here, should he?"

"No!" The pain in her voice was clear. "How is it that my brother rides openly into Cusack's stronghold?"

Christopher hated to ask, given what was at stake, but he had to know. "What's his story? Has he been at odds with your father lately?"

"I wouldn't have said so." She gave a quick shake of her head. "But then, if Matha intended to betray our father, he would have made sure we didn't question his loyalty."

There was already a rock in Christopher's stomach at the scale of what they were facing, but now it grew bigger and colder for her sake. They would all be lucky to get out of Ireland in one piece.

Huw arrived at the wall. "All the more reason to leave this area, don't you think?"

Christopher glanced back to see William's white face and shock of blond hair poking around the bush. He'd been left with both horses—undoubtedly against his will. Christopher reminded himself that William had just discovered his uncle had been murdered, and that Christopher should give him a break. He jerked his head, indicating that everyone should return to deeper cover.

Once at William's side, he related to William and Huw who it was that had come. "We'll wait until the last of the column passes, and then we'll head west to Roscommon Castle as we planned."

"We cannot! Christopher, you must see that we cannot," William said. "If Matha O'Reilly is with the rebels, too much has gone wrong, and we can't trust any of these Irish lords."

"But—" That was Aine, naturally rising to her countrymen's defense.

William shook his head at her, almost pleadingly. "Riding west is the wrong choice. I'm ready to admit that Trim was the right place to go earlier, but I'm more convinced than ever that now we should go to my aunt at Castle Roche. She has men loyal to her. She will be an ally for David, and right now she doesn't know that she needs to be."

"We will never get there," Aine said. "The lands between here and there are held against us."

"The same could be said of where you want to go," William said. "Nobody knows which side I'm on, do they? I'm a nobleman. I can travel through the Pale most of the way there, and you all would be safe with me. Please."

Aine looked like she was about to cry. "I can't."

Christopher hated the idea of splitting up again, but William was looking more determined than usual, which was saying something, and Christopher didn't have the authority to tell either him or Aine what to do. "I can agree that finding two allies instead of one might be worth the risk." He took in a breath. "Do you know the way to Castle Roche, William?"

"I've been there before." William swallowed hard and blinked away the wetness that had come into his eyes.

Christopher's tone softened, though perhaps gentle understanding was not what William needed right now if he was going to hold it together. "Where exactly is it?"

"It's a few miles to the northwest of Dundalk, so some thirty miles from here."

Aine looked at Christopher. "Less than I have to ride to Roscommon."

"But possibly more dangerous," Christopher said. "We *know* there's a war going on between here and there."

"As I said, nobody will bother me. And I won't be riding." William handed the reins of his horse to Aine. "Where I'm going, there will be opportunity to purchase a horse, and I'll be just one man."

Christopher pressed his lips together and looked at Huw, who sighed. "Two."

Now that he had the destination he wanted, William no longer looked mutinous, and he nodded. "Okay. Two." His attention went again to Aine. "Please come with me."

"I can't," Aine said again.

William looked at Christopher, who lifted one shoulder. "I'll keep her safe."

There wasn't really anything left to say after that, and Christopher genuinely wasn't sorry to think that William might achieve as much by going to Castle Roche as he and Aine might by riding to Roscommon. As business-like as possible, Christopher sent the stable boy home, and the four of them pooled their few valuables and provisions, splitting all but the money evenly. Christopher and Aine were taking both horses, so William needed enough to buy two more if he came upon them. Plus, William and Huw would be traveling through predominantly English territory, where cash for services was more normal. They'd have to pay for food and shelter. For Aine and Christopher, Irish hospitality was supposed to be like Welsh—sacred once given. Aine assured him that they wouldn't starve.

Christopher was so worried about his friends, however, that he took Huw aside before they set off in opposite directions. "Sorry about this."

"It's okay." Huw sucked on his upper teeth, his eyes surveying the road back through Kells. Matha's company was no longer visible, having disappeared through the castle gateway, effectively answering whatever lingering questions Christopher might have had about their allegiance. "I don't envy your road any more than you envy mine."

"I'm worried that William is going to lead you into a situation you can't get out of."

Huw tipped his head. "He is less reckless than he once was. And he may be right about his aunt. His cousin will be the heir. How old is he?"

"Seventeen, with a sixteen-year-old younger brother." Christopher knew this only because William had spoken of them several times in the last few weeks.

Huw grunted. "Within Norman society, no matter how talented, a seventeen-year-old won't be viewed as a leader. If William's uncle is really dead, his aunt will need William, if not to lead her army, then to be her advocate to the eventual victors."

Christopher desperately wanted that victor to be David, but things weren't looking too good for him right now. While Huw went through the pack one more time, Christopher walked back to William, who'd just boosted Aine onto her horse. "You're a brave man."

It was both the best and the worst thing he could have said, because it made William swallow hard again. Still, he stuck out his hand to Christopher. "Take care of her."

"I told you I would." Christopher shook his friend's forearm. "If you see David, tell him where we've gone."

William managed a laugh. "That won't be an easy conversation."

"If O'Connor doesn't throw in with us, then the country may really be lost. It's worth finding out how much that's worth to him."

William studied Christopher for a moment. "I'm almost jealous."

Christopher frowned, realizing how dense he'd been not to see that William was interested in Aine. He shouldn't have been surprised, given how pretty and smart she was. "You can still come with us."

William dismissed the idea with a gesture. "I know, but I don't mean that. You're already the Hero of Westminster. If the O'Connors bring Connaught marching to David's defense, you'll be the Hero of Ireland too."

Christopher scoffed. "It's equally likely that I'll end up dead."

William raised his eyebrows. "And that's why you'll deserve it." Before Christopher could marshal an adequate response, William put his heels together and bowed. Then he lifted a hand to Aine and set off down the trail.

Huw followed, commenting as he passed Christopher, "Good luck, my lord. We're all going to need it."

Christopher couldn't disagree. Truthfully, he didn't think any place in Ireland was safe right now for any of them.

20

Within the Pale
Llywelyn

"Were we right to separate?" Meg asked her husband. Before setting out in their respective directions, Llywelyn and Dafydd had ridden close enough to Trim to see Dafydd's flag still flying from the castle's towers and Comyn's men set up around it, out of bowshot of the walls. To know that their men held Trim caused a rush of emotion in Llywelyn as if he'd just sunk into a warm bath. His hands had shaken for a moment—in relief and pride. While they couldn't get in and their men couldn't get out, that Trim held made Dafydd's plan all the stronger. No army could maintain a siege when an enemy came behind them, which meant that if Dafydd could gather an army, Comyn and whoever allied with him would be forced to break off the siege and come out to meet them.

"Our son knows what he's doing, and I trust Callum as much as any man."

"Callum didn't stop the violence at Trim," Meg said.

"But he planned for it, and it's because of him that we all got out alive." Llywelyn brought his horse closer to Meg's. Their guide, a monk named Robert, rode just ahead of them. The rain had let up, and now that sunset was near, a patch of blue sky was starting to form in the west where Llywelyn hadn't seen blue sky since they'd arrived in Ireland.

"What if we're wrong about the people's support? What if—"

"We're not wrong." Llywelyn gave Meg a concerned look. "You are worrying needlessly ... but even if it isn't needless, we can't do anything about it. We have enough on our trencher without borrowing trouble, as you so often say."

Meg looked down and shook her head. "I can't seem to help it. I have this—" she put her fist near her stomach and rubbed, "—ache that I can't get rid of."

Llywelyn's voice gentled. "I know, *cariad*. This is hard, but we are still in one piece ourselves, and we can't allow the deaths of all those men at Trim to go unanswered."

"I'm glad you didn't say *unavenged*."

Now it was Llywelyn's turn to shake his head. "This cannot be about revenge. Governing never can."

"Our son knows it too." Meg lifted her head and gazed into the distance. The land was green and rolling, all the way to the sea, though they weren't going that far.

"Maud de Geneville is now a widow," Llywelyn said, "and who better than we to speak with her about what has happened."

"Will she believe us? Will *she* support David? She was as loyal to Edward once upon a time as Geoffrey."

"While she was born in Dublin, she's lived much of her life in England and the March. She and I are of an age and have the same understandings about the world and how it works." He paused. "And she has resources to draw upon—resources that can help us. It is to Skryne that Geoffrey sent the bulk of Trim's garrison. That's several dozen men right there."

Maud de Geneville, formerly Maud de Lacy, was a descendant of many of the great families of England and the March. She had chosen to wait out the conference at Richard de Feypo's castle of Skryne, a stone's throw to the east of the Hill of Tara. While Dafydd had worried that Feypo might have led off his rebellion by making Maud a prisoner rather than a guest, there was a good possibility that he wouldn't have wanted to give away the game too soon. With the carnage at Trim occurring only that morning, and Feypo himself dead on the floor with a bullet in his head, a rider might not yet have been sent to Skryne.

And if one had ... well, Meg and Llywelyn were hardly a threat. Making sure that the people of Ireland—English, Danish, and Irish—were on Dafydd's side was of paramount importance. But such were the resources of Maud de Geneville—not to mention Richard's wife, Anais, the ruler of Skryne now that he was dead—that it was worth finding out if even one castle was still loyal.

Meg still had her hand pressed to her belly. Llywelyn hated that she'd been caught up in this. He had known from that first night at Criccieth when she'd attacked him with a poorly wielded knife that he wanted to spend the rest of his life protecting her. When she'd disappeared just before Dafydd's birth, his life had all but unraveled, and it hadn't been put right again until Dafydd and Anna, and then she, returned. What was a rebellion in Ireland compared to that?

"Geoffrey was one of the greatest landowners in Ireland," Llywelyn said. "I have no idea if his people loved him, but they won't want their lands to fall to someone like Comyn or—worse by their standards—an Irishman. They will fight for Dafydd if they know he's asking. The key is to ask. At this point, it doesn't matter why they fight—only that they do."

The road they were on was one of the king's roads, built shortly after the initial Norman conquest. As prescribed by law for such roads, it was wide enough for two carts to pass and drained outward, so even with the rain, the puddles were minimal. The open fields around the castle ahead of them ensured that anyone watching would know that three riders were coming towards them. The castle itself had been improved upon since Adam de Feypo had built it. No longer situated on a motte, which had been left as it was, the keep had been rebuilt in stone on level ground and was surrounded by a high stone wall.

"This is making me nervous," Meg said. "We're walking into a trap."

"It can't be a trap for us if nobody knows we're coming." Then Llywelyn put out a hand to her, in case she felt he'd spoken abruptly. "I have a good feeling about this."

Meg laughed, finally, the joyful sound ringing around them. "So often what we have is *a bad feeling about this*, so I will take you at your word." She straightened her shoulders. "We can brazen it out together, come what may."

"That's my girl." Llywelyn reached for her hand and squeezed. "We always do."

Meg was right that the long road up to the castle exposed them uncomfortably to the battlement, but they arrived at the gate unmolested, and immediately a helmeted head poked out between two merlons. "Who goes there?"

"I am Llywelyn ap Gruffydd, the King of Wales. I would ask to speak to the lady within, Maud de Geneville."

The guard, who was hardly more than a boy to Llywelyn's eyes, gasped once and then disappeared. Feet thundered on wooden steps behind the wall. Then the great double doors swung open to admit them.

But Llywelyn and Meg neither dismounted nor entered. For a moment, they looked at the guard, and he looked back at them. He was standing at the far end of the barbican and had taken off his helmet to reveal a sweaty blond head, his brows furrowed in confusion. He took a hesitant step forward. "My lord?"

"Llywelyn! What are you doing here?" Maud de Geneville's voice rang out from the bailey of the castle. At sixty years old, she still cut a striking figure, with a straight back and iron gray hair wound into a bun on the top of her head and adorned with cloth and lace in the latest style from London. Lifting up her skirts, she strode forward like a man, never mind her esteemed pedigree or that she'd been a baroness for forty years as Geoffrey's wife. She didn't stand on ceremony. Neither did she suffer fools, and she seemed to think the guard was one for not admitting Llywelyn and Meg. "Let them in!"

Llywelyn shot Meg a grin and urged his horse beneath the gatehouse. The barbican had two portcullises, and, despite his smile, when neither dropped to cage them within the barbican, he heaved a sigh of relief. With Maud coming out to greet them so heartily, he'd assumed she thought all was well, but he was glad to be certain.

He dismounted on flagstones that had been swept clean of mud since the last rainstorm ended. The bailey was huge—far larger than the size of the keep might normally have demanded—but it had to be large to enclose the modern keep plus the abandoned motte and bailey castle that had preceded it.

It took a number of long strides, but Maud reached them a few moments after Llywelyn set Meg on her feet, and then she surprised Meg with an embrace. Meg, being Meg, hugged her back.

Then Maud turned to Llywelyn, and instantly her initial bright demeanor and enthusiasm were extinguished. "What is wrong? I have felt a storm coming all day, but nobody could tell me anything, and we've had no news. You wouldn't be here if all was well."

Meg squeezed Maud's hand, and Llywelyn bent his head and spoke under his breath. "Things are very bad, Maud. That's why we have come. How loyal are these men?"

"They're my men." Maud was momentarily affronted. "Richard took the whole of his garrison off yesterday without saying why or where he was going. I didn't like it, and it was unbecoming behavior in a vassal, but I could do nothing about it. All he left me of his men were dunces like Robert." She gestured to the blond guard, who'd put on his helmet again and returned to his post. "Fortunately, I have my own men whom Geoffrey sent with me from Trim."

"That's actually the best news we've heard all day," Meg said. "How many men do you have?"

"Thirty garrison, and another twenty who aren't soldiers." She sniffed. "As you may recall, Lord Callum replaced Trim's servants and workers with *your* men."

"Can they hold Skryne?" Llywelyn said.

Again the affronted look. "Of course. But against whom?"

Meg was looking around at the walls. "You seem somewhat lightly guarded to me."

Maud waved a hand dismissively. "They're there. You just can't see them."

Llywelyn chose to take her at her word, though if he and Meg stayed, he would inspect the defenses personally. He gestured with his head towards the keep. "Can we confer alone?"

For the first time, Maud seemed to hesitate. "Of course. Follow me."

She led the way into the keep, across the hall, which was as spotless as the bailey, and up the twisting stairs to the next floor, where her private apartments lay. These must normally have belonged to Richard de Feypo.

Once inside, Meg gestured to a chair near the fire, which was burning brightly in its hearth. "Please, sit, Maud."

Maud's hands clenched into fists, and she didn't take Meg's suggestion. "He's dead, isn't he?"

Llywelyn took in a harsh breath. "There has been an insurrection. A portion of the delegates to the conference turned on the rest. I survived thanks to the quick thinking of Earl Callum. Dozens are dead." He bent his head. "Including your husband."

"Who is responsible?" Maud's voice was completely level, and she wasn't showing any emotion other than in her hands, which were now clenched so tightly they'd gone white. "Is one of them Richard?"

"Yes," Meg said. "Why would you think so?"

"He sent Anais and the children to visit her family in France." She shrugged. "I chose not to view it as a snub."

"Callum killed him," Llywelyn said.

"Good!" She began to pace as Llywelyn related who was involved and who was dead.

When he finished, Maud turned away, her fist to her lips, and gazed at the fire. Llywelyn and Meg let the silence lengthen, and when Maud still did not speak, Llywelyn said, "We have a plan—Dafydd has a plan—and he would like your help implementing it."

Maud held the silence through another count of five, and then she turned back to face them. Tears lay on her cheeks, but they fell silently, and she wiped at them with the backs of her hands. "Whatever I can do."

"If your men are truly loyal, then Dafydd asks that you prepare them for war. This castle must be held, and with such a large bailey, we can house any additional recruits when they arrive. He has asked that every man able to wield a weapon join the fight."

Maud bobbed her head in curt agreement. "Of course. I will speak to my men at once." And without further ado, she opened the door to her apartments and descended to the great hall. By the time Meg and Llywelyn followed, she had announced that she wanted everyone to gather, servants and soldiers alike. Some of them were, as Maud had said, Richard de Feypo's people, and Llywelyn found his eyes moving from face to face, looking for the one or two who already knew the news and thus couldn't be trusted.

It took a quarter of an hour for the meeting to begin, and all the while Maud stood unmoving in front of the dais, watching the people come in, greet her, and then take their places at the tables. Even if they entered speaking to one another, the moment they laid eyes on her, they fell silent, and it was a grave group of a hundred or more that gazed up at her, holding their breath and waiting for her to speak.

By now they knew that something was very wrong, and Maud didn't make them wait any longer to hear it. "I have gathered you here today to speak to you of war. David, King of England, Lord of Ireland, and your liege lord, has called us to battle."

A whisper swept through the hall and was immediately silenced by a raised hand from Maud.

"A treasonous alliance was formed among a number of lords all across Ireland, from Dublin to Connaught. These turned on the rest of the justiciars at Trim and killed them. Both Geoffrey, my husband, and Richard, your lord, are dead."

Meg's eyes found the floor, and Llywelyn held his clasped hands before his mouth. Maud had just implied that Richard had not been one of the traitors. Llywelyn's impulse was to expose the lie, but he did not. The truth could wait. Maud was right that what Dafydd needed were people prepared to fight, not ones suffering from conflicting loyalties.

Maud had just put into words the cold truth: civil war had come to Ireland.

21

Navan

William

Almost immediately after parting from Christopher and Aine, William began to regret not so much the decision itself, but that he hadn't done more to persuade Aine to come to Castle Roche. She had no business wandering the countryside with only Christopher to protect her. In the last day, Christopher had proved himself capable, but ever since James had left, things had gone awry. Nothing about the next few hours made him feel any better about it either.

Admittedly, at first they'd made good time on foot, following the same track the stable boy had led them along, but going the other way and eventually reaching the road on the far side of Kells by which they'd come in. William and Huw had hiked along well all the way to Navan, a good eight miles, which had taken them over two hours.

Now, however, he was looking at yet another inn and finding himself missing Christopher's perspective. At Kells, they'd marched right in and demanded service. He was tempted to do the same here, but it wasn't morning anymore, and it was hours now since Trim had fallen.

"Are we going or not?" Huw said from William's right shoulder.

"I don't know. What do you think?"

Huw paused, probably surprised that William had asked him. Honestly, it wasn't that William didn't respect Huw's opinion. He knew that Huw had been a charter member in the now-defunct Order of the Pendragon, and that he'd been instrumental in rescuing Queen Lili from Westminster last year.

But for all that William had been David's squire for many years, Huw still didn't trust him. William blamed himself for the presence of Gilbert de Clare in David's company, and he was pretty sure that Huw not only blamed William for that, but distrusted him for falling ill at Dover and not traveling to France with David last year. Of course, if William had gone, he would have been killed along with everyone else. Nobody had ever accused the Welsh of being logical, however, and Huw was nothing if not Welsh.

"I don't trust anyone here," Huw said, entirely proving William's point.

Huw's doubt also decided William, and he straightened from his hiding place at the edge of one of the houses on the other side of the road from the inn and set off towards it. Huw followed, not protesting, but William could feel his disapproval hanging over him like a cloud.

"We need food and drink. More importantly, we need to buy horses if we're going to get anywhere at all. Much more walking, and I will wear right through the soles of my boots."

Huw grunted, for once agreeing, if not outright. "Let me go in first."

William acquiesced to that, waiting in the doorway while Huw stood in front of him and surveyed the room. After a moment, Huw took a step forward, and William followed. Several men sat in the common room, nursing cups of beer and eating trenchers of bread, cheese, and onions. William's mouth watered, and he happily went with Huw to the bar.

"May I help you, my lord?" The innkeeper ducked his head, recognizing a lord when he saw one and correctly deducing that Huw was William's inferior. Huw also leaned his bow against the edge of the table, and its length marked him not only as a foreigner, but as a Welshman.

William put a single coin on the table between them. "Food and drink. The best you have." Then, after a moment, he added, "Please." Christopher really was rubbing off on him. William's father would have left it as a demand.

The man tugged his forelock. "Yes, sir. Perhaps you'd like to step into the parlor?"

William hesitated, tempted to hide himself from the villagers in the common room, but he decided that he didn't want to separate himself from Huw. "We will eat here."

The innkeeper pulled two large cups of beer, and Huw carried them to a table near the fire. The warmth spread across William, and he dropped his head for a moment, longing to lay it down on his arms right then and there and sleep. Instead, Huw nudged one of the cups towards William, and he picked it up and drank down half of it in one go. Huw did the same.

Brighter-eyed, they welcomed the food the innkeeper brought a moment later and set to.

"I have never tasted anything so good in my life," Huw said, as the last of the bread and cheese disappeared down his throat.

"Nor I." William's spirits had risen considerably, and he told himself to remember how he felt before walking into the inn compared to how he felt now. *An army marches on its stomach* was something David had said to him more than once. And so, apparently, did William himself.

"Horses." Huw stood and headed past the bar to the back door.

William drained the last of his drink and followed.

Which turned out to be absolutely the worst thing he could have done.

"You there!"

William had taken two steps into the yard when the shout came from the front gate where a man stood near his horse, talking to the proprietor. It was the only way out of the yard, which otherwise had a high wooden fence all the way around it.

"He's David's squire!"

Huw had stopped at the man's initial shout, but now he returned to William in two strides, grabbed William's arm, and spun him around to head back through the door to the inn through which William had just come.

Unfortunately, two men-at-arms, who did not look friendly, were already there, blocking the way, and two heartbeats later, the yard was full of men just like them.

"Well, well." From out of the stables strolled a tall man with a sword belted at his waist. "If it isn't William de Bohun, David's pet."

William filled himself with all the dignity he could muster. "What is it to you?"

The man sneered. "It seems we're about the same business you are—looking for horses. Too bad we got here first." He lifted his chin to point to the two men behind William and Huw. "Bind their hands. They can join Matha's father at Drogheda."

22

Beyond the Pale
Christopher

Now that Christopher and Aine were alone and both on horseback, they could travel more quickly. These horses weren't going to set any speed records, and Christopher had never expected to make this journey at a gallop like David had across France, but at least they could move at a canter some of the time.

"When we meet someone, what are you going to say about me?" Christopher asked Aine. "I don't know much, but I do know that you and I shouldn't be traveling together without a chaperone." He swallowed hard. "Sorry about that."

She looked him up and down. "You look Irish and could easily be my cousin. Nobody will ask." And then she tipped her head. "And if they do, I will tell the truth. You are Christopher of Westminster."

"Do you think that's smart? Bad enough that I'm English, but it will tie me to David."

Aine directed a disparaging tsk at him. "Haven't you learned by now that your cousin is admired here? And even were that not true, I assure you that every Irishman hated Gilbert de Clare more."

"We're also bringing news of the massacre at Trim. Nobody will love us for that."

"But again, we're bringing the news. They will admire a Saxon of your stature who is willing to ride through Ireland without a guard."

Aine spoke so unconcernedly that Christopher didn't know how to reply. Still, he wasn't going to suggest that they say anything different either, and they were moving along pretty nicely at the moment as they were. They'd already come ten miles. Admittedly, it was late afternoon by now, but since it wasn't raining, they could ride into the evening and night. With luck, they could reach the castle by midnight, if not sooner.

Of course, luck had been in short supply up until now—and that proved to be the case again.

"I hear hooves!" Aine said.

They'd been riding through mixed farmland and pastureland, and up until now they'd seen a few farmers and homesteads, but nothing that would cause them to panic. The stone wall to Christopher's left was shoulder height to keep in the livestock, and when a side path appeared ten yards in front of him, Christopher didn't hesitate to veer down it.

He didn't keep going, however, not wanting to add a single extra yard to their journey if he didn't have to. Instead, he reined in and turned the horse back the way they'd come. Aine had followed him down the path, and he dismounted, tossed the reins to her, and dashed back to the intersection. The hoof beats grew louder. Now that they were closer, he realized that they belonged to a single horse.

Aine had remained standing uncertainly in the path, and he motioned that she should wait where she was, out of sight of the intersecting road thanks to the stone wall and trees that lined it. He himself crept as close to the corner as he could, pressed his right shoulder into the wall, and crouched so that his head didn't stick up above the wall and the rider couldn't see him. Then he waited.

Thirty seconds later, the rider flashed past at a gallop. Christopher straightened and stepped into the middle of the road to watch the rider disappear off to the right where the road Y'ed. The undyed white robe flapping behind him was unmistakably churchy.

"Was that a monk?" Aine said.

"Could be he was a Templar," Christopher said.

She shook her head. "We have few Templars here and even fewer who are Irish. Templars are brave, it's true, but he rides alone, which Templars never do."

Christopher chose not to contradict her, since the occasion of David's ride through France and England had been unprecedented—and it was true that he hadn't ridden alone. "Whoever it was, his mission looks urgent."

"I have never seen a monk ride like that," Aine said, "and I can think of only one piece of news that could be so important that an abbot might send out riders. He's bringing news of Trim."

Christopher nodded and returned to his horse. "He went right. Are we going the same way?"

"Our fork is the left one."

"Good. Maybe we can still make it to Roscommon before he does."

23

Beyond the Pale

James

The farthest journey had fallen to Robbie and James, who had the unfortunate task of bringing the news of the death of James's brother-in-law, the Earl of Ulster, to Richard's wife and sister at Carrickfergus, a hundred miles away. First, however, they had to stop at the Verdun castle of Roche and tell Margery, William de Bohun's aunt, that she was now a widow.

The unpleasantness of the task had James recalling a conversation he'd overheard between David and Christopher not long ago, where they'd been reciting quotes to each other from a pageant called *The Princess Bride,* which was apparently popular enough in Avalon that they both knew it well. Christopher had told his cousin that life and pain were inextricably intertwined, and not to believe anyone who told a man differently. Or something like that.

David had laughed and replied with another quote, which James couldn't recall at the moment. James had been struck by the laughter and the idea that anyone wouldn't know that life was pain. Though the Church insisted that pain only made the moments of joy all the more remarkable and that redemption lay in the next life, he was having a hard time convincing himself of it today. He hadn't known his brother-in-law well, but he'd liked him, and he already missed him. It would be much worse for Gilles, who'd truly loved Richard.

Unfortunately, so far, he and Robbie hadn't made nearly as much progress as James would have liked. From Bective Abbey, they'd taken the road to Navan and turned northeast from there, but their passage through the town had been hampered by the occupation of the road by a combined Irish and English force—mostly cavalry, but some on foot too. The Cusack rag flew next to the O'Reilly bleeding hand, one of the more ominous banners James had ever seen. He would have hoped that the company was bound for Drogheda to rescue Gilla, but their general high spirits denied that presumption and didn't inspire confidence. James and Robbie made sure to keep their distance.

"All of Ireland is on the move and not in a good way," Robbie said.

"You learned that phrase from Christopher," James said, "but to mimic him too, since our army cannot yet be mobilized, the only reason for such great numbers of men marching through the countryside has to be because they are *up to no good*."

Robbie laughed. "I would never have thought the word *good* could have quite so many uses."

James shook his head, laughing too, despite the urgency of the moment. In their short acquaintance, Christopher's vocabulary had had a greater impact on James than David's—not so much in his use of complicated words, at which David excelled, but at Christopher's constantly inventive turn of phrase. Though to hear him tell it, everyone in Avalon spoke that way. Someday, in a quiet moment, James would have to take up the issue with Callum to confirm Christopher's assertion.

"They do seem to be heading east." Robbie was frowning. "I don't understand the O'Reilly banner unless someone in the clan has turned against Gilla."

"Is that so surprising?" James had come to the same conclusion himself: one of the O'Reillys had betrayed Gilla, and he'd joined with Cusack to do it. "It happened at Trim. It's happening all across Ireland."

"I suppose it's no less than one would expect among the nobility of Scotland," Robbie said. "Brothers betray brothers at home as a matter of course."

James eyed his young charge. "We can hope that Padraig never betrays King David in that way."

Robbie shivered. "Don't speak of it." He was still frowning. "I don't understand why the English never suffer so."

James scoffed. "Wasn't one of the Bastard's sons killed in a hunting accident with his brother? The English just hide their animosity better. And, truth be told, few kings have had more than one son *to* inherit. The Welsh have suffered the most because they make the mistake of giving a bastard the same chance as a legitimate son."

From Navan, they managed to avoid the enemy soldiers by cutting across fields and taking side tracks that kept the main road in sight but made it less likely that anybody would wonder what they were doing. Then, at Slane, they encountered the same army again, having apparently been riding parallel to them all afternoon and making no better time. Robbie and James managed to cut across the road ahead of them, finally turning north towards Castle Roche.

Their escape was made easier by the fact that the company included prisoners, who were bound at the wrists and forced to run behind the horses. James couldn't see the prisoners' faces from this distance, but he told himself that whoever they were, he and Robbie could best help them by completing the task David had given them.

From Slane, the road remained clear. Because they were obviously two knights, few were going to trouble them. James was relieved to see no more armies on the march, and they arrived at Castle Roche several hours after sunset. The castle, as befitted its French name, was perched on a rock that gave it commanding views of the surrounding countryside. The Irish called it something else: *Dún am Gall*, fort of the foreigner.

James had resolved to deliver his news and then continue on his way north, no matter how tired he was and how much both he and Robbie needed sleep. But from the moment they set foot inside Castle Roche, he realized that he would have to change his plans. The whole castle was in an uproar because Margery de Verdun was in the midst of labor to deliver a child. Thus, James had no choice but to give the news of their father's death directly to her two eldest sons, John and Theobald.

Few tasks had ever been as difficult. John brought James and Robbie into the receiving room of the castle, just off the great hall. Castle Roche had been built on a grand scale. A curtain wall enclosed an enormous bailey in front of the castle, which then required visitors to cross a ditch to reach the two D-shaped towers that guarded the inner ward. It wasn't Trim, but from its hill, it more than adequately guarded the South Armagh pass between Gaelic Ulster and English-controlled lands. According to James's wife, a not-so-secret tunnel lay underneath the castle that led to an outpost tower.

None of which was of the least concern right now to the white-faced boys who stared back at James, having learned that their world had crashed down around their ears. Six younger brothers sat at the table with John and Theobald to hear the news, and the youngest, a boy of four, burst into tears.

John pulled him into his lap, but he didn't calm him with platitudes. He simply held him while the boy sobbed into his chest. Then a servant entered the room with wine and food, placing the dishes between James and John, who sat at the head of the table in what had been his father's chair. While she laid out the dishes, effectively giving John a chance to collect himself, James took stock of his surroundings. As he would have expected from the sister of Humphrey de Bohun, everything at Roche was tidy, the men well-behaved for the most part, and fresh rush mats had been laid on the floor with the departure of winter.

As the servant left, John drew in a breath. "Tell me that David has a plan."

James bent his head. "He does."

In one of those unfortunate twists of fate, John was thin and pale, while his younger brother, Theobald, was far more robust and clearly the warrior in the family. He wasn't the thinker, however, and after a quick assessment of what he was dealing with, James added, "King David has confirmed you in your holdings and asks that you muster your men and march to the Hill of Tara."

John leaned forward slightly, though he was hampered in his movements by the presence of his little brother on his lap. "David intends to claim the High Kingship?"

"He has claimed it."

John sat back. "Good. It's about time."

Theobald finally spoke, and true to his calling, his words were belligerent. "Why should we believe any of this? Perhaps you conspire with the men who killed our father, and once we march away, you will take our castle!"

That he wouldn't be believed had not occurred to James. Margery would have believed him, but these two didn't know who he was, not really. "I assure you, that's the farthest thing from my mind. My brother-in-law died too, you know."

"Perhaps you killed him! You're married to his sister. With him gone, you could rule Ulster!"

John put out a hand to his brother. "Quiet, Theobald. James is the Steward of Scotland and trusted by David. I heard Father speak of it."

To James surprise, Theobald subsided, though he still looked mutinous. Robbie had set to his food with enthusiasm, but he stopped chewing and said, "I was at Trim when it happened. Men died, and if we are not to lose Ireland entirely, then you need to act."

"We are safe behind these walls," Theobald said.

"You are not wrong," James said as mildly as he could, "but if you are to remain safe, you will need allies. King David is offering himself. Do you truly wish to deny him?"

"We do not," John said, though his eyes were on Theobald, who pushed to his feet and began to pace before the fire. It had been a long time since James himself had had that kind of restless energy, but he remembered it—that feeling that if he didn't move, he would jump right out of his skin.

John watched him for a moment, and then he turned back to James and Robbie. He had more color in his face now, but his eyes had aged ten years since he'd learned of his father's death. His gaze was steady, however. "My father instructed me on what to do if we were attacked in his absence. Theobald is better with a sword than I am, but we are both ready. I would be grateful if you could stay to assist us in preparing to march."

It was no less than James had expected, once he'd learned of Margery's confinement, but he was nonetheless pleased that John had the wherewithal to ask for help. He wasn't a warrior, but he had a presence about him, even within the short while he'd had to absorb his new station, that was encouraging.

"We will stay. I would ask, however, that you choose two among your men to send to my wife at Carrickfergus. She needs to know of her brother's death and be prepared for a fight—if that castle isn't already under siege." James's stomach twisted sickeningly at the thought of what could be happening at Carrickfergus. But he couldn't in good conscience leave these two boys to their own devices either.

"If our enemies had planned better, they would have sent armies to the home castles of every man they intended to kill," John said. "I would have let them in, not knowing their intent."

"On our way here, we saw a combined O'Reilly/Cusack cavalry riding through Navan and then Slane," Robbie said.

"Gilla has allied with the Cusacks?" John said.

"Not Gilla," Robbie said. "It can't be Gilla. Thomas de Clare and Auliffe O'Rourke attacked his fort at Drumconrath last night, burning it to the ground and taking Gilla prisoner."

James nodded. "Most of the leaders of this rebellion were at Trim for the meeting of Parliament, which meant that they had to rely on others—captains or brothers—to marshal their men. They may have wanted to wait to ensure that Trim had fallen and their opponents were dead before acting."

John stood. "Well, we won't wait. We can act."

Theobald had been staring at the fire, but he swung around. "I will send word to all the households in the region that we muster at dawn at the castle, though we must leave some defense for my mother."

"We will, though I understand that Castle Roche is nearly impregnable and has never been taken or even assaulted," James said.

"It has not." Theobald looked again at his brother. "I suggest that you stay here."

John's chin stuck out defiantly. "No. I am the new Lord Verdun. Our father is dead, but you know our family's motto as well as I, Theobald."

"Never falter," Theobald said.

"And we shall not," John said.

24

Navan

Huw

Huw would have screamed to get their attention if it hadn't meant putting Robbie and James at risk. Letting them go—together, praise the Lord—was one of the most difficult things he'd ever done.

But seeing as how he and William were surrounded by enemies, he thought it best not to call attention to either himself or them. His own life, Huw assumed, was forfeit, but the fact that James and Robbie had found each other gave him hope that all was not entirely lost.

Like Huw, William's hands were tied in front of him, and he stumbled along behind the horses at the rear of the company. "Did you see them?"

"I did." They were speaking Welsh, which was not one of the languages commonly spoken in Ireland, and thus there was little chance they would be understood. "They're headed north."

William ground his teeth. "As we should be!"

"James knows what he's doing," Huw said soothingly, "and if Robbie is with him, that means they have a plan."

"We need one. I've been a fool."

Privately, Huw couldn't disagree, but William had admitted to being wrong—again—and Huw took heart from it. He liked William, when he wasn't grinding his teeth at his stubborn, misguided, misbegotten Marcher pride. "We took a chance, and it went against us."

They continued on foot for another hour, more exhausted than Huw had ever been in his life, and finally the captain called a halt. He arrived at Huw's side and slashed the rope that attached him to the saddle of the horse in front of him. "You don't deserve to ride, but you're too slow."

William was boosted onto a horse, and one of the O'Reillys helped Huw to mount behind him. William's chin was already on his chest, and Huw had to prod him awake when his captor offered him a flask. "Drink!"

William did, and then so did Huw, though without hands, more wine ended up on his shirt than in his mouth. He'd been stripped of his armor, arrows, and bow, of course, but at least none of them had been discarded beside the road. He could see his bow strapped to the saddle bags of Matha O'Reilly's horse.

They rode through the afternoon and evening. Eventually, it was William who roused Huw. "At least he told the truth about where we were going."

Huw lifted his chin to look. Against all odds, they'd arrived back at Drogheda. "Perhaps Aine's father really is alive."

As when Huw had been here with Christopher and the others, they were approaching the town from the west. At Navan, while the army had crossed a river that fed the Boyne, they hadn't bothered crossing the Boyne itself. Huw had thought that was because the captain had lied and later they would be turning north, but now he understood they could simply use the bridge at Drogheda, seeing as how the company was in the favor of the castellan.

Entering by the west gate, they were immediately thrown into the hubbub of a busy commercial center, not unlike portions of London or Shrewsbury. The streets were laid out in a grid pattern, so they rode straight east until taking a right onto the street that led to the bridge.

Though Comyn's ships remained moored at the dock, the riverboats were gone. Huw wished again that he could have spoken to James or Robbie, because he was desperate for more information about what was happening. Had Robbie made it to Trim? How was it that Matha O'Reilly was marching with men who served Cusack, unless he had betrayed his father and sister? Betraying a father Huw could understand, though he got on well with his own. But risking a sister's life or wellbeing? That was unforgivable.

They crossed the bridge, traversed the smaller half of the town of Drogheda, and then entered Drogheda Castle by the main gate. Huw didn't have much of a chance to look around, just a quick glance amidst the flurry of dismounting soldiers. His right leg was crushed between an adjacent horse and his own, but since his hands were tied, he could do little but kick out with his foot. A man with an air of authority walked down the steps that led from the keep to greet the leader of the Cusack party, who apparently wasn't Cusack himself.

Meanwhile, Matha O'Reilly shooed away the other horses around Huw and William and said in a commanding voice, "Off!"

William had been riding in front of Huw, so he obeyed first, swinging his leg over the horse's head and dropping elegantly to the ground. The angle was wrong for Huw to attempt that move, even if he had been skilled enough to do it (which he wasn't), so he leaned forward awkwardly, his foot still in the stirrup, and swung his leg over the back of the horse.

Once they were on the ground, Matha O'Reilly grasped the back of Huw's neck with one hand and William's with the other and pushed them forward, past the men-at-arms and knights who filled the bailey, and fetched up in front of the keep.

The man on the bottom step frowned at Matha's approach. "The last thing we need is more prisoners, Matha."

"Lord Butler." Matha bowed and then straightened. "We picked them up on the road. They are known companions to David. We thought they might be useful."

Huw's heart sank as Matha named the man they faced. Here was the youngest Butler son, Thomas, turning against his brothers as surely as Cain had murdered Abel.

Thomas sneered. "Put him with your father. He's in the corner tower." He pointed with his chin to indicate a tower near the gatehouse. "Give him my regards."

"I will do that." With his hands still gripping their necks, Matha turned Huw and William in the direction Thomas had indicated, and the three of them slogged through the muddy bailey. At one point Huw stumbled on an unseen stone, finding his legs were so tired they were barely functioning, and Matha hauled him upright.

The tower where they were to be imprisoned was located where the town wall met the castle wall, and thus it overlooked the town, the castle, and the exterior ditch that was the town's first layer of defense.

Castle prison cells came in all sizes and locations. The two usual choices were to put prisoners in a tower basement, accessed by a trap door, or in a tower room too high above the ground to get out.

To Huw's great relief, this tower did not have a basement, perhaps because, with the river nearby, the groundwater level was too high. They entered straight into the guardroom, where two men lounged, leaning back in their chairs with their feet on a table.

Matha looked at them disdainfully, but he didn't berate them for their lack of discipline. These men were not Irish, so they wouldn't have listened to Matha anyway. Two of Matha's own men had entered the guardroom after Matha, Huw, and William, and with a gesture, Matha directed them to stand guard on either side of the door. In French, he asked one of the tower guards for the key to Gilla's room, which he was given.

Then he urged William and Huw up the stairs in front of him. Many circuits around the tower later, having bypassed the second and third floors, they arrived at the top of the tower, which was well above the level of the curtain wall and a good seventy feet above the ground outside. Huw had been keeping track of their progress through the arrow slits.

No guard sat outside Gilla O'Reilly's room. Matha grunted, seemingly disapproving, and went to the only door. A window with three iron bars allowed Huw to see through the door to a man standing at a window, looking outward.

Matha put a key into the lock. "Athair." Pronounced *ah-her,* it was Gaelic for *father*, one of the words Huw knew. David said Gaelic and Welsh had the same roots, but they were so unalike, Huw didn't know if he believed him.

At their entrance, the man, who had to be Gilla O'Reilly, swung around. Seeing who it was, he strode towards Matha, speaking rapidly in Gaelic. Matha answered, and then to Huw's utter astonishment, the two men embraced.

Frustrated that he didn't understand what they'd said, but thinking that things were looking up, Huw made an attention-getting gesture with his conjoined hands.

Matha waved at Huw and William and said in French. "They are friends."

Gilla looked them up and down, though he soon returned his attention to Matha, and Huw wasn't sure he had really taken in much about Huw or William. "What is happening? Nobody will tell me anything."

"Are you aware of the massacre at Trim?" At Gilla's curt nod, Matha continued, "While many are dead, David's men overcame Feypo's, and King Llywelyn and David escaped. The castle, however, remains besieged by a combined force of Cusack's and Red Comyn's men."

"So that's what Comyn was here for." Gilla clenched his right hand into a fist and slapped it into his left. "You could have warned me that Clare and O'Rourke were coming to Drumconrath."

"I'm sorry. I didn't know." Matha looked intently at his father. "Besides which, we agreed that I would do nothing to betray my true allegiance."

Gilla grunted his assent. "I just didn't expect them to burn Drumconrath to the ground."

Matha's face fell, turning first white and then gray. "Where's Aine?"

Gilla put out a hand to his son. "She was alive last I saw, though in the company of Christopher of Westminster. I can only pray that she still lives, but I can tell you no more than that."

"Christoph—" Matha's mouth dropped open, and he seemed unable to speak.

Huw would have interrupted right then and there to tell them of Aine, but Gilla spoke again before he could. "The story is too long to tell. How are you planning on freeing me?"

"My men are ready to turn on Butler's and Cusack's men. At midnight, someone will let the three of you out."

Finally, Gilla looked at Huw and William, though again his words were for Matha. "Why do you trust them?"

"This is William de Bohun and Huw ap Aeddan. David's men."

Huw had no idea how Matha had learned his name, but William scoffed. "More than that, we are friends of Christopher. Last I saw, he and your daughter were riding west to Roscommon Castle."

Gilla stared at William with the look of a man who was inches away from total collapse, so Huw stepped in to pick up the tale. No man wanted to hear that his unwed daughter was traveling through the countryside alone with a stranger who may or may not be a friend, but Huw resolved to do his best. "As Christopher's companions, we noted his absence and tracked your company back to Drumconrath. We were nearby when it fell and met Christopher and your daughter as they escaped the fort. We traveled with them to Kells, where we learned of the events at Trim and that the conspirators included both English and Irish lords. William and I determined that we should set out for Castle Roche, to seek aid from William's family, and Christopher and Aine rode to enlist the support of the King of Connaught."

As Huw was talking, a diverse series of expressions crossed Gilla's face, from suspicion at first, to joy, relief, and then a growing horror.

But Matha dropped a hand on Huw's shoulder. "How could you let them go?"

Huw jerked his head. "We spent only a day in her company, sir, but you should know by now that Aine could not be stopped, not when she'd made up her mind."

"You're saying that riding to Connaught was her idea?" Gilla said.

"It was," William put in. "Christopher went with her because otherwise she would have gone alone."

Gilla looked ruefully at his son. "That does sound like Aine."

Matha let out an audible sigh. "Why Roscommon?"

"Because O'Connor is the last unallied lord in Ireland. If King David is to quell this rebellion, he needs O'Connor and his men," Huw said.

Matha still wasn't convinced. "What of this Christopher? Is he an honorable man?"

William snorted. "To a fault, just like his cousin. Don't worry, your sister is safe with him."

25

Beyond the Pale
Christopher

Two Christmases ago when Christopher and his family had flown to Wales, he had experienced for the first time the kind of time zone difference that made him want to puke. Their flight had arrived at ten in the morning, and they'd been determined to stay up all day, so they could go to sleep at a normal time. But by mid-afternoon that first day, Christopher had longed with every part of himself to be horizontal.

Now that darkness had fallen, he was feeling that way again. His head ached, probably still from the concussion, which had been only a little over twenty-four hours earlier. Coupled with the lack of sleep the night before, he was feeling more than a little off-kilter and was having trouble focusing. Blinking back some of the blurry vision, he looked up to find the usual spectacular starscape of the Middle Ages spread across the sky. The stars were so close and so bright, he felt as if all he had to do was reach up and touch them. With light pollution everywhere but a few places in the modern world, people had no idea what they were missing. And conveniently for Aine and

Christopher, between the stars and the moon, which had risen too and was two-thirds full, the sky was so bright they didn't need a torch.

An hour ago they'd ridden past a hilltop monastery when its bells were tolling. Christopher didn't think it would be too far off to say that *every* hill in Ireland had an abbey or a church on top of it. Aine said the bells had to be for compline, the prayers before the monks retired for bed—roughly at nine o'clock in the evening.

Soon after, they crossed the Shannon River, which flowed into a big lake on their left that Aine called Lough Ree, *lough*, apparently, being the Gaelic word for *lake*. Truthfully, now that it was dark, Christopher could see very little beyond what immediately surrounded the road. It went up and down hills and through valleys— which pretty much described Ireland from top to bottom as far as he could tell.

Since they'd left Kells around noon, they'd been traveling for at least ten hours. Christopher was just about to wonder out loud how many more miles they had to go when they rounded a bend in the road to find the brightly lit battlement of a castle clearly visible in the distance.

"We're here," Aine said, relief in her voice.

Christopher pulled up in surprise at the size of it. "I thought this was an Irish castle."

"It is," Aine said, "but the O'Connors took it from the Saxons, who built it."

That explained why it looked as it did. It was rectangular in shape, with towers on each corner, a double-towered gatehouse, and a massive curtain wall—and was surrounded on all four sides by water. The moat protected the southern, eastern, and northern sides of the castle and was fed by a large lake that lay behind the castle to the west. The setup wasn't exactly like Trim, but the overall vibe was similar, and the castle itself appeared to be similar in size to Trim.

Then Christopher's attention was drawn to lights that had appeared in the distance, behind a ridge to the north of the road where they'd halted. He pointed them out to Aine, and she frowned, her eyes going from the dozens of lights where a few minutes before there had been none, to the castle in the distance. "What are they here for?"

"It looks like they just arrived too, but I don't—" He broke off, looking like Aine from the castle to the lights, his brow furrowed. "I don't think anyone on the battlements can see them."

"You were right not to light a torch, Christopher," she said. "It means nobody can see us either."

More lights were arriving every second. Christopher drew in a breath. "It's an army. What are the chances it's friendly?"

"Not high! Come on, before they discover that we're here!" Aine dug in her heels, and her horse leapt forward.

Christopher couldn't do anything but follow, even though inside he was asking himself if this was really the right choice. They were riding towards a castle, the owner of which might really not like them, and if the army that had arrived was intent on besieging the castle, entering it could trap them for the foreseeable future. He really didn't want to be trapped.

But by the time he caught up with Aine, they'd traveled the last mile to the castle at a gallop. The drawbridge was down, the gate open, and the portcullis up, since a farm cart was just crossing underneath it on its way to dispose of the pile of refuse in its bed—never mind that it was ten o'clock at night. Maybe that's when the castle was cleaned, which Christopher supposed made sense. Like the latrines, it was best to do the cleaning when fewer people were around.

By the time they got close, the guard on the battlement could hear them, even if he couldn't yet see them clearly. They'd come straight down the road from the east, so it wasn't like he could have missed them if he was at all good at his job. As they slowed, he appeared in the entrance to the castle behind the cart. Before Aine could ride across the drawbridge, he spread his arms wide, telling them in Gaelic to stop ("Fai!"). Then he caught the bridle of Aine's horse as she reined in, speaking more Gaelic to her. She answered.

As Christopher reined in too, he noted the wide-eyed look the guard sent him and said in an undertone to Aine, "Did you tell him that we need to speak to King O'Connor right now?"

"I told him that you are the Hero of Westminster and that you've come to warn them of an army on their doorstep."

Christopher almost laughed aloud. "That should do it." He turned to look at the guard and said in English. "Let us in. I must speak to your lord immediately."

The guard probably didn't understand Christopher any more than Christopher had understood the guard, but Christopher had spoken commandingly, and the guard bobbed his head. He turned into the gatehouse, tugging on the bridle of Aine's horse with her still astride. Christopher followed. Now that they were up close, the castle was even bigger than he'd thought. The giant curtain wall, which fronted the moat, was thirty feet high and at least ten feet thick.

Once through the gatehouse, Christopher put out a hand. "Can you tell them to pull up the drawbridge and drop the portcullis? It makes me antsy to think of the army out there."

Aine responded immediately, speaking to the man in Gaelic. He frowned, looking like he was going to argue, but then Christopher made an impatient movement with his hand. The guard nodded his head again and spoke sharply to a companion still in the gatehouse, who then ran to do his bidding.

They entered the outer ward only to be faced with a second, massive gatehouse, and it was only after they passed through that final defense that they reached the inner ward of the castle.

The ward wasn't busy at this hour of the night, though several men-at-arms came down from the interior wall to bolster the guard in case Christopher decided to arbitrarily attack someone. Reaching up to Aine, he helped her to dismount. Once her feet were on the stones of the inner ward and someone was leading away their horses, he turned with her towards the keep. The building was long and relatively low, built into the north wall of the inner ward. The guard gestured to them with one hand and a bit of a bow, and they followed him up the steps and through the door.

A wave of warmth hit them. Despite the inherent tension of the moment, Christopher felt his shoulders relax, and Aine took in a breath and let it out. But then, to Christopher's dismay, a guard appeared, bowing and apologetic, and motioned that Christopher must give up his sword. As in England, nobody was allowed to enter the presence of the king wearing one.

Christopher had known from the very first day in the Middle Ages how important it was for him to wear a sword as a sign of his station. But until today, he hadn't wanted one for its own sake. He certainly hadn't appreciated how clearly having a sword defined him. It told every man here that Christopher was a nobleman and worthy of respect. So while it was hard to give up, he did so willingly. It was clear that the sword had gotten them in the door, and because he was the Hero of Westminster, there was a good chance they were going to bypass all the underlings and speak directly to the king himself.

An older man with a white beard, wearing a long tunic belted at the waist (but without a sword), met them a few paces from the door. He and the guard conferred in low tones. Christopher tried to wait patiently, but he couldn't get the image of the lights behind the ridge out of his mind. An enemy army was here, and the longer these two men talked, the less time they would have to come up with a plan to deal with it.

Which was absurd, really, since Christopher had never fought in a battle and had no business being part of any kind of planning.

But then again, nobody here knew that. He found his right knee jiggling restlessly and forced himself to relax. Finally, the second man, the castle steward by Christopher's guess, dismissed the guard and gestured that they should come with him. He led them down the long hall, mostly empty of diners at this hour, to a stairway in the back corner. They went up one flight, and the steward knocked at the door, opening it at a command from someone inside.

The steward held up a hand to indicate that Christopher and Aine should wait in the corridor, and he entered the room first, leaving the door partially open so Christopher could see him conferring with a man who sat in a chair by the fire. He was thick around the shoulders, but not overweight, and from the gray at his temples, he appeared to be in his late thirties or early forties.

As with the guard, they conferred in Gaelic, but then the man looked towards the door, and Christopher inadvertently met his eyes.

There was an uncomfortable moment, but Christopher didn't look away so much as bob his head in greeting. That seemed to go over okay, because the man waved Christopher and Aine into the room.

Up until now, the only Irish house Christopher had visited belonged to Aine's father. The decorations in this room were hardly different from what he had seen at Westminster Palace—probably because when the O'Connors had taken Roscommon, the English who'd surrendered the castle had left most of their stuff behind.

This particular room appeared to be the king's private chambers. A door at the far end of the room was open, allowing Christopher to see beyond it to a canopied bed with red curtains. The office had two tables, one with chairs around it, implying that people might eat at it more privately than in the great hall below, and a second table that was stacked with papers. The fire was burning brightly, and Hugh O'Connor had been reading a rolled parchment.

As Christopher and Aine entered, Christopher couldn't help but grin to see the King of Connaught holding a pair of Benjamin Franklin-type reading glasses in his right hand.

"My steward gave me your names," he said in French. "What brings the Hero of Westminster to Connaught?"

Aine glanced at Christopher, as if waiting for him to speak. She was pretty outspoken with him and his friends, but this was the Middle Ages, and they were in the presence of a king.

"Will you translate for me?" Christopher said. "My French really isn't that good."

"You would prefer English?" Hugh said.

Christopher gave a sigh of relief. "Yes, please. I'm sorry that I can't return the favor. I speak no Gaelic."

"No matter. I had tutors." He eyed Christopher for a moment. "To defeat one's enemy, one must first know him, yes?" Then, ignoring Christopher's startled look, he gestured towards several chairs placed against the wall, and the steward hastily moved them so Christopher and Aine could sit near the fire. Then the steward departed. Christopher dared to hope for food and drink, because he was starving.

Clearing his throat, hoping that they hadn't made a huge mistake in coming here, Christopher glanced once at Aine and then related as clearly as he could how the day had gone for them and why they had come to Roscommon.

After the first startled curse at what had happened at Trim, Hugh listened intently, leaning slightly forward.

"And now you have an army on your doorstep," Christopher concluded. "I don't know who leads it, but it's here, and you have very little time to decide what you're going to do about it."

"We defend, of course. What else?"

Christopher had an idea of what else, actually, but before he could say it, someone knocked at the door.

Hugh surged to his feet, revealing himself to be the same height as Christopher, and went to open it. "What?"

The steward was waiting on the other side, wringing his hands. "I'm sorry to disturb you, my lord, but you have another visitor: a monk from Bective Abbey has brought a message from David!"

26

Dublin
Callum

Having dined with Magnus Godfridson in Oxmantown, they'd left him preparing his people to march. Thus, it was well into evening by the time David and Callum approached the first defense of Dublin: the gate that protected the bridge across the Liffey River. The moon shone brightly, reflecting off the water and lighting up the night as much as the torches on the gatehouse tower. A guard came down from the top of the wall to meet them.

"What's your bet?" David said. "They gonna admit us? Maybe we shouldn't tell them who we are."

"As I've been telling you over and over, you haven't a hope of remaining anonymous. You will be recognized."

Before David could deny this obvious truth, a rider came pounding up the road behind him and called to the watchers on the gatehouse tower. "David is dead! David is dead! Trim Castle is controlled by rebels, and all of Ireland is about to fall!" He reined in before the astonished guard at the gate and dismounted.

"Not again," Callum said.

David sighed and trotted up to the gatehouse. Reining in beside the messenger, he pushed back his hood and spoke while the rider and the guard were still trying to catch their breaths. "I am not dead, and all of Ireland has not fallen. You do your countrymen a great disservice to be spreading such falsehoods."

Both the messenger and the guard gaped at David, who was still astride his horse, but then they bowed deeply. "I apologize, my lord," the rider said. "I reported only what I was told."

David canted his head, graciously accepting the apology, though his eyes were intent. "That does not mean, however, that we aren't in danger and don't have work to do."

Callum looked at the guard. "Are we three the first to bring you news of Trim? Has there been a change in authority at Dublin Castle?"

"No, my lord! Lord Falkes remains in charge."

"We will go to him now," Callum said. "You need to drop the portcullis behind us and let nobody in until you hear from me again. Is that clear?"

"Yes, my lord!" The guard nodded fervently.

David jerked his head to the rider. "Come with us."

The rider's eyes were too wide, but he did as David asked, and they rode across the bridge to the gate that would allow them entrance to the city proper. Dublin had started out hundreds of years ago as a Danish city—the main Danish center in Ireland, in fact, along with Waterford and Wexford. Through these three towns, the

Danes had carved out a small kingdom for themselves and worked to expand their influence in Ireland. It was from here too that they'd established a mercantile empire that stretched from Ireland to Rome. They'd been similar to the Templars in that, except they hadn't been Christian and one of their biggest exports had been slaves.

The power of the Danes began to wane by the twelfth century, and the coming of the Normans broke it entirely. Two years after Strongbow's arrival, King Henry II of England showed up and demanded allegiance and land. Henry became Lord of Ireland, and Strongbow gave him Waterford and Dublin (in exchange for his life). The Danes who'd remained in Dublin under Strongbow's rule were moved to Oxmantown, across the Liffey River, and eastern Ireland was filled with English settlers. Henry gave his loyal barons the rest of the country, provided they could wrest it from the Irish lords who controlled it. Strongbow died soon after.

David, in turn, had found his rule of Ireland so unpalatable that one of his first acts after he'd become king was to devolve much of the authority for Dublin and Waterford to the people who lived there. Once David granted them status as free market towns, they had the right of self-governance, on par with any other free market English town—though David still held ultimate authority.

He retained Dublin Castle too, and in a move that could have been construed as both shrewd and risky, he'd placed John de Falkes in charge of it, in an attempt to find someone who was a good administrator but had no stake himself in how things went in Ireland. Since the border with Scotland had been at peace for many years—though with Comyn involved in the rebellion in Ireland that might be about to change—David had considered Falkes wasted at Carlisle. And David had needed someone whose loyalty was unassailable. Between Falkes and their two hundred archers, David had a formidable force at his disposal, if they could just get to it.

Callum's eyes remained fixed on the watchtower up ahead. "I hope what the guard just told us is true."

"You're the one who taught me how to brazen things out and act like I know what I am doing," David said. "Don't fail me now."

Callum tsked under his breath. "Never."

"I know you won't."

Callum turned his head to look at David, who was regarding him with a grave expression, the joking put aside. Callum returned David's look with a quick nod. Then, as they reached the gatehouse, Callum lifted his chin and bellowed, "David, King of England and Lord of Ireland, demands entry!" In borrowed clothes, without a single flag or banner indicating who they were, words would have to do.

A flurry of activity was evident from the other side of the portcullis, which slowly began to ratchet up. Shouts and calls came from inside the city, and a bell in the gatehouse tower rang a warning. Callum's stomach clenched, and he almost grabbed the bridle of David's horse and made him turn around. But then, through the portcullis, he could see people coming out of their houses and shops, despite the late hour. One woman pointed at them, a hand to her mouth, and a father swung his toddler onto his shoulders so he could see better. The people weren't shouting in fear. They were genuinely eager to see David.

By the time Callum and David passed underneath the gatehouse, the street was full of people. Lines formed on either side of the gatehouse. Without even trying, David had worked his magic here too. Even though Callum had just explained that reality to David, he still had to shake his head in disbelief. David might argue that he hadn't *done* anything. He had argued, in fact, that in Ireland he'd done all the wrong things. But his reputation had preceded him, grown, and expanded over the years, and he would use it, as he had used it in England, when he needed to.

While in a cynical moment David might have said that the people of Dublin liked him because he allowed them to keep most of the money they made, these people clearly didn't have any cynical feelings about him. As they entered the streets of Dublin, the welcoming cheers felt genuine. David laughed, and then he reached down and began to shake the hands of the people who lined the road.

While David was occupied, Callum's eyes went to the surrounding houses and shops, looking for threats, though mostly he saw people smiling and waving, hanging out of windows and scrambling on rooftops in order to see the king.

So he turned to the messenger, whose name was Tom and had been born and bred in Dublin. "Why did you say that David was dead?"

"That's-that's what I was told."

"By whom?"

"By—" He paused, and then his expression grew thoughtful. "My captain sent me here on the orders of Lord Cusack, who is one of the besiegers of Trim."

Callum growled under his breath. "Cusack." If he had been truly medieval, he might have spat on the ground. "You are from Kells?"

The rider ducked his head. "Killeen." That was one of the Cusack strongholds east of Trim and south of Skryne and Tara.

"What did he say about who it was that murdered the men at Trim?"

"It was the bastard Irish, that's who, my lord! They were to meet in peace without weapons, and the Irish delegates turned on our lords without warning! They now hold Trim against the king!"

"How is it that men like the O'Brien chief ended up dead, then?"

"Well, we fought back, didn't we?"

Callum definitely had a headache coming on. The story the boy was telling was a twisted mass of untruths and deception. That Cusack would want it told was confusing too. Informing the men of Dublin that the Irish delegates had turned on their English counterparts appealed to their biases, but Cusack *was* aligned with Irish lords. How was he going to explain that when it came time to ask the men of Dublin to fight alongside them? "Did he say what the people of Dublin were supposed to do?"

"He believes that the Irish of Leinster, led by Niall MacMurrough, are marching north as we speak. Aymer de Valence has joined the Irish cause, and I was to warn Lord Falkes of their coming so he could prepare to hold the city against them."

Callum stared at Tom. "The MacMurroughs and Valence are themselves allied with Cusack. They have to be, since Cusack besieges Trim with Red Comyn, Valence's brother-in-law."

Tom frowned. "That can't be true. My lord had nothing to do with the uprising at Trim."

Callum scratched the back of his head, not answering and not knowing what to say. He supposed there was no point in arguing with the young man, since whether or not Cusack was involved changed nothing about their immediate future. The truth would come out in time. Maybe it was just as well that Callum wouldn't be the one to tell it.

As they passed under Dublin Castle's stone gatehouse, Callum gave David the rundown on what Tom had just told him.

Rather than showing consternation, however, David's expression lightened. "Really? That's excellent."

"What could be excellent about Valence and MacMurrough marching to Dublin?"

Already on a high from the greeting the people of Dublin had given him, David responded with a smile, and laughter bubbled up in his throat. "My mom always talks about how the English, wherever they went in the world, pursued an overt policy of divide and conquer. They won Ireland initially by exploiting the already established animosities among Irish chieftains. But our enemies are dividing themselves up before we even meet them."

"You think that Cusack is already separating himself from Valence and MacMurrough?" Callum said.

"What else could Tom's message mean?"

"What is Comyn going to think about that?"

"Maybe he's in on it. You have to admit that Valence has proved himself to be something of a liability in recent years." David tipped his head. "Then again, maybe Comyn doesn't know."

Callum grimaced. "Falkes would have fought anyway."

"Yes, but this way, after Falkes takes care of MacMurrough and Valence, he will then send men to help Cusack."

Disgust rose in Callum's throat. "It's a diabolical plan."

"Yeah." David grunted. "It may be, however, that what Cusack is doing now wasn't the original plan. You killed Richard de Feypo, the highest ranking of Geoffrey de Geneville's vassals. Cusack wasn't at Trim because he was of a lower rank, but if he's stepping into the breach you made, Callum, he may be making this up as he goes along."

"I don't disagree, but I'm still not sure why you're so happy about it."

David grinned. "I'm going to get Valence and MacMurrough to fight for me!"

"You're going to—" Callum broke off, completely incapable of finishing his sentence at the audacity of what David was proposing. He cleared his throat, determined to bring David back to earth. "How?"

But David had been distracted by the arrival of Falkes, who'd been given enough warning that David was on his way to be in the bailey of Dublin Castle to greet him, Darren Jeffries at his side. David dismounted and strode forward to embrace Falkes as he came out of his bow.

"Great to see you!" David pounded the older man on the back. Then he greeted Jeffries with another hug, which Jeffries accepted, accustomed to David's American enthusiasm. "Come on. We have some serious planning to do."

In his middle forties, Falkes was as fit as when Callum had met him nearly five years before. He wasn't very tall—a good six inches shorter than David—but he was well-muscled, with a military bearing that was so ingrained he probably slept flat on his back so he wouldn't have to bend his spine. His hair had turned steel gray, but his blue eyes were as intelligent as ever. "Of course, my lord. What are we planning?"

"I need you to collect for me a company of men under the flag of peace, and I need this man—" he turned to point to Tom, whose face went blank with shock to be singled out by the king, "—under guard and protected."

"Me, my lord?" Tom said.

"You." David's eyes were bright. "In the morning, you and Lord Callum are going to ride to Valence's lines and tell them everything you told us."

Callum barked a laugh. "You have far more faith in my negotiating skills than I do, my lord."

David switched to straight American English. "It is unlike you to sell yourself short. You turned a war in Scotland into peace that has lasted until now. It gave me breathing room that I desperately needed. I know you think trusting Aymer de Valence to do anything good is dangerous, not to say foolhardy, but *we need more men*, and I don't have a lot of time to find them."

"You don't think the people will come?"

"I think many will come, but we have all of Ireland to win, and Valence and MacMurrough will be leading an army that I'd rather have on my side than fighting against me. Valence wants his lands and his honor back. Only I can give them to him. He will hate me for it, and he will plot against me in the future, but he knows as well as I do that the plotting will succeed only if he is campaigning from a position of strength."

Callum nodded, though with extreme reluctance. "You're hoping that he will choose an unsavory alliance with you over being stabbed in the back by Cusack and his cronies." He pursed his lips. "What if he turns around and stabs *you* in the middle of battle?"

"First he has to ally with us," David said.

Callum took a step closer, lowering his voice. "What about Comyn? Are you hoping that Valence will bring him to your side? I'm stunned that they're working together again at all, seeing as how Red turned on him back in Whittington."

"As I said, maybe they're not. But they are brothers-in-law and power-hungry. I'd be offering Red the same deal if he were here, but I think Feypo lured him to Ireland with the promise of the High Kingship if they win. He won't give up that chance easily."

"That's what the Irish promised Edward Bruce twenty years from now in Avalon," Callum said.

"Yup." David lifted one shoulder. "I was just talking to my mom, right before all hell broke loose, about how this world has diverged from Avalon's history. But I've also been thinking as this day has unfolded how the more things change, the more they stay the same."

Callum rubbed his chin. "It's still a crazy idea, but I will do my best."

David clapped Callum on the shoulder. "Bring 'em in, Callum. If anyone can do it, you can."

27

Roscommon Castle

Aine

"I have to protect my people," Hugh said.

Christopher leaned forward. "I know you do. But fighting for King David is the best way to do that."

The messenger who'd brought word of the gathering at Tara was eating in the hall below them. They'd gone over his message a dozen times already. In Aine's opinion, Christopher's conclusion remained the correct one. It was a huge relief to know for certain that David lived. Even better, he had a plan. The fact that he claimed the High Kingship for himself had set Hugh back a pace at first, but he hadn't dismissed Christopher and Aine. Even more, the arrival of the messenger had confirmed that everything Christopher had so far told him was true.

Still, Hugh's eyes narrowed to thin blue slits. "You're asking me to risk everything on a man I do not know—a man who has never set foot in Ireland before this month."

"He would have come sooner, but he's been busy," Christopher said, pushing back. "And since he's been here, you have to give him points for trying."

Hugh held his gaze for a moment, and then he barked a laugh. "I grant you that, and I admit that one of the reasons he is in this position now is because he did not come here with an army. While I felt that the conference at Trim was misguided, no king of England has ever before tried to bring a peace to Ireland that included the Irish."

"That's why you must help him," Christopher said, back to his former urgency. "Your army is wasted here. Nobody is coming to relieve a siege, and by the time you either win out here or whoever comes against you gets sick or gives up, all of Ireland could be lost, and then you will lose your lands anyway."

"It's Thomas de Clare and Auliffe O'Rourke!" Breathless, with a hand to his chest, a young man leaned against the doorframe. Dark-haired and blue-eyed, he was a younger and smaller version of Hugh. He was also soaked from the top of his head to his muddy boots and was shedding water from his cloak on the threshold. Unless he'd gone for a swim in the lake, Aine could only conclude that the rain had started again.

Hugh rose slowly to his feet. "Are you sure, Felimid?"

"I led the scouting party."

"How many?" Hugh said.

"Hundreds. Ten times what we have here."

Then Hugh waved Felimid forward and introduced him to Christopher and Aine as his son. Christopher stood and held out his hand, no longer denying—or even blinking twice—at being introduced over and over again as the Hero of Westminster. Aine canted her head as Felimid bowed over her hand and said, "Word of your beauty preceded you, though rumor didn't do you justice."

Aine couldn't help but smile at the flattery, and she could have said the same thing about him. She'd known of Felimid, of course, since he was the son of the King of Connaught and just her age, but had never met him before.

Christopher rolled his eyes, though only so Aine could see, prompting her to turn back to Hugh. "If Clare is here, it's because either he's already taken Thomond, or he's been told to keep you occupied until such time as you are isolated and his allies have grown too powerful for you to fight. Otherwise, he would be sitting at Thomond, gloating over his victory. With Turlough O'Brien dead in Trim's hall, the O'Briens have no leader."

"Likely, it's his job to hold the west." Hugh sat heavily in his chair, with an elbow on the arm and a finger to his lips. "These are the same men who burned Drumconrath?"

"Yes," Aine said.

Hugh flicked out two of his fingers to Christopher. "I will hear what you propose."

Aine drew in a breath. During a lull while Hugh had been seeing to the messenger, Christopher had shared his idea with her in full, and it was breathtaking in its audacity. Maybe that made it no good, but if he said nothing and the king sat here, Ireland would be lost.

"I propose something of a reverse Trojan Horse," Christopher said.

Hugh leaned forward, showing real interest. "How so? The Trojan Horse allowed Troy's enemy to take the city from the inside."

"That's why I suggest a reverse of one. We leave now—all of us, all of your men, but a small handful. When Clare's men knock on the door tomorrow morning, your men surrender the castle on the condition of their own freedom."

Felimid was aghast. "You're asking my father to give up his castle. Do you think him a fool? Nobody would do that."

"A player would in a game of chess," Aine said.

"This isn't chess," Felimid shot back.

"That's where you're wrong," Christopher said.

Hugh motioned to his son to desist. "Hear him out." Then he nodded to Christopher. "Go on."

"Your men will say that you aren't in residence and that you made the mistake of leaving a small garrison. The man who surrenders needs to be convincing, even to the point of making a case for his own advancement."

"Pretend to be a traitor, you mean?" Felimid's expression remained fierce. "Again, why would he?"

Christopher kept his focus on Hugh. "He can tell Clare that he knows of Trim, thanks to the monks spreading the news across Ireland. If Clare doesn't already know of David's plan, he can tell him.

That will infect Clare and O'Rourke with a sense of urgency and make them more likely to accept the surrender."

"Clare would suspect a trick," Hugh said.

"Why would he?" Christopher said. "As Felimid said, only a fool would give up his castle."

"At that point, only a fool wouldn't accept the bargain, and Clare isn't a fool," Aine said, remembering his coolness in her father's hall. "He will be jubilant that he took the castle without a fight."

Hugh studied them both, his eyes going from Christopher to Aine and back again. "What happens next? I've just given up my castle to Clare and O'Rourke. Where's the Trojan Horse?"

"I propose that you leave a half-dozen men—more or less, depending on how you can make this work—hidden somewhere in the castle, somewhere nobody is going to look. Then, tomorrow night, after the enemy is drunk on your stores of beer and wine, they come out and open the gates for your army. You take your castle back with the added bonus of eliminating the army that took it."

Hugh and his son stared at Christopher. Aine didn't know at first if they were overcome by his audacity (as she was), or horrified at the foolishness of his plan (as she also was). Then Hugh visibly swallowed. "The castle is the Trojan Horse."

"Yes, sir," Christopher canted his head, "or your beer."

Hugh guffawed. "I will see that it is not watered down."

"My lord, do you have the means to get the bulk of the residents of Roscommon out tonight without Clare knowing?" Aine said.

"I have an outpost on the far side of the lake. I can send a small company around to the men there immediately to warn them of what is afoot, and meanwhile we can evacuate the castle by boat."

Felimid's expression had changed from one of distrust to calculation. "I know of a place to hide."

His father turned to him. "Where?"

"In the chapel," Felimid said. "I don't know why it was built, but if you inspect the width of the side wall of the vestry, in front of which the priest stores the sacred relics and his robes, it is thicker than it ought to be."

"What is hidden there?" Hugh said.

"Nothing," Felimid shrugged, "at least not anymore. It is accessed through a cupboard. The space is large enough for five or six men to stand or sit, though it won't be comfortable. I found it when I was playing hide and seek with little Ciara and the cousins. Then the priest came and—" He stopped, his face coloring. "It's a good place to hide," he concluded lamely.

Aine didn't want to know what the priest had been doing that embarrassed Felimid to recount. She raised a hand hesitantly. "We should hide men in more than one place, in case one group is caught. Clare will think he has them all and not look further."

"Not the latrines," Christopher said. "They always look in the latrines."

Aine frowned at him, thinking she'd misunderstood his English. "Did you mean to say *they*? Who's *they*?"

Christopher blinked. "Oh—I've read it in the histories."

Aine had read no such histories, and by their puzzled looks, neither had the O'Connors.

"We have no more time to talk," Christopher said. "If we are to do this, it must be done now."

Felimid had continued to stand throughout their conversation, and he clenched his hands into fists. "I volunteer, Father."

Hugh rubbed his chin, still not committed.

"I do too," Christopher said.

Aine gasped. "No—"

He put out a hand to her. "It's my plan. I should be one of the men to implement it." Then he looked at Hugh. "You need to start evacuating the castle. Clare's and O'Rourke's army could be moving to surround it even now."

Hugh studied Christopher's face for a long moment, and he must have liked what he saw because he finally nodded and rose to his feet. Looking at Aine, he said, "You have a few moments to say your goodbyes. The women and children will be the first to leave."

He left the room with Felimid. Meanwhile, Aine's hand had gone to her mouth, and she sat frozen in her seat. Throughout their conversation, it hadn't occurred to her that implementing the plan meant that Christopher would be among those fighting. He wasn't ready. He'd said so himself. She had a sudden fear that she would have to be the one to tell David that Christopher had died because she had dragged him to Roscommon.

Christopher watched the O'Connors go, unaware at first of her emotions, but when he turned to speak to her, his expression became one of concern. He'd been sitting a few feet away, but now he brought his chair forward and sat so they faced each other. "I won't lie and tell you it's going to be okay, but honestly, I think it will be."

She dropped her hand from her mouth. "A man of your station should be with Hugh."

He gave her a rueful look. "What you really mean is a man of my inexperience."

Aine opened her mouth to deny it, but then she closed it again, because he was right.

"Did you notice that even after Felimid volunteered, Hugh still didn't commit to the plan until I volunteered too?" Christopher shook his head. "You can't lead from behind."

"This is my fault. It was my idea to come here." Aine's fingers worked at the side seam of her cloak as she struggled for composure. "What if it doesn't work?"

"It may not. Maybe I've misread Clare entirely, in which case, as at your father's fort, my life is forfeit."

"But you don't think you've misread him," she said, not as a question.

Christopher pointed a finger straight up. "Listen."

Aine did, but all she could hear was the drumming of rain on the roof, and she said so.

"Exactly. Clare's men took Drumconrath yesterday evening. They then marched all day to get here. They're going to spend a wet and sleepless night outside the castle, and when it surrenders tomorrow, it will be such a relief for everyone to be warm and dry that they will be more careless than they might otherwise have been."

Aine swallowed hard and said in a small voice. "I hope you're not doing this because you're trying to prove you deserve to be the Hero of Westminster."

Christopher rose to his feet, restlessness in every line of his body. "It isn't something to live up to or prove. I *am* the Hero of Westminster. I can't change that, even if I wanted to. And I've realized today that I don't. What's more, part of being that man is doing this."

28

Roscommon Castle

14 March 1294

Aine

Aine clutched her cloak tightly around herself as the rain pummeled the top of her head. She held a sleeping two-year-old in her arms, and they were scrunched in the bow of the boat, pressed up against the rail to allow the greatest number of people to fit inside.

By the time she'd left Christopher, the evacuation was in full swing. The first boat had already left the dock, and a second one was filling with Hugh's people. She'd waited for the third boat, which amounted to waiting until the first boat returned, a matter of an hour or so. With the wind and the rain, the journey wasn't an easy one, but Hugh's boats weren't typical river boats. This one resembled nothing more nor less than a Danish longboat, and his prescience in acquiring such a vessel implied that he deserved to be one of the most powerful men in Ireland.

"Sorry, lass." The old man next to her had twisted in his seat to look towards shore and in so doing jostled her in the ribs with his elbow. "Almost there."

The wind had picked up, and the rain was now blowing horizontally across the lake from west to east. The force of it would aid the longboat's journey back to the castle, but they were fighting the weather the whole way to the O'Connor outpost on the opposite shore. Still, a quarter of an hour later, they docked at the square, three-story watchtower that guarded this side of the lake for Hugh.

Aine got out of the boat to find one of Felimid's cousins, Rory, standing before her. "Himself wants to see you."

Aine blinked, surprised to hear it since she hadn't realized that Hugh had left the castle already. Of course, Felimid and Christopher had stayed behind. Deciding he must have ridden around the lake with his guard, which made sense since that was the only way to get horses out of the castle, she handed off the child to its father and went with Rory up the watchtower's staircase to a door ten feet above the ground. When he pulled it open, the wind almost took it right out of his hand. She hustled into the tower so he could pull the door closed behind them, and ended up in a dimly lit anteroom, far wider than it was deep, where boots, clothes, weapons, and who-knew-what-all were stored.

"*Whoo.*" Rory pushed back his hood. "This way." He led her through the only other door into a much larger room that took up the rest of the floor of the tower. It was empty of people, though a fire burned brightly in the hearth on the far wall, venting up a chimney that seemed to be drawing well enough to send most of the smoke out of the room.

She walked to the fire and put her hands out to it. She was incredibly cold, and the wet cloak wasn't helping, so she unhooked it and hung it on the rack before the fire.

"Thank you for coming." Hugh appeared out of the corner stairwell.

"Thank you for the fire." She curtseyed.

Hugh went to a table and poured wine from a carafe into two cups, giving one to her and keeping the second for himself. She took a sip, and the warmth seeped through her as if she'd just sunk into a hot bath.

"So. Gilla O'Reilly's daughter. I never thought I'd see the day one of the O'Reillys came to me for help."

Aine swallowed her sip. "It is true that my father isn't one to ask for anything."

"And yet you came to me. Why?"

"We—" She coughed. "We told you why."

"Ah yes. Because I am the last king standing." He regarded her over the rim of his cup.

She shifted uncomfortably. "We came to you because you rule Connaught. You're a king in your own right, and David needs you on his side to overcome the forces that face him. If I am being honest, we had few choices."

"You could have ridden to Dublin. You could have gone with your friend William to Castle Roche. But you didn't. So again I ask, why me?"

Aine had never felt so much on the spot. Up until now, she'd kept house for her father, waiting for the time when her father decided on an appropriate marriage. She hadn't questioned that fate, not ever, but having set out into the world this last day, she wasn't going back to Cloughoughter. The world was a much bigger place than she'd imagined, and she could see possibilities for herself that she'd never seen before. "We came here because my father sees in David a future that requires all of us to make different choices."

Hugh set down his cup. "David wants the High Kingship."

"I don't think he does, actually."

Hugh scoffed. "He has claimed it."

"Only because it is the only way to get everyone to stop fighting each other and work together."

Hugh canted his head as he looked at her. "Why do you think what you say is true? Have you ever met him?"

"No." Aine felt her jaw firming. "But I know Christopher and his friends, and that's what they say."

"Christopher of Westminster. The Hero of Westminster." Hugh turned back to the table and poured another cup of wine.

In that moment, she realized she'd lost his attention because he thought she was in love with Christopher. Curiosity had turned into dismissiveness. She took a step forward, wanting his attention back. "You misunderstand."

"Do I?" Hugh drank the wine he'd poured in one go rather than sipping it as he'd been. He was finding courage in a carafe. It wasn't what she'd expected to see.

"Five years ago, I heard you speak at the meeting of the clans. You were on fire with the desire to take back Connaught from the Saxons, but when you finally achieved your goal, you didn't slaughter Roscommon's garrison. You didn't allow your men to give in to revenge and retribution." She gestured to the tapestries on the walls. "Your castle is decorated in the English style."

Hugh growled. "To remind me of those years of exile; to ensure that I never forget what's at stake."

Aine risked one more step closer. "Like my father, among all the kings of Ireland, you have the wisdom to understand David's vision. I think you want to be standing at his side when he wins. Which he's going to do, with or without you."

Hugh looked up at that. "Is he." It was less a question than a deadpan response.

Aine looked down at the ground. What she had to say next was so risky that she couldn't look at Hugh when she spoke. "You're wondering now if, after you take back your castle tomorrow, it wouldn't be smarter to stay in Connaught and not march to David's aid as you promised Christopher you would."

Hugh was silent a moment, and then he snorted. "It's a thought."

"Maybe it would be wise to hold Christopher hostage and trade him for a place in David's new Ireland? Or, if Cusack's faction wins, hand him over to Clare to do with as he wishes?"

"You think so little of me, do you, girl?"

Aine's head came up. "Quite the opposite. You said that you didn't go to David's conference because you thought it was misguided, but perhaps that isn't it at all. Maybe you weren't meant to go, so you could be here now."

"You think my doubt is God's hand at work?" Hugh said. "That it was God's will for those men to die at Trim?"

Aine shook her head vehemently. "Those men died because other men were greedy."

The door to the tower opened behind her, and Rory appeared in the doorway. "My lord." He bowed. "The last of the boats has reached shore."

"And Clare?"

"He has moved his army forward, though his men remain out of bowshot of the walls. We got out just in time."

"God's will, you say?" Hugh's eyes were still on Aine. "Thank you, Rory."

Rory left.

Then, still watching Aine, Hugh said, "They say David is the return of Arthur. Do you believe it?"

"Yes!" Aine's chin came up defiantly.

Hugh scoffed. "It's a bard's tale, meant to entertain a hall on a long winter's night." But then he turned away to look towards the fire, and when he spoke next, it seemed as if his words were not for Aine as much as for himself. "And yet, David lives, and every man who has gone against him has found himself defeated, disgraced, or dead."

"My lord?" Aine couldn't bear the uncertainty a moment longer. "What will you do?"

Hugh's hand clenched into a fist. "What I must."

29

Drogheda Castle
William

"Do not be ashamed to be afraid. I am."

William had been looking out the high thin window at the activity—or lack thereof, now that midnight had come and gone—in the bailey of the castle, and he swung around to stare at Gilla. He didn't even have the spit in his mouth to say *what?*

If Gilla hadn't spoken in English, he might have thought the Irish chief's words weren't meant to be overheard, but in that case he would have spoken in Gaelic, which William's ear had long since stopped trying to decipher. The words of that language were a hopeless mess of vowels and sounds that shouldn't exist, even to a Marcher lord with a head for languages, and one who'd been accused many times by his English friends of entirely making up the pronunciations of Welsh.

Gilla went on, apparently not needing an answer. "You are young enough still that I see it in your eyes. The fear. We all have it. With time, most of us grow more accomplished at hiding it."

Gilla was right that fear had been slowly twisting its knife into William's gut while they'd been waiting for Matha to return and release them. He'd confessed once to his father how afraid of failure he sometimes was. He was more afraid of failing than of dying. His father had given him a typically stout answer, clapping him on the shoulder and telling him that if a man wasn't afraid, then he wasn't alive. He'd told William that everybody was afraid.

William hadn't believed him. He didn't believe Gilla. "My father is never afraid."

Gilla guffawed. "What do you think he is, then—angry?"

William's eyes flicked to Huw, who was deliberately not looking at either of them, having removed his whetstone from his pocket and busied himself with sharpening one of his tiny knives. Huw had been inordinately pleased when the patting down he'd received had failed to discover either tool.

William brought his attention back to Gilla. "Yes, he's angry."

Gilla nodded. "Then he is afraid. Most men hide it with rage."

"Not King David." For some reason, William wanted to argue with Gilla.

"Is that so?" Gilla canted his head. "He isn't angry, or he isn't afraid?"

As David himself had confessed to being afraid at times, William was struggling to maintain his thesis that he was the only one who felt this way. He hadn't believed David, but David wasn't angry either. Gilla was certainly right, however, that all was not well with William. While treachery had surrounded William (and his father) his whole life, even the intrigue surrounding the fight over the English throne and finding out that his intended bride would rather be a nun than marry him hadn't set William back on his heels quite as much as today.

Huw swept his blade across the whetstone again. "You can be courageous and afraid at the same time. You were David's squire. How could you not have learned this?"

William grimaced, and when he didn't have an answer, Huw added, "You've fought in battles. Back at Windsor when you were a boy, you charged into the fray and almost got yourself killed. How did you manage that?"

"It was an act," William said. "Bravado."

Gilla put up one finger. "Precisely."

"Fake it 'til you make it," Huw said. And then when both William and Gilla looked at him, he shrugged. "So says Queen Meg."

"I have never heard that phrase before, but if I understand it, it is a good one." Gilla turned back to William. "I tell you this now because I am a father of a son of whom I am very proud, and because I was once such a son. We are all afraid. What we cannot do, however, is let our fear drive our actions or our decisions."

David would have said the same thing. He probably had, if William had been listening. Still, he argued. "We are about to take back this castle because all Ireland will fall and we will die if we don't. Fear *is* driving our actions."

"Is it really? I am afraid of that outcome, but that is not why I fight," Gilla said patiently. "Nor is it why you do."

William felt his chin jutting out, and he fought the impulse. They were lecturing him, and he hated being lectured, but he knew that they were trying to help him too. Unfortunately, he wasn't understanding what they were getting at. So, everyone was afraid. So what? They didn't show it, and they certainly didn't have the knife-twisting uncertainty and watery bowels that afflicted William. He threw up his hands, feeling stupid, but knowing he needed to be told the answer.

With a sigh Huw stopped his sharpening and looked at William. "You're doing it not because you fear what is behind you. You act because you have hope for something bett—"

A footfall outside the door stopped Huw in mid-sentence, and a heartbeat later he was on his feet, his knife in his hand and a finger to his lips. He moved to one side of the doorway and signaled that William should take up a post on the other. Gilla faced the door, legs braced for whoever might come through it, but then Matha's face appeared behind the iron bars of the window, and he put his key into the lock. The door swung wide on greased hinges.

Gilla accepted the sword Matha handed him and followed him from the room towards the stairwell. "I don't understand. Why is there no fighting?"

"Many of our enemies should be insensible with poppy juice by now, but we couldn't dose your guards in case their captain noticed and sounded the alarm too soon," Matha said. "Cusack's and Butler's men were more alert than I counted on them being, so I decided to wait to attack until you were free. Three more fighting men might be the difference between success and failure."

William gripped the unfamiliar sword Matha had brought him. The weighting of it was a little off, but beggars couldn't be choosers. Somewhere in this castle was his own sword, given to him by his father, and he wanted it back. *His father would kill him if—*

He swallowed down the thought, reviewing what Huw and Gilla had told him. Fear of disappointing his father had driven William for his entire life. He remembered standing in the nave of the church at Valle Crucis Abbey, being given over to David to protect. At the time it had felt as if his father had abandoned him and that he was relieved to no longer be burdened by the responsibility of a son like William.

When they'd found his father in a cell at Painscastle, William had hoped that, at long last, he would have done something to make his father proud. Instead, his father had only expected more, forcing him to agree to the marriage to Princess Joan and put in his claim for the throne of England. His relief when Joan had chosen the Church over him had been immeasurable, overcoming his fear of his father's disappointment.

And still his father pushed and pushed, and nothing William ever did was good enough. How could Gilla think that William's father was actually *afraid*?

Worse, what if Gilla was right and fear drove his father too? Did that make his father weak like William?

Leaving Gilla, William, and Huw behind a curve of the stairwell, Matha was the first one into the guardroom. He made a joke in French, something about what happens when you put an Irishman, a Welshman, and a Saxon in a cell together, and the guards laughed. It was the cue for the three of them to descend the stairs the rest of the way.

Matha had already plunged his knife into the chest of the nearest guard, and he could apparently move so quickly and well that he had the second guard on the ground with the same knife to his throat before the first one was even dead.

"You seem to have this well in hand, son." Gilla spoke affably, but he bent to look into the face of the guard on the ground, who was still alive.

"We were told you would betray us, and here you are," the guard said.

Matha glowered. "What are you going on about?"

The guard puckered his mouth to spit, but then as Matha increased the pressure of the blade on his throat, seemed to think better of it. "Lord Cusack warned us that you Irish would never stay true to our cause."

Matha's face reddened, but Gilla's expression turned thoughtful. "When were you going to turn on my son's men?"

"I don't know the exact moment. We were just to be prepared when our captain gave the word."

Gilla straightened, though he still looked down at the guard. "As that will not happen now, you can die here, or you can aid us. Your choice."

The guard sneered. "Aid you? Why should I believe anything you say? I could help you, and you'll turn around and murder me in my sleep."

"If you do not want to aid us—" Gilla glanced at Huw and William and then looked back to the man. "Would you serve David?"

"He's dead!"

"He is not."

"Lord Cusack—"

"Lies."

William had a moment of fear that *they* were the ones telling lies, but instead of swallowing the fear down like he always had, he allowed it to take him over for a moment. His whole being filled with that sweating, shaking fear that was something to be feared in and of itself. Had his father ever felt this way?

Then Huw's hand came down on his shoulder and, as if on command, William took in a deep breath and let it out. By some miracle, the fear began to drain away with his breath, just like David had said it would, years ago. William was so amazed, he felt lightheaded—and like laughing.

He didn't though, just shook himself and muttered to Huw under his breath. "Thanks."

"We're going to win, William. David's alive, and we're going to take back this castle. And then Ireland."

William had never seen Huw so determined, and he took heart from that too.

"What's your decision?" Gilla was still speaking to the downed guard. To William it felt like an hour had passed, though it had been only heartbeats.

"I'd like to live."

Gilla jerked his head at his son, who removed the knife and took a step back. Gilla reached down to the guard, who, after a moment's hesitation, clasped his hand and allowed himself to be pulled to his feet.

"Why did you offer me my life?"

"Where were you born?" Gilla said.

The guard hesitated, clearly wondering why Gilla was asking. "In a hamlet near Dublin."

"I was born thirty miles away," Gilla said. "Why do I have more right to be here than you?"

"You sound like David," the guard blurted out.

William was also shocked to hear an Irishman saying such a thing. It would be like a Welshman welcoming a Norman to Wales. Or a Jew. Then he paused and took a breath, realizing that's exactly what King Llywelyn had done. And King David too. And they'd done it over and over again until people had started to believe that they actually meant what they said.

"Do I?" Gilla said. "Good. I meant to."

Could that be what Gilla and Huw had been trying to tell him? Gilla had said that he was afraid, and yet he'd entered the guardroom with casual aplomb, accepting the death of one enemy at the hands of his son and offering another his life despite fear of failure, of losing his family's lands and honors, of making the wrong choices. For the first time, William saw his father's act of giving him up to David in a new light.

It might actually mean that his father loved him.

30

Roscommon Castle
Christopher

What Christopher had neglected to mention to anyone before hiding in this closet was that he was not extraordinarily fond of tight spaces. Maybe he hadn't really known it until now. David had once told him about fitting his entire guard, full armor and all, into Christopher's mom's minivan. David had laughed as he'd told the story, but Christopher couldn't think about his mom's minivan without feeling ill at the memory of that awful day when David and Anna had disappeared.

Everyone was uncomfortable here too—and they'd been so for the last six hours, ever since the castle had surrendered at sunset, making it now nearly midnight. Clare and O'Rourke hadn't liked waiting all day for the castle, but the deal was so good, they'd agreed. The castellan had arranged for the delay out of fear that the men with Christopher wouldn't be able to bear being in the cupboard for longer than six hours. They'd been unable to see anything in the near total darkness, and were forbidden to speak, cough, or eat for fear of being found out. They dared to drink only enough water to wet the tongue out of fear of needing to pee. At times they'd managed to shift position—moving from a standing position to a crouch—but the closet was all of three feet deep, which didn't leave a lot of room for stretching. Mostly, they sweated.

The stakes were as high today as they'd been for David in his minivan too. Then, he'd been moments away from being caught by the English. David had been younger that day than Christopher was now, though more experienced in war. As Christopher eased out a breath and put an ear to the wall in front of him to listen for footfalls, he acknowledged that he was gaining experience by the second.

Felimid touched Christopher's arm. They were pressed so close together that he'd needed to move his fingers less than an inch to reach him. "My lord, it's time."

"Thank God." Christopher tapped the shoulder of the man next to him, who was crouched in front of the entrance to the hiding place. In order to get in here, they'd had to crawl through a cupboard, part of a ten-foot-wide and eight-foot-tall wardrobe that took up the side wall of the vestry. It was like one of those do-it-yourself closets you could buy from Ikea, except this one had been built by hand in solid oak instead of pressboard.

The man slid aside the back panel of the cupboard. Though Christopher couldn't see them from where he was standing, altar cloths were stacked in the opening, put there to convince Clare's men that nothing untoward was going on behind the back wall. As it turned out, they'd been in little danger of discovery except for one minute when a guard had desultorily opened the cupboards only to anticlimactically close them again. That had been hours ago.

The first man crawled through the hole, followed by two more, before Christopher could sidle sideways and get on his hands and knees himself. Once in the vestry, he wiped the sweat from his brow. Six armored men in a closet heated things up pretty quickly, and it was a relief to breathe the cool fresh air of the church.

"This way. Let's hope everyone's drunk like they're supposed to be." Felimid opened the vestry door, which led directly into the priest's house, a one-room affair that was as empty as the church. If only everything else about the night went as well. The priest himself had argued that, even with the changing ownership of the castle, he should stay behind, but Hugh had convinced him that nothing could be more foolish. Clare and O'Rourke would expect him to go, and the last thing they wanted to do was anything unexpected.

Aine had suggested that they poison the food and drink before they left. It was a good idea, but Hugh had decided that it posed too much risk. Those who didn't partake would notice that something was wrong with their companions, and Clare would realize that there was treachery afoot. For that same reason, they hadn't left two parties of men behind, even though, despite Christopher's warnings, Hugh had thought the latrine idea was an excellent one. Their sole mission was to open the main gate. Six men would have to be enough.

Unfortunately, the chapel was located on the exact opposite side of the bailey from the front gate, which meant they had to cross the inner ward to get there. At least it was still raining, so they didn't have to watch every step. With no cameras to avoid, their primary concern was evading the guards. The first test came at the approach to the rear gate, which led to the dock by which the majority of the castle's inhabitants had escaped the previous night.

They'd gone over their plan a dozen times before entering the cupboard, but for some reason it hadn't occurred to Felimid or his father that the door to the guardroom at the base of the tower might be left open. A square of light shone on the ground at the base of the steps. Felimid and Christopher looked at each other, debating whether to go ahead and kill the guards or to attempt to evade detection.

Christopher made a circling motion with his hand and whispered in Felimid's ear: "They have no night vision." It would be stupid to try to kill every guard on duty. Better to simply pass on by.

Felimid nodded and set off first, avoiding the square of light and the puddle it illumined. Christopher took up the rear. Taking a cue from Callum, with whom he'd trained for a time, he kept his focus behind him, walking backwards every few yards to make sure that they weren't spotted.

They skirted the craft halls and stables on the inside perimeter of the curtain wall, all the while blessing the smothering darkness outside the circle of the torchlights on the walls and the rain that was keeping everyone inside.

Ten yards from the gatehouse, their luck ran out. Christopher heard a man say in English, "Who are—"

Being in the rear, Christopher could see very little, but he couldn't miss the indrawn breath of recognition on the part of the two soldiers who'd come out of the barracks. The first died on Felimid's blade, and the second was brought to the stones of the bailey with a thud and a crunch, underneath the weight of one of Hugh's men-at-arms, a man named Sean. They'd considered not including him tonight because of his bulk and the tight conditions of the closet, but Hugh had insisted that he was his best man in a fight. After that display, Christopher had no cause to doubt.

For all that Felimid appeared to be an accomplished warrior, he still hadn't moved from his position above the body of the man he'd killed. Christopher went to grab the dead man's ankles. "It's okay, Felimid," he said, though it really wasn't and never could be. "We need to move the body."

After another moment's hesitation, Felimid came to his senses, reaching down to lift the man by the arms, and two more men came to help. They dumped the body between two nearby huts. If Hugh had still been in residence, the huts would have held sleeping craft workers, but they'd all gone, either in the first wave or (to bolster the authenticity of the deception) that evening when the castle had surrendered to Clare, the entirety of which Christopher had missed, since he'd been hidden in the closet.

Christopher couldn't believe that Felimid had never killed a man before, but he still seemed to be catching his breath, so Christopher clapped him on the shoulder and said, "Come on."

He took the front position now and led the way towards the front of the castle, keeping as close to the shadows as he could until they were actually approaching the gatehouse of the inner ward. Squatting to stay out of anyone's line of sight, he peeked around the corner. It was after midnight, but the portcullis was up and the door open, undoubtedly to facilitate movement within the confines of the castle itself. Beyond the inner gatehouse lay the outer ward and the gatehouse that fronted the moat. Unlike when Christopher and Aine had arrived, that portcullis there was down and the great wooden door closed, just as they'd expected them to be.

Two men stood together twenty yards away in the gatehouse archway.

Christopher pulled back his head, muttering, "No plan survives contact with the enemy."

"What?" Felimid asked under his breath.

"Just something someone said." Christopher leaned his head back against the wall. They were slightly sheltered from the rain here, and all five of Hugh's men were lined up beside Christopher to his left. An ache in Christopher's belly told him that a lot more than five men were going to die before they were done, and he prayed that they wouldn't be his five. But he couldn't change the plan now, and if they failed to open the main gate and the portcullis, they were all dead anyway.

"Remember that the armory is on the right, the guardroom on the left," Felimid said. "We'll need to take out those guards first so they can't lock us out of the inner ward."

Christopher nodded. "Some of the men who took the castle should be Englishmen, right?"

"Should be."

It was bad to make assumptions, especially today when they had no idea who was really allied with whom, but sometimes you had to. "Okay. I'm going to pretend to be drunk and walk right up to them. I'll distract them while a couple of you get to this guardroom. Once the men in there are down, we'll need to take care of the guards at the outer gatehouse. You're just going to have to kill everyone."

"I know." Felimid's grip tightened on the sword in his hand.

"And you have to put that away for the moment, or you'll give the game away," Christopher said.

"They're going to know you're not one of them," Felimid said.

"Probably, but it's dark, and hopefully I won't have to fool them for more than a few seconds." *Seconds* wasn't a word used in English much yet, though the twenty-firsters used it all the time. Christopher thought Felimid could figure out what he meant.

While Felimid dried his sword on his cloak and sheathed it, Christopher checked around the corner again. The second soldier had gone back inside, leaving just one still in the gateway. A huge relief. Thankful that in real life, a sword or knife made no sound when it was drawn, he pulled his belt knife from the sheath at his waist and stood. Taking a breath, he stepped into the archway—and immediately lost his footing because he'd stepped on an uneven stone he couldn't see in the dark.

Christopher staggered to the left, throwing out a hand for balance, and though he righted himself, he couldn't have looked more drunk. Taking courage from the fortuitous mistake, he continued to weave towards the guard, adding to the deception by launching into a sea shanty he'd learned from some of the men in David's company. He found it easier to mimic the medieval English accent when he was singing—because he was just parroting the song—than when he was talking.

Go to the helm!
What ho! no near!
Steward, fellow! a pot of beer!
Ye shall have, Sir, with good cheer,
Anon all of the best.

Christopher's voice was nothing like David's, which was perhaps one of the reasons the guard waved his hand, trying to get him to stop. Belatedly, Christopher realized that it might not have been wise to sing, even in such a mumbling tone, since his voice echoed around the stones of the gatehouse. He could only hope that he was also distracting the guard from the movement of his companions towards the guardroom.

Whatever the guard's objection, he hastened forward, making shushing sounds. As he approached, Christopher put a hand out to his shoulder, implying that he needed to steady himself, and then he drove the knife he held in his right hand into the guard's chest. He died right there at Christopher's feet, just as the man at Drumconrath had done.

There couldn't have been many guards in the guardroom, because Felimid's men were inside for only thirty seconds before three of them were back, passing Christopher and heading for the outer gatehouse. Christopher dragged the dead man into the shadow of a side wall, and then he followed, not to the other guardroom but to the winch that controlled the portcullis. Breathlessly, he began winding it up. Hugh had assured him that it was well balanced and that one man could do it alone.

Once it was up, he wound the rope tightly around the grommet, knotted it, and yanked on it so it would stay. All someone would have to do to drop it again was untie it or cut the rope. That was why the men in the guardrooms had to be taken care of as quickly as possible, to prevent them from sounding the alarm or dropping the defenses again.

Next Christopher ran to the gate, which was blocked by a wooden bar the width of his thigh. Again, this defense needed only one man to open it, but a second later there were two, because Sean, the big man-at-arms, was beside him, and he lifted the bar out of its cradle as if it were a twig. While Sean pushed the door open, Christopher grabbed a torch from a sconce on the wall and ran out the gate with it into the wind and rain. The drawbridge, the last defense of the castle, was still down. Christopher stood in the center of the bridge and waved the torch above his head.

He didn't know how Hugh had gotten his men so close without anyone on the battlements knowing, but all of a sudden there they were—and included more than the hundred or so fighting men he'd had when Christopher had last seen him. Hugh had called the men of the countryside to him, and they had come.

They filed past Christopher, their boots thudding on the wood of the drawbridge but otherwise making no other sound—or not one that could be heard over the rain. Once inside, they split into pre-arranged companies. Christopher had turned his head to watch them enter the castle, so he didn't realize Hugh was beside him until he felt the king's hand on his shoulder.

"Thank you, Hero of Connaught."

And then he was past, and the fight was truly on.

Christopher stayed where he was. The rain drummed on his head, but he didn't care. He didn't want to fight anymore, and, in that moment, he didn't see why he should. All of Hugh's men were inside the castle. Christopher's inexperienced sword wouldn't make any difference at all. He heard the moment Clare's men raised the alarm, however, and realized that he needed to do something other than stand on the drawbridge. Someone could drop the portcullis and lock him out.

He hurried back the way he'd come, but instead of entering the inner ward, he decided to see what had become of Felimid, whom he hadn't seen leave that first guardroom. He was anxious all of a sudden about the fate of the man with whom he'd spent the last six hours.

Only two remained inside: Felimid and Padric, the youngest of the five. Felimid's right arm hung uselessly at his side, and he was sitting on the edge of a table, cursing the wound while Padric tried to bandage it.

At the scrape of Christopher's boot on the threshold, both men turned to look, weapons at the ready, though Felimid's sword was in his left hand. Christopher waved, and Felimid sat back down on the table. His face was incredibly pale, but he jerked his chin at Padric. "Find out what's happening, will you?"

"Yes, my lord."

Sword in hand, Padric left the guardroom, and Christopher closed the door behind him, not wanting to be surprised by a stray soldier from Clare's army. "Let me get that." He continued where Padric had left off, wrapping the bandage twice more around Felimid's upper arm and then tying it off.

Felimid grimaced, but accepted the help from Christopher with more patience than he'd been showing Padric. "You've put my father in quite a bind."

Christopher stepped back, surveying his handiwork and only half listening. "How is that?"

"He's going to have to fight for your David now."

That got Christopher's attention. "He already said he would."

A look of surprise crossed Felimid's face before his eyes narrowed. "You can't be that naïve."

Christopher looked down at his hands. They were covered in blood, as much from Felimid's wound as from the man he'd killed.

Felimid was right that he was naïve. He had taken Hugh at face value. He'd killed for him—and for David—because of it.

Then the door to the guardroom swung open, revealing the King of Connaught himself. "Where's Thomas de Clare?"

Christopher spread his hands wide. "I haven't seen him."

"Nobody has." Hugh swore loud and long. "His men are dead, but somehow he got away."

31

South of Dublin

15 March 1294

Callum

"This is a trick!" Aymer de Valence's face was red with fury as he shouted at Niall MacMurrough.

A guard shoved Callum from behind so he landed on his knees and almost fell forward onto his face. Since his hands were tied behind his back, he couldn't catch himself.

Aymer was still in full spate. "David is unworthy to lick my boots! He murdered my father! If we march to Tara, his armies will turn on us!" He swore and kicked a camp stool so it soared across the tent and hit a side wall.

As Callum got his feet under him again, he could have been cursing David too. He had known before setting out that this task David had given him ranked up there with sending him to Scotland as one of the least desirable jobs on the planet. Callum had consoled himself with the idea that *that* particular trip had turned out well in the end.

What Callum hadn't quite anticipated was Aymer's fury and disbelief. Even worse, like an idiot, instead of turning tail and riding away as fast as he could, he'd been the one to offer himself up as ransom to David's sincerity. Jeffries had argued vociferously against it, but eventually let him go, along with Tom, into the enemy camp. Jeffries said he would remain outside, and if Callum didn't return by dawn, he would come in and get him.

Noon had come and gone by the time they'd found Aymer's camp. With few cavalry, the army had been marching north, heading, as Tom the messenger had informed David he would be, to Dublin. Although Callum had allowed Tom to explain word-for-word what Cusack had told him, Aymer had refused to believe him, which had prompted Callum to make this foolhardy gesture.

He should have realized that Aymer wasn't to be reasoned with. Reasonable men, once they were provided with the necessary information, could be relied upon to make good decisions. Unfortunately, Aymer had never displayed any of those characteristics, and it had been foolish of David to think he would start now.

"That is remarkably unlikely, Aymer. If you would put aside your pride and look at the facts, you would see it." Niall sat on a camp stool before a brazier with his elbows on his knees and a cup of wine held lazily in two fingers. He was a large, dark-haired man with a full black beard and blue eyes, the consummate Celt, in contrast to Aymer's olive skin and dark eyes. "We know Cusack besieges Trim with Comyn's men. All of David's allies are dead. Why would he turn to us if he wasn't desperate?"

"Red would never betray me," Aymer said.

Niall turned his head slowly to look up at the Frenchman, pinning him with a gaze that was as disdainful as it was disbelieving.

Aymer made a scoffing noise and swung around to look at Callum, who'd of course been following their argument with interest. They'd been speaking French rather than Gaelic, so he'd understood every word. Though Callum spoke Scots Gaelic with some fluency, it was only a cousin to Irish Gaelic, not the same, and he'd had to work hard these last three weeks he'd been in Ireland to make heads or tails of what the Irish were saying when they spoke quickly.

"You offer me nothing! Nothing!" Aymer strode up to Callum and shook his fist in his face. "Only what I already should have!"

"Your father rebelled against the king," Callum said calmly. "What kind of king would David be if he hadn't confiscated your father's lands?"

"See. Exactly my point." Niall gestured with his cup. "If David has shown us anything these last five years it's that he knows how to *be* a king." Again the circling gesture with his cup. "Not like these jumped-up Saxons, thinking that because they inherited their titles they deserve to rule." He took a long sip.

Callum nodded to himself, understanding Niall's point even if Aymer didn't. English law willed that eldest sons inherited everything, regardless of their age or qualifications. But the Irish, like the Scots, looked to the clan to choose the next leader. Sons might be incompetent or spoiled—or simply too young—to rule. In those cases, the clan voted in an uncle or cousin. Niall was such a leader, and the difference in maturity between him and Aymer was striking.

"I will *not* listen to this!" Aymer spun on his heel and marched from the tent.

Callum had been positioned near the tent opening, and Aymer childishly knocked into his shoulder as he went by.

Niall let him go and then signaled with his cup to the other men in the tent. "Leave us."

As Niall's lieutenants filed out the doorway, Callum settled more comfortably into parade rest, bracing for whatever might come next. Niall was a much wiser man than Aymer, but rather than making him less dangerous, it made him more. Aymer might have drawn his sword and run Callum through in a fit of pique, but Niall would do it without hesitation as part of a cold-eyed strategy.

And when Niall's next move was to draw his belt knife, rise to his feet with a sigh, and advance towards Callum, he had a moment of panic. But, sensibly, all Niall did was move around behind Callum to saw at the rope that bound Callum's wrists. "Pardon the temper tantrum. One cannot always choose one's allies."

That was an opening Callum couldn't pass up. "Actually, you can."

Behind Callum, Niall froze for a second, and then he barked a laugh and dropped the rope to the floor. Returning to his stool, he wagged a finger at Callum. "I like you. I do. I see why your king sent you." Then he indicated the abused stool that Aymer had left against the wall of the tent ten feet away. "Please. Sit."

Callum picked up the stool and set it by the fire across from Niall. He would have preferred to stand, but negotiations had begun, and he was wary of making a wrong move.

"Tell me why I should listen to you."

"Because David is going to win, and I think you want to be on the winning side."

Niall snorted and leaned back a little. "Just like that? He's going to win?"

"Yes."

Niall pointed with his chin towards the doorway behind Callum. "That's not what Aymer says."

It was Callum's turn to snort. "Because Aymer knows so much? He's a good judge of character?"

Niall stared at Callum. "Character does not win battles."

"No, it doesn't. But judge for yourself. Does David win battles?"

"He has never lost."

"Not in the end, no. Not yet. Who would you rather be betting against? Aymer or David?"

"Cusack says that all the clans are allied with him. The O'Rourkes ally with the O'Reillys. I'd never thought I'd see that in my lifetime."

Callum grunted his disagreement. "Gilla O'Reilly's fort at Drumconrath was burned to the ground by the allied forces of Thomas de Clare and Auliffe O'Rourke."

Niall pursed his lips for a second before answering. "That can't be true."

"I spoke to witnesses—several of them—including James Stewart, who was there."

"And Gilla?"

"Captured and held at Drogheda."

At that news, Niall couldn't remain seated any longer. While Aymer might have cursed Callum and claimed it wasn't true, Niall took a turn around the tent, his arms folded across his chest and his head bent, thinking. Still pacing, he said, "What do you propose?"

"I realize now that it was a fool's errand to speak to Aymer."

"He would rather die than ally with David." The thought prompted Niall to stop walking and look directly at Callum. "You realize this? The wound in Aymer is mortal."

"Yes. I realize this. Now."

"My wound, however—" Niall canted his head. "Let's just say that I am a more practical man. What does he offer me?"

Callum took in a breath, knowing this was his chance and not wanting to blow it. "What do you want?"

"Leinster for starters. And a chance, like you gave the lords of Scotland, for the throne."

"David understands that every lord who aids him will want to be rewarded with land," Callum said straightforwardly, "but you must understand that the king will hold the reins. You aren't going to rule Leinster like a fiefdom as before. King David will be the ultimate authority, and he will take that seriously."

Niall's eyes grew even warier.

"I can promise you a genuine, fair vote for overlordship of Ireland sometime in the future, but for now, the High Kingship is not for sale. Not to Cusack, who we are sure wants it. Not to Red Comyn, to whom I suspect Feypo promised it. Not to anyone."

A stillness came over Niall. "David reserves it for himself?"

"He is of the blood of Brian Boru, is he not?"

There came a faint grinding sound from Niall's jaw, and he gave Callum a curt nod. "He is."

"David will not allow Ireland to descend into another two hundred years of anarchy. There will be order. There will be a Parliament. And both Irish and English will have a say." Callum leaned forward. "An equal say. One man, one vote."

"Irishmen will be named as justiciars?"

In the past, it was through the rule of justiciars that the Irish government had functioned without a king in residence, but they had all been English.

"Yes. And you will be one of them."

Niall's eyes remained narrowed. It wasn't enough, Callum knew, but it was all he had to offer. David had declared outright that he was not giving out favors like those boxes of chocolates he'd bought (or rather, Callum had bought) in Avalon. This was about the stewardship of Ireland. On one hand, he really did want Niall's support, but he wasn't going to be held hostage to it either. Callum was, in effect, telling Niall that he could get on board or get run over.

"What if I say no?"

Callum lifted one shoulder in a half-shrug that was genuinely casual. "I would hope you would release me to deliver that news to David." He found himself referring to David without his title, just like everyone in Ireland seemed to. It would be easy to get used to, but he would have to remember to add *king* again when he returned home to England.

"What if I were to have an alternate suggestion?"

"I'm listening."

"I stay with Aymer, and we join forces with Cusack and the rest. Once the two armies are engaged, my men will show their true colors and fight for David."

Callum laughed at Niall's audacity, though he supposed the proposal wasn't any more outrageous than Callum's own. "That leaves you to decide at the last moment which way the wind is blowing. How do we know you will do as you say?"

"As a measure of my good faith, I will convince Aymer to go directly to Trim and not to march on Dublin."

"Heh." If Callum's stool had had a backrest he would have leaned into it. "That alone is a gift, I admit. It frees the men of Dublin to come to Tara."

Callum stood and went to the doorway of the tent to look out. The rain continued to fall, though Niall had pitched his tent on the leeward side of a sheltered valley. Callum stared at the weather for a few more moments, watching the men huddle against the wind and rain. Most didn't have tents but had constructed makeshift shelters under cloaks and tarps. Niall commanded a larger army than Valence, whose sole contribution seemed to be a company of mounted knights. There were no men with bows or crossbows that Callum could see, though they wouldn't be showing with the weather so wet. Still, nearly a thousand men were gathered before him.

He swung around. "We accept. What will you tell Valence?"

"That I sent you back to Dublin with your tail between your legs. He would have preferred to send your head back to David on a pike, but as you can see, most of the men here are mine."

"What will you tell Cusack about why you didn't attack Dublin?" Callum asked.

"I will tell him about your offer, laughing at the absurdity of it, and say we changed direction because of the gathering of David's armies at Tara. Cusack will hear the full story from Aymer anyway."

"Will Cusack come out?"

"He will have to. The last thing he wants is to be trapped between your forces and Trim Castle. Better to meet head on, on ground he chooses. Yes, he will come out. He will not be able to resist."

It was a risky game they were playing, with no guarantee—and perhaps no hope—of success. So far, David's army consisted of the men of Dublin and Oxmantown and nobody else. Niall's army would have made David's force imposing. At least men of Ireland, be they English, Danish, or Irish, were no strangers to battle. It would have to do, and it appeared to be all that he was going to get.

"Then I guess I'll see you on the battlefield," Callum said.

"You will."

Callum tipped his head to Niall MacMurrough and walked out of the tent into the rain.

32

Drogheda Castle

16 March 1294

Huw

"**M**y lord, news has come that all men are to gather at Tara!" A man-at-arms practically threw himself through the front door of Drogheda's great hall, so overcome with his news that he couldn't contain it. What he should have done was tell the steward, who would then have whispered it in Gilla's ear. Huw would have thought such discipline would be the first quality a messenger would cultivate, but that rarely seemed to be the case, especially when the news was as momentous as this.

It was moving on towards noon, and the new leadership at Drogheda had gathered at the high table. Since they'd overcome Butler's and Cusack's men, the hours had been spent consolidating their hold on the castle and adjacent town; sleeping, since everyone was quite short of sleep; and, frankly, wondering what to do next. Things had to be happening elsewhere in the country, but here at Drogheda, they'd had no news. The absence was aggravating in the extreme.

Although the citizens of Drogheda town, once told of the events at Trim, had submitted easily enough, the O'Reillys found themselves in something of a bind. Even with William and Huw insisting that King David would stand by them if they would stand with him, nobody knew where he was. Thus, the arrival of the messenger came as a huge relief.

Gilla stepped off the dais and walked towards the newcomer. "Calm down, son," he said in Gaelic, which Huw's ear was finally starting to get the hang of. At least he understood such a simple phrase. Then Gilla switched to French. "Speak so we all can understand."

The man swallowed hard. "The whole countryside is on the move, marching to Tara."

William stepped closer. "Who, exactly, is marching?"

"Everyone, my lord. Farmers, merchants, Irish, Saxons. Everyone."

"Why are they going to Tara?" Matha had stood too and came to stand beside his father.

"David is claiming the High Kingship!"

"But—" Matha began.

Gilla made a slicing motion with one hand to silence his son. Then he lifted his chin and turned back to the messenger, who'd watched that brief exchange with rapt attention. "Is he now?"

The messenger straightened his spine, his eyes alight. "He's called for an army and is himself marching from Dublin. They say that the O'Connors have already defeated an army of rebels and even now are marching from Connaught."

William punched the air. "They made it!"

Matha wasn't so easy to please. "How did you come by this news?" Since they'd taken the castle, Matha had been much more accepting of William's and Huw's presence, as well as their confidence that Christopher was to be trusted, though he apparently remained suspicious of David and his motives.

The messenger looked affronted. "The roads are full of men." He gestured towards the door of the hall. "On the road here, I met a monk from Bective Abbey. He'd been sent to call all Ireland to arms, with the exception of Drogheda, which David thought loyal to Tuyt. I assured him that you'd taken the castle, and the town is in an uproar with the preparations for war."

Matha frowned. "You say that O'Connor marches for David. Who else?"

"The whole of the north has risen. The Verduns, the Burghs, and the O'Neills are all on the march, though the O'Neills have the farthest to come and may arrive too late. You sent me to scout all the way to Dundalk if need be, and that is what I did."

Gilla's eyes grew bright as he looked at his son. "It is as I said would happen. Do you remember?"

Matha's brow furrowed. "What did you say?"

Rather than answer Matha directly, Gilla made a broad gesture to include everyone in the hall. "Five years ago, after the death of William de Valence, I spoke at the meeting of the clans. They did not listen, of course, thinking only of the advantage they might have now that one of the most powerful lords in Ireland was dead. I gave the same warning again last year when Gilbert de Clare was killed." He bobbed his head, as if confirming his words in his own mind. "Could they not see who had come into their midst? David, *Beloved of God*."

Huw found himself holding his breath as the Irishman spoke. He had believed in David from that very first day when he'd arrived, desperate and exhausted, at his father's hut. Out of that meeting, Huw's family had risen in rank to the point that Huw was one of David's most trusted men, as evidenced by the fact that David had given him the responsibility of looking after his cousin, though Christopher had proved himself no longer in need of looking after.

"No greater king did Israel ever see than King David. Scotland too. And now England," Gilla said. "But it isn't the name, of course, that makes the man. The name is only the outer manifestation of what—" he clenched his fist before him, "—defines the inner man. I saw this coming. I warned them. We could have worked out our problems among ourselves. We could have seen the way the wind was blowing and created an Ireland that David would not have meddled in. Now we have no choice. He has come, and since we did not bring peace upon ourselves, he will bring it for us."

"So we march for Tara?" Matha said. "We will fight for David? Why? This is a man who hadn't set foot in Ireland before three weeks ago!"

Gilla looked directly into his son's face, but he pointed at William. "Had this man? Or that one?" His pointing finger was now directed at Huw.

When Matha didn't answer, Gilla snapped his fingers at Huw. "Why did you come to Ireland? Did David promise you an estate? Riches? A landed wife?"

Huw couldn't help it. He scoffed. "No."

Gilla swung around to look at William. "And you? Do you hope to carve out a kingdom here as reward for your loyalty?"

William's mouth dropped open, surprised at the suggestion. "I—" He stopped. "Of course not."

"Of course not," Gilla repeated and looked back to his son. "Do you see their faces? My questions were ones *they never even asked.* David has a hundred men like this around him, and you ask why he will win? We took this castle from David's enemies, and yet you question the decision to keep fighting them?"

"No, Father." Matha bowed. "No, I don't."

Gilla jerked his head in a nod. "Leave a skeleton guard to hold the castle. Otherwise, roust the townspeople and our men. We march for Tara in one hour."

33

Hill of Tara

18 March 1294

Meg

Meg knew that she and Llywelyn were early, but she couldn't help herself. She'd arrived at the field of Tara at dawn to stand with her husband and await the arrival of the armies they were hoping would come.

Except no men had.

Well, that wasn't fair. Twelve men had come. From the road she could see them encamped in the center of the meadow—clearly a prime location—with their horses picketed twenty yards away. The double-ringed hill fort and standing stone on the Hill of Tara, where Ireland's high kings traditionally were crowned, was just to the west. If she looked east, she could see the church tower of the abbey at Skryne, perched on its hill. Skryne castle was hidden from view just down the rise. The men of Skryne were on their way, but as most were walking, they'd fallen behind Llywelyn and Meg.

Llywelyn leaned into her. "We are early, Meg. Dafydd said *today*. He didn't say *at dawn*."

"I know but—"

"They will come."

"You don't know that!"

Llywelyn tipped his head as he looked at her. "It isn't like you to lose faith like this." He urged his horse towards the small party of men.

Frustrated with the situation and with herself, Meg followed. "I haven't. You know I haven't."

One of the men rose to his feet at Llywelyn's approach. He was in his twenties, David's age or younger, with blond hair still tousled from sleep. He wore a mail vest, but none of his companions were well-armored. When the Normans had come a hundred years ago, their armor had given them a huge advantage against the Irish, who hadn't adopted armor yet, not even after so many years of fighting the Danes. In the intervening century, however, some Irish lords had come to see its advantages, and Meg hoped these had armor somewhere in their saddlebags.

Upon arriving in the center of the field, Llywelyn dismounted and spoke in halting Gaelic. "From whence have you come?"

The young man threw back his shoulders and raised his chin. It looked like he was expecting a fight. "I am Cian O'Neill."

To an outsider, answering Llywelyn's question with his name might not make sense, but it told Meg and Llywelyn what they needed to know: he was an O'Neill and had ridden here from the northwest.

Llywelyn stuck out his hand and introduced himself. "Welcome." He pointed with his chin to Cian's men. "Am I to assume that more are coming?"

Cian laughed, switching to English, though heaven knew how he'd learned it. "Coming? Your David has raised the whole bloody north."

Meg leaned down. "How soon?"

Cian glanced to his left as if he might see armies marching towards him at any moment. "Soon."

Meg, who was still astride, looked too, but she saw no men, only birds in the trees and an unusually clear sky.

Then Cian shrugged. "You could ask the O'Connors."

Llywelyn swung his head to look at Cian. "Where are they?"

"Around the other side, of course. We're only here because it's full over there." He grinned. "Who knew we'd end up getting the best spot!"

While Meg stared at him, trying to convince herself that she'd heard him correctly, Llywelyn said. "Will you show us?"

Cian bobbed his head in a nod. "Of course." The young man spoke English like one born to it. "All we need now is David."

"He sent a rider ahead," Meg said. "He's coming with the men of Dublin and Oxmantown."

For the first time, Cian's face took on a less than joyful expression. "Danes." Before Meg could put in a good word for working together, however, his expression cleared. "They can fight; I'll give them that, and David's descended from Sigtrygg Silkbeard as much as Brian Boru. A man of all Ireland, he is."

Then he whistled to his men, speaking to them in Gaelic. One nodded and moved to accompany him. "Cousins." Cian gestured to them. "With my uncle dead, we're all rivals now. Each thinks he's fit to lead, but I've been leading my family since my father died four years ago. It should be me."

"Your uncle was the clan chief?" Meg said. They were mounted now and heading south along the road around the Hill of Tara.

"Dead on the floor of the hall at Trim." And this time it was anger that sparked in Cian's eyes.

"I was there." Llywelyn gestured to Meg. "We both were."

Cian's attention focused on Llywelyn. "You saw him fall?"

"I did."

"How did you escape?"

Meg didn't think she was mistaken that she heard a hint of suspicion in Cian's voice.

"Earl Callum killed five of the attackers all by himself. I was lucky to have him beside me."

That got a grunt of acceptance. Llywelyn didn't mention that Callum had used a gun, which made the deaths a far different accomplishment than if he had used a sword, but the less said about the modern weapon the better.

When they reached the crest of the hill below Tara and stopped, Meg was thankful for her glasses because she was able to see the spectacle before her. If this was the O'Connor clan, they'd come in force and marched a long way through enemy territory to do it.

"A thousand men. He's brought a thousand men." Llywelyn breathed out the words, as if he didn't dare believe them.

"At least." Cian grinned. Maybe it was because he was looking forward to battle, or simply the change in the weather, but Cian was the happiest Irishman Meg had met. "They left Roscommon at noon three days ago, hours after he took back his castle. Seventy miles in three days." He shook his head, marveling at the feat, which wouldn't have been that amazing on horseback, but O'Connor had moved a thousand men on foot.

"Thank you for showing us," Meg said. "Good luck tomorrow."

"Madam." He put his hand to his forehead. "Tomorrow it is. Tell your son, when he comes, that the Tyrone O'Neills send their regards."

Meg let him go, even though her instinct was to put out a hand to stop him and ask *why? Why fight for David?*

But she didn't stop him, and she didn't ask. She knew the answer already: Cian wanted land and power, as every man did. The clans were in disarray at the loss of their chiefs, but Cusack, Tuyt, and the others had grossly underestimated the resolve of those left alive. Even if Cusack's band won and one of them claimed the High Kingship, they would still have a lifelong guerilla war on their hands.

They should have known better than to think killing the chieftains would be enough to break the backs of the clans. Or David.

A great shout went up from the camp below them. At first Meg thought it had something to do with her and Llywelyn, since men were pointing in their general direction.

But then a *whoop* came from behind her, and she turned in the saddle to see Cian riding back towards them. He reined in beside Llywelyn. "My apologies, my lord, if I implied any moment of doubt! He comes!" He swung an arm and pointed, as the men below them were doing, to the southeast.

An army was marching towards them, equal to or larger than the one already camped at Tara. Flags and banners waved above the heads of the marchers, including the biggest dragon banner Meg had ever seen. "How—" She broke off and laughed as she realized what David had done. "It's a sail." From the looks, he had raided the boats they'd come in on, which were still docked in Dublin harbor, for every flag, banner, and piece of sailcloth in their holds.

"If Cusack didn't know we were coming, he does now," Cian said.

"That's the point, I think." Llywelyn had been smiling too, but now he studied the oncoming force. "Dafydd intends to meet him in open battle. He wants the fight."

"That's so … unlike him," Meg said. "This whole time I've been assuming that he intended to find a way out before it came to that, like he did at Windsor."

Llywelyn shook his head. "I'm sorry, *cariad*. Not this time."

34

Hill of Tara

David

His mother was right that, as a rule, David avoided battle, and whenever he set up for one, he wanted to figure out a way for it not to be a battle at all. He prided himself on his ability to think his way out of problems rather than to use his fists.

But this fight, this army, and this battle were different from any he'd encountered before. For starters, the men who'd marched with him from Dublin formed a real army. And as they'd taken to the road, the men who'd joined them along the way were also fighters. Never mind that they were farmers too. History wasn't kidding (to take a page from William, who'd arrived with the O'Reillys, of all people) when it said that war was a way of life in Ireland. Whether Irish, Danish, or English, a man knew how to defend himself and his family or he and they died. Sometimes it was just that simple.

He'd followed Callum towards the open entrance to the pavilion, set up below the stone of Tara, but he stopped as Christopher stepped into his path. "David."

"I'd heard you were here." David laughed and grabbed his cousin up in a hug. "You had my mother worried."

"I've already seen her and had my ear talked off." Christopher turned slightly, gesturing to a girl about his age that she should approach. "I'd like to introduce you to Aine O'Reilly. She and I rode to Roscommon together. We wouldn't have O'Connor's support if it wasn't for her."

Aine curtseyed deeply, her pale face coloring so that her skin tone almost matched her hair. "It was only my duty, my lord."

"It was far more than that." David reached for her elbow to encourage her to rise. "Thank you also for keeping an eye on Christopher for me."

Aine straightened, though she hadn't yet looked him directly in the face. David raised his eyebrows at Christopher, who shrugged. There were undercurrents here that David wasn't getting, but unfortunately, he didn't have time to figure them out. Callum had halted in the entrance to the pavilion, waiting for him. That Christopher had not only convinced the O'Connors to throw in with David but had eliminated the combined Clare and O'Rourke army in the process was almost too much to be believed. All of a sudden, his cousin had grown up, not an unheard of effect of living in the Middle Ages. David himself had experienced that process live and in color.

So, for the moment, David simply put a hand on his cousin's shoulder. "We are going to talk, just as soon as this meeting ends."

"It's okay," Christopher said. "I'm okay."

From what he'd heard about what had transpired over the last few days, David wasn't sure that was true, but for now he had to take Christopher at his word. With a jerk of his head, asking Christopher and Aine to follow, he headed inside where the lords of Ireland waited.

At David's approach, the men quieted, and Callum raised a hand to announce David's presence with his full name and title. Even David couldn't deny the necessity of ceremony in this instance. He'd been King of England long enough to know how to look good on the outside despite uncertainty on the inside. Not that he was fundamentally uncertain about this fight, even if he still wasn't entirely sure about leading it. These men were looking to him, and he'd all but declared himself High King of Ireland, so at this point he either had to go through with it or return to England with his tail between his legs, leaving the various lords of Ireland to duke it out amongst themselves. He'd already said that he couldn't do that, so that left leading as the only alternative.

David beckoned the highest-ranking lords to come to the table upon which a map, taken from Bective Abbey, lay. The abbot to whom the map belonged was here too, standing in a far corner, his eyes somewhat hollowed. None of them were getting enough sleep.

"Abbot John, a prayer, if you will." David had already coached the abbot about what he wanted him to pray for, namely the Will of God, along with, if possible, few casualties, torrential rain overnight, and, most importantly, unity of purpose.

After the prayer, David gazed around at the assembled men and women. The latter included not only Mom and Aine, but also Maud de Geneville, who would not be left behind. From what James had said, Margery de Verdun would have come too if she hadn't just given birth to a daughter. She'd sent her two eldest sons instead.

"Thank you for coming. It should be obvious that I mean that sincerely, but let me say it again: *Thank you for coming.* I stand before you because Ireland is at a crossroads. By coming here today, you have chosen a path that your forefathers did not. I say to you that by doing so you have changed the course of Ireland's history forever."

David spread his hands wide. "Before I say more, I must confirm for you what you are *not* doing here: first of all, you are not fighting for lands or rewards. At the end of the day, you may end up with more than you had. You may end up with less. We may all lose our lives."

He had their full attention, speaking in French, so everyone could understand, with the exception perhaps of Christopher, who was watching closely anyway. He and Aine were standing on either side of William de Bohun, who was perfectly capable of translating if needed.

"Secondly, you are not fighting for me. That may come as news to some of you, but it's the truth, as I see it. I am the Lord of Ireland but—" here he waved a hand dismissively, "—it's hardly ever been more than a paper title, and most of you didn't respect it anyway."

Out of the corner of his eye, David saw Callum shake his head at David's honesty. David knew this was a risky strategy. Callum had told him that it would be safer to give a rah-rah speech rather than something that amounted to more of a lecture, but David had argued against it, saying it wasn't honest. He didn't want the men here fighting tomorrow under false pretenses. David needed to get to the heart of the matter, lay it bare, and then dismiss it.

"Most importantly, you are not fighting for yourselves, either as individuals or as clans." David paused. "So what are you fighting for?"

Silence had descended on the pavilion when David had started speaking, but now even the side comments and fidgeting ceased. Both William and Christopher looked to be on the verge of speaking, but Callum came up behind them to put a hand on each of their shoulders, telling him without words that the question wasn't directed at them.

"Tell us, sire," John de Falkes said at the same moment that Aine said, "Ireland."

David pointed at her. "Thank you, John, but she has said it." He looked gravely at the audience. "Ireland."

Aine wasn't done, and David was glad to see that she seemed to have recovered from whatever had held her tongue earlier. "More than that, we're fighting for the people, Irish, Danish, and Saxon, who live here and want nothing more than to live in a land where war is not the only constant."

Christopher had settled back on his heels, but his chin was up, and he was grinning. William's eyes were alight too, and they brightened further when Maud de Geneville stepped to Aine's side and hooked her arm through the girl's. "How many years have we fought over the same fields and valleys, the same castles? And now my husband is dead by the hand of a man he would have called a friend." She turned her gaze away from David towards the men assembled before her.

"I am an old woman and cannot fight, but only a fool is blind to the future that faces us." She gestured to David without looking at him. "When the barons of England asked David, an outsider, to take up the crown, they did so because the bickering and the carnage had gone on too long, and the price of disagreement had finally been deemed too high. Our patience has been far greater. Two hundred years ago, Leinster invited Strongbow to Ireland. In so doing, he set us on a path of destruction from which we have hardly deviated. I say, *enough!*" She paused, and now her eyes met David's. "What say you?"

Nobody stirred. Nobody spoke—until Hugh O'Connor stepped to the fore at the same instant as John Verdun. The two men looked at each other—the older Irishman and the young Anglo-Norman, who had never met before this day. And as if they were twins they canted their heads and said together, "We say yes."

* * * * *

You did the right thing," Mom said the next morning, "talking that way. You had to tell them the truth, and they did agree to fight." She should have remained back at Tara, but she refused to be left behind to learn their fate after the fact. Though the rain that had fallen all night had ceased with the dawn, she was dressed appropriately for it in a simple dress with leggings underneath, boots, and a thick cloak. She also had a long knife belted at her waist. David didn't know that he'd ever seen such a determined look on her face, and his mom had spent a lot of her life being plenty determined.

David put down the binoculars he was holding. "They were browbeaten into it."

"Peer pressure can be a powerful tool," Mom said.

"They were right that winning is by no means a certainty."

"If they don't fight, losing is a certainty, so in the end they had no choice."

"They could have joined Cusack."

Mom laughed. "And pigs could fly."

Whether she intended it or not, her comment garnered a laugh from David, who put the binoculars back in front of his eyes. "What's your bet? Will MacMurrough side with us?"

"I don't believe in betting." Then she shook her head, modifying her flip comment. "Trust has to be earned. If he does as Callum asked, then he will have earned it. If he doesn't ... well, then we'll know."

Callum appeared at David's side. "Your horse is ready, my lord."

David glanced quickly at him, surprised by Callum's formality with only his mother present. Callum gave a rueful smile and tipped his head towards the horse, which was waiting near the company of men who would accompany David into battle. David turned back to his mother to tell her that he had to go and found her eyes swimming with tears.

"I'm sorry! I'm sorry!" She flung her arms around him. "I know I'm not supposed to do this!"

David handed his binoculars to Callum, bent, and wrapped his arms around his mom in a fully body hug. "It's going to be okay." He gave her a quick squeeze. "We've got this."

Mom gripped him tightly for another second, and then she stepped back, wiping at her cheeks with the fingers of both hands. "I love you."

"I love you too."

Twenty-five wasn't fourteen or even eighteen. At one time, while David wouldn't necessarily have underplayed her concerns, he wouldn't have entirely understood them either. Now, however, he too was a parent, and though his sons were still small people, he knew how much of himself was wrapped up in them. Because of who he was, he could surround his boys with people to watch them and pretend to himself that he had some control over whether they lived or died. His mom, on the other hand, had just knowingly sent her son into battle. Necessity or not, Mom was never going to do that without tears and an aching nausea that wouldn't go away until he stood before her, whole and alive, again.

Still, she put a brave face on it, waving and smiling as he rode away. David waved one last time and then turned to face front. Callum nodded, all business too. "I didn't see a change in their order of battle. Did you?"

"No." As David had just observed through his binoculars, the enemy cavalry occupied the vanguard—those front and center of the combined force that faced them. If the cavalry were placed behind the spearmen and needed to charge, they would run right over their own men. "Comyn and Cusack occupy the center, Valence is on the right, and various and sundry others are on the left, including MacMurrough."

"So, what's the trick?"

David shook his head. "I don't know. The scouts don't report reinforcements anywhere?"

"No."

Once everyone had decided to stand together, the talk had turned to strategy. On one hand, David still preferred to negotiate rather than fight. Today, however, even if he was so inclined, negotiation wasn't an option. They were going to fight. The key was to win.

"How's the terrain?" David said when they reached the command tent where the captains were gathered.

"Wet, my lord." That was James Stewart, who'd arrived with the Verdun boys.

"It's hardly better than a bog, so it be," Gilla O'Reilly stated flatly. "We should have chosen better ground."

"Given the rain, better ground isn't to be had," James said. "I've ridden across half of Ireland this week, and every field in the country is like this."

David motioned with one hand to stop the argument. "We discussed this already. This ground is just as I wanted it."

"Pardon, my lord." O'Reilly remained unconvinced. "This field is too narrow."

"It's perfect for our purposes."

While David had been speaking to O'Reilly, Dad had entered the tent, accompanied by a soldier wearing Comyn's colors. David held up his hand to silence everyone and then moved to the doorway to confront the newcomer. "What is this?"

The man bowed stiffly. "My lord Comyn asks that you meet him to speak of peace."

"Really?" David swung around to look at the men who surrounded him. Most had a stubborn set to their chins that told him they weren't willing to talk. He wasn't either. David turned back to the messenger. "Why?"

The man looked taken aback. "Why what?"

"Why negotiate? You have us outnumbered." David gestured to indicate the world outside the pavilion. "Your scouts must have told you that we have three thousand men. You have four thousand."

"Five." It was boastful of the messenger to correct David, which only showed how secure Comyn and Cusack were feeling. But then the messenger cleared his throat, finally answering David's question. "My lords are feeling merciful."

The men at David's back didn't like that. Nor did David.

"He seeks to delay us," Hugh O'Connor said in an undertone. "He hopes that some of us will defect to his side. Or perhaps he hopes to give more armies time to reach *him*."

David nodded. Men were going to die, and David was going to let them rather than allow Comyn and Cusack to delay. He tilted his head to look at the messenger, with the implication that he was a bug in a jar. "Tell your master that while we appreciate his benevolence, we will continue as we are."

The messenger blinked, and David flicked out his fingers, indicating that the man was dismissed. Callum took him away, and David turned back to the assembled men. Placing both hands on the table, he leaned heavily on them. "Gentlemen, we are committed."

35

Near Tara
19 March 1294
Christopher

For better or for worse, Christopher had chosen to fight among the O'Connors rather than the O'Reillys. But as Hugh O'Connor's soldiers were currently standing next to Gilla O'Reilly's, and Christopher and William had somehow been maneuvered next to their sons, in the end the decision hadn't amounted to much.

Still, it felt important to Christopher. Gilla O'Reilly had conveniently forgotten that, only a few days before, his men had given Christopher a concussion, abducted him, and hauled him twenty miles hanging over a horse's withers. Even with David's campaign of peace, love, and unity among the factions supporting him, Christopher hadn't forgotten that. He'd kind of been holding out for a *sorry*. Maybe even a *thank you* for getting Aine out of Drumconrath. One hadn't been forthcoming yet, however, and now he was thinking that one never would.

"It's okay to be afraid," William said from beside him. "I am."

Christopher turned to look at his friend, astonished that he'd been so honest. It made it easy for Christopher to be honest too. "I think everyone is."

They stood in what looked like the rearguard, but was actually going to become the vanguard soon enough. David had placed a solid block of five hundred foot soldiers in the front of the army, standing shoulder to shoulder with their shields locked together. Behind them stood six phalanxes of archers, arranged in wedges, with the point of the triangle aimed at the enemy.

Ten more wedges were arrayed on the left and right flanks (five on each side), near the base of the treed hills that formed something of a bowl around the valley. Those archers had carefully planted a forest of tall stakes in front of them to protect them from Cusack's cavalry and ensure that the enemy horses, when they charged, would swerve away, towards the center of the field. To use stakes for stationary archers was a standard Welsh tactic, but according to Aunt Meg, it hadn't become typical for the English army until the battle of Agincourt a hundred years from now.

According to her too, when Strongbow had come to Ireland, his Welsh bowmen had mown through the ranks of the lightly armored Irish like a medieval version of a machine gun. These bowmen hadn't stayed in Ireland, however, being discriminated against by the English as a matter of course. And while a few archers continued to be deployed both within and without the Pale, neither the English nor the Irish were devotees of archery to the degree the Welsh were.

Cavalry (dismounted to disguise their numbers) were placed in three blocks between and slightly behind each of the central wedges of bowmen, so that if or when they mounted and charged forward, they wouldn't run over their own archers. To the left and right, behind the archers and the cavalry, Irish spearmen waited.

David had expressed concern that, with no tradition of fighting on horseback and too few of them wearing armor, if the enemy cavalry tried to flank the main body of the army, they might not be enough to stop them. But the O'Neills and their O'Donnell allies were proud and insisted that they would stand their ground. Privately, David had said to Callum (in a conversation Christopher had overheard) that he wasn't worried about them standing. It was them falling.

For the moment, it was all Christopher could do to stand his own ground and stay in line. He gripped his horse's bridle, telling himself that he was ready for this. Then a hand came down on his shoulder, and he turned to see Huw standing between him and William. "No one in Ireland has ever seen Welsh bowmen go up against a cavalry charge before—and neither has Comyn or Cusack. We will stand our ground until our arrows run out."

"That is a lesson my forefathers learned to their detriment." William eyed Huw. "It's good to know that you're among them."

"As I am glad to know your sword will ride." His hands gripping their shoulders, Huw shook them both. "I must return to my line."

William watched him go. "He had my back."

"That surprises you?" Christopher said.

"No, but we have not been natural friends." William paused. "Thank you for bringing Aine back safely."

Christopher almost laughed that the thanks he'd been seeking had come from William rather than Gilla. "I had very little to do with it." He tipped his head. "But you're welcome."

Their conversation had taken Christopher's mind off the battle, but now a trumpet sounded, signaling that the foot soldiers should start forward. They were to march until Cusack's army responded. This was the trickiest part—the trick, in fact—and if it didn't work, then this battle might be over way more quickly than David wanted—and not end in his favor.

Hundreds of men began to march forward down the slight slope they'd set up on, heading towards the center of the field. Comyn and Cusack had put their cavalry in the front of their force and, as David hoped, the sight of those locked shields coming towards them was too much to resist. They *knew* that there was no way five hundred foot soldiers armed with spear and shield could withstand a comparable number of cavalry pounding toward them. They *knew* it.

Someone gave the order to charge. The roar of excitement—of battle engaged—echoed throughout the field. Meanwhile, the foot soldiers marched on. As they were much slower, not being mounted, the first rank of cavalry was a third of the way across the field before the foot soldiers reached the bottom of their own slope.

Because he was in the front row of David's cavalry, Christopher had a good view of what happened next, and it was the most terrifying thing he'd ever seen: the foot soldiers broke ranks and ran like hell. They shouted and screamed, threw down their shields, and all in all sold their panic really well. They almost had Christopher thinking they were terrified—and he had been in on the trick.

More importantly, it looked like utter panic to their enemies, and a great cheer went up from Cusack's men. They thought they'd won the battle after only five minutes. All that waiting, all that expectation, and they were going to rout their enemies before lunch. Five hundred cavalry became fifteen hundred men and horses, charging directly towards Christopher.

But David had set a trap. He, Aunt Meg, and Callum had cooked up this formation and until this morning hadn't told anyone else what was going to happen, out of fear that a traitor in their ranks would inform the opposing army what they were up to. According to David, once the foot soldiers ran, the rest of the plan came straight out of the battle of Agincourt, one of the greatest English victories ever, where Henry V had been outnumbered ten to one. It was unfair, really, that David had thousands of years of history to draw upon—or it would have been unfair if it wasn't so important that he win.

Because, of course, the foot soldiers hadn't actually run away. Instead, they'd made for the sides of the field, racing for gaps deliberately left open between the last rank of archers in the central body of the army and the first rank of archers on the flank. And it was those archers who started shooting first.

Outpost in Time

Uncle Llywelyn called to the cavalry, and the word went among the riders: *mount your horses, but wait for the signal to charge.*

Christopher scrambled into the saddle, his heart pounding furiously. But the signal wasn't given, and instead of joining the fray, he gaped at the carnage. He hadn't ever been in a battle before, so what he was seeing was all new to him, and from the looks on the faces of Felimid and Matha, it was new to them too.

As David had promised everyone they would, the Welsh archers had gone to work with brutal efficiency. Christopher had been told over and over again that a good archer could fire six arrows a minute—and a great one more like eight to ten. Well, David's archers were the best, handpicked and experienced, and led by a grizzled man named Morgan whose brown arms were so similar in color to the bow he held that it looked like the bow was growing out of his hands.

His voice could be heard bellowing above the screams of men and horses, counting out the beats in Welsh, which sounded to Christopher like *Een! Die! Tree!* Over and over again.

There were only two hundred archers, but in one minute they'd fired nearly two thousand arrows. Purportedly, Cusack had brought archers too, but if so, they'd been posted at the back, and couldn't fire at David's army without hitting their own cavalry.

The death was ungodly. Wave after wave of cavalry went down under the barrage of arrows. So far, none of David's own men had set foot on the field, but the enemy cavalry was mired in mud, and with each man and horse that fell, it became harder and harder for those living to escape. It had rained all night, and the field was as wet as Gilla O'Reilly had told them it was. Worse for the cavalry, the fake panic among David's foot soldiers had emboldened more cavalry to enter the field in hopes of participating in the rout, and they'd been followed by hundreds of Cusack's foot soldiers.

Thus, the cavalry in the front were struggling over their fallen comrades, while many in the back were trying to retreat. But by now their way was blocked by their own men, who had no idea what was happening ahead of them and continued to push forward, even as they were being run over by their own men and horses.

That put the next phase of David's plan into effect—namely the return of the lightly armored foot soldiers, who were less likely to sink into the mud than horses, men-at-arms, and knights in armor. They raced back into battle, their numbers nearly tripled by men who'd been held back behind Christopher in the far rearguard. The Irish fought predominantly on foot, and Hugh O'Connor led one of these groups, as did Magnus Godfridson, the mayor of Oxmantown.

"We need to move! We need to move now! They're flanking us!" Callum reined his horse between two blocks of cavalry.

"What about them?" Christopher pointed ahead to the fight in front of them.

"Don't worry about them. Nobody's getting through that. It's the ones behind us I'm worried about."

As one, four hundred cavalry swung around to look, and what Christopher saw made his breath seize in his throat. Fifty yards away,

David was standing in the stirrups twirling his sword above his head. A football field beyond him, enemy riders were pouring towards them from the left, having circled around the entire field and the woods to come at David's army from behind. The O'Neills were supposed to have stopped them, but they hadn't.

"Follow me!" David spurred his horse directly at the lead riders, typically miles ahead of any of his men.

Blindly obeying and infected by the urgency of the moment, Christopher followed in the midst of all the others. He could hardly run away at this point, and he was thankful he'd devoted so much time to riding these last nine months. He might never have swung his sword in battle, but at least he wasn't going to fall off.

No archers could help them in this direction, since they would be shooting into the backs of their own cavalry. Christopher felt lightheaded, sweating and cold at the same time, and he clenched his jaw and told himself to focus. He could have mentioned to David at any time in the last day that he thought he was concussed and that his head still hurt, but somehow the conversation had never happened. Christopher hadn't wanted to fight, but he'd felt like he needed to, and if David had known about the concussion, he would have stopped him.

The opposing sides of cavalry hit like they were two semi-trucks playing chicken, except nobody swerved. Christopher's helmet prevented him from seeing anything but what was directly in front of him. All he was trying to do was stay on his horse and not kill any of his own men as he flailed about with his sword at anyone who came close. He was trying to live.

The only sounds he could hear were his own breathing and the thudding of his heart. He was literally seeing red, as if he'd burst all the blood vessels in his eyes and they were pulsing at him like a cheap neon sign. He slashed his sword at some poor schmuck wearing Comyn's colors—not red as they ought to be, but three sheaves of wheat on blue—who subsequently fell off his horse. Christopher was pretty sure he'd killed him, but he didn't have time to make sure before he had to slash at someone else.

Twenty seconds later, someone on the ground stabbed upward at Christopher's horse, who stumbled, and Christopher only just managed to clear his feet from the stirrups before the horse went down. Sweat poured into Christopher's eyes. Terrified that he was going to be struck down from behind, he flung off his helmet so he could see better, but when he turned, his sword out, desperate to keep all comers at bay, he found himself forming a defensive triangle with William and Felimid. The Irishman was singing—actually singing—in Gaelic at the top of his lungs, which had the added benefit of letting Christopher know at all times exactly where he was.

Before the charge, Christopher had had some sense of what was going on. He'd seen that first cavalry charge and the lines of men fall to the archers' arrows. Now, having participated in a charge for the first time himself, he understood why the initial assault had gone down as it had. He had no sense of anything happening outside a ten-foot radius. He was standing on a sloping grassy field, fighting for his life, and the battle could be all but over twenty yards away, and he wouldn't know it.

If this were a movie, the three of them would have been exchanging witty banter between slashes at enemy soldiers, but the only thing Christopher could think about was what he was doing with his sword and his absolute desperation to keep them all upright and alive.

Then a roar came from somewhere in the distance, the kind of sound made when a stadium full of people open their throats and yell. Whatever they said was beyond Christopher, but William gave a cheer of his own, and behind him Felimid interrupted his singing to whoop exultantly. "MacMurrough comes!"

It was as if a wind had swept across the battlefield, and instead of being in the center of the fighting, Christopher suddenly found himself on the edge of it. At last, he had more friends around him than enemies.

"He's fallen! He's fallen!" These words came in French. For a terrified second, Christopher thought whoever had cried out meant David, but William elbowed Christopher in the back and told him to look. Cusack's banner had been planted a hundred feet away near a stone wall that separated this pasture from an adjacent field to the west. As Christopher watched, it wavered and then fell to the ground.

And all of a sudden, men were flowing past him, many moving at a dead run if they could manage it, with real panic in their faces as opposed to what the foot soldiers had shown a lifetime ago when the battle began. Two minutes later, Christopher, William, and Felimid were alone, standing upright amidst corpses.

Christopher couldn't breathe. He tugged on his collar, trying to loosen it so it didn't press on his throat. He weaved on his feet for a few seconds, looking at Felimid, who had a huge smile on his face. "My father was right to trust you!"

Christopher didn't have the wherewithal to respond. Then, still grinning, Felimid dropped with a plop to the ground. Christopher and William joined him. Maybe that was stupid, and in a second somebody was going to come along and stick his sword in them, but Christopher was too tired to care.

36

Near Tara
David

David flung himself off his horse after Robbie. Since David had been focused on his own battle, it had taken him a second to realize what Robbie's purpose was. David rolled underneath the blade of an oncoming cavalryman and left him for Theobald Verdun to take out. Which he did. The rest of David's guard formed a circle around him, though the battle was winding down now that MacMurrough had joined the fray, and most of Cusack's and Comyn's men were surrendering rather than fighting.

Robbie, meanwhile, sat astride the body of Red Comyn and was choking the life out of him. David could understand why he wanted to, but he couldn't let him.

"Stop." He scooped his arms underneath Robbie's armpits and hauled him backwards.

"No! He deserves to die!" Robbie fought his forced retreat, to the point that he lifted Red's head off the ground rather than let go of him. Then Comyn swung an arm at Robbie's wrists and forced his hands away.

James had arrived by that time, and he grasped Red by the shoulders and pulled him out from underneath Robbie's legs.

David held onto Robbie until Comyn was clear and then shoved him to one side. Robbie fell to his knees, gasping for breath, a match to Red, who'd been genuinely desperate.

"You should have let me kill him," Robbie said.

"That may be." David went to crouch in front of Red, who'd managed to get himself into a sitting position. James had already relieved him of his knives and now picked up his sword, which had been flung from his hand when Robbie had thrown himself at him. "What am I going to do with you?"

Red spat on the ground. "Like he said, you should have let him kill me."

David tsked through his teeth. "You don't mean that. You're a survivor."

Red turned his head to look directly at David. It was probably the first time that the two men had ever exchanged an honest look. David didn't know what Red saw in David's eyes, though what David felt within himself was sadness at the waste of human life and regret at what could have been. He had a sick sense too that somehow in saving Comyn, he'd subverted Robbie's fate. He'd never felt that kind of fatalism before and hoped he never would again.

Red, by contrast, displayed disdain, wearing a sneer that implied that David couldn't possibly understand him or know what was going on inside his head. Any fool, however, could see that what Red was really feeling was anger, a not uncommon go-to emotion for any man, even those who hadn't spent their life fighting.

But Red's anger wasn't driven by remorse or fear or physical pain. His eyes weren't looking at the dead men and horses around him and feeling regret. He was mad because he'd taken a chance and chosen the wrong side. He was angry at himself for almost dying at Robbie's hands and that he was going to have to face his wife and his uncle with the utter failure of the Irish venture.

Red was embarrassed.

Knowing now that he would have to think long and hard about what to do with him, David got to his feet and turned away. Red was the kind of medieval man who could no more understand David's purpose or the reasoning behind his actions than he could fly. And if Red ever did understand David, he would mock him for his naiveté. David could spend his life trying to make the world a better place, and the moment his back was turned or he died, men like Red would be there to put everything back the way it had been.

Men like Red made David despair ... and feel very, very tired.

* * * * *

He found Christopher sitting between William de Bohun and Felimid O'Connor, dead men all around them. The fact that they weren't lying flat on the ground told him that they were alive, but that didn't mean they were whole.

He knelt in front of his cousin. "Are you wounded?"

David still didn't know how the *hell* Cusack's cavalry had managed to roll over the O'Neill rearguard so easily, but he cursed the carnage it had caused. Twenty minutes earlier, Cian O'Neill, who'd survived after putting up a better fight than his elders, had come to him on bended knee and apologized. It was more than his rivals had done. David didn't think he'd been complacent, but it revealed a weakness in his plan. At the very least, it showed him the stupidity of asking men to fight after marching through the night.

Christopher looked up blearily. "My head hurts."

"I can imagine."

Huw loped over and came to a halt in front of the trio, looking down at them with his hands on his hips. "You live, then."

"It seems so." William reached up a hand so Huw could pull him to his feet. They lifted Christopher next, and with Christopher's arms around their shoulders, the three of them limped from the field. Two dozen paces on, they encountered Aine, who was among the women who'd come to look for loved ones. She shook her head at the sight of them, and then ducked under William's free arm to walk with her new friends to the medical tent.

David watched them go, breathing a little easier. He wasn't ready to talk to anyone else yet, however, or make any of the decisions that everyone was waiting for him to make—the first of which had to be what they were going to do with all the prisoners, not just Red Comyn.

The system of ransoms was long established by now. Men of wealth and power who were captured in battle were ransomed back to their families for whatever the captor could get out of them. David found the whole enterprise distasteful, but the alternative was either keeping the man in prison for some length of time or killing him.

It was the problem Henry V had faced after Agincourt: his prisoners had outnumbered his army—and he feared that if the French realized it, they would overwhelm his men. So he'd ordered all but the wealthiest killed. History reported that many of his own men refused the order and, in the end, 'only' several hundred were killed instead of several thousand. Regardless, it wasn't a path David was willing to go down.

But as many of the men they'd captured were genuinely dangerous, they remained a problem. He didn't want to just let them go back to their families only to wreak the same havoc on Ireland the moment David's back was turned. He'd already arranged for Comyn to be marched to Skryne Castle where Maud de Geneville could look after him. Cusack's death had broken the back of much of the resistance, but, unfortunately, Valence was missing—as were Auliffe O'Rourke and Thomas de Clare, both of whom had somehow escaped Hugh O'Connor's net.

Meanwhile, David had death and destruction on his hands the likes of which he'd never seen. The main battlefield was churned up from thousands of men's feet and horses' hooves, littered with discarded armor and weapons, and the bodies of the dead were only now starting to be distinguished from the wounded. Not far from where David stood lay a discarded helmet, blood marring the interior and just starting to run from the rain that had started falling. Again.

When David had conceived the battle plan with the help of his mother and Callum, he'd believed in what he was doing. It had been this or surrender.

But he hadn't understood. *God forgive him,* he hadn't known.

He started down the slope, which wasn't steep, though it had felt like it was as steep as Mt. Hood a few hours ago as he'd charged up it towards Comyn's cavalry.

Callum arrived at his right shoulder. "My lord."

David shook his head. "What a terrible, bloody waste."

"Comyn and Cusack should have known better."

Unable to speak for the rage that consumed him, David clenched his fists and bent back his head to look up at the sky. Raindrops pelted onto his face, and he let them for a moment before dropping his chin again. "You were right."

David could feel the wariness emanating from Callum. "What was I right about?"

"That everyone came here to fight for himself. Nobody cares about Ireland. They care about power and wealth. That's what this was about." He kicked at a clod of dirt and it exploded like a mini bomb in front of him, reminding him again of the extent to which he'd neglected his responsibilities to Ireland. This battle had been entirely devoid of the technologies that David had brought to England. There'd been no cannon. No early warning systems. No guns.

"They're men, David. That's what men care about."

"Well it's about time they stopped!"

Callum's laugh was immediate and genuine. "That isn't going to happen, David. Not now. Not a thousand years from now." David looked morosely at his friend, who added, "You're going to have to give Leinster to MacMurrough."

"And Breifne to O'Reilly, and Ulster to the O'Neills and the Burghs, who will have to be convinced to accept my decision and not fight among themselves when they think I'm not looking. Believe me, I know."

"You can't expect to change Ireland overnight."

"Maybe not, but I can wish for it. At least half of the new justiciars I'm going to appoint are going to be women," David said. "I'm not going to screw around with anyone's sensibilities this time."

"I agree, though Maud de Geneville may be no less prideful or cutthroat than Geoffrey was."

"I don't care. If there's even a slight chance that appointing women will mean less of this—" He broke off, gesturing to the carnage in front of him. He counted fourteen dead horses within a hundred feet of where he stood. Thankfully, the men had already been moved, "—then I'll consider it a win."

Callum's hands were on his hips as he surveyed the field. It was clear he wanted to say something else, but he wasn't quite sure how to go about it.

"Spit it out, Callum. Let's have it."

"Scotland."

David scoffed. "I am well aware that Comyn and Valence weren't here entirely on their own behalf. Balliol had to have had something to do with it. On top of which, Clare and Valence are in the wind. That's not going to turn out well."

"I can't disagree." Callum hesitated again, but before David could snap a *What!* at him, he added, "Back in Avalon, Balliol was viewed as a somewhat ineffective king, not helped by the fact that Edward constantly undermined him."

"You're implying that I have not done that—and now look where it's got me?"

"I didn't say that. It's just that history might be repeating itself here, though not on the same timeline as in Avalon, or the same in all particulars."

David had been thinking exactly the same thing for days, not just when he'd hauled Robbie off Red Comyn. Red might come to regret the favor, seeing how he was now facing a long prison sentence. David couldn't ransom him back to his family. He had forgiven him once. He couldn't again.

"And one more thing," Callum said, "which I can't believe I'm suggesting, but I think might be the end game here, and you're really going to like it."

"That would be a switch."

Callum snorted laughter before saying, "What if you suggest, or speak to some like-minded people who could suggest to your new Parliament, that they make a rule that to own lands in Ireland requires giving up all lands in any other country. A man—or woman—would have to choose one or the other."

David gaped at him. "I would too."

"Yes, you would. You couldn't be High King of Ireland and King of England."

David let out a burst of air that became a laugh, and then he clapped Callum on the shoulder. "You, my friend, are a genius."

"But only when you deem the country ready," Callum hastened to add. "Let's not be hasty."

"Oh no, you don't." David laughed again. "You've got me thinking now—"

He broke off as Callum nudged him with his elbow. David looked over to see a mixed delegation of Irish and English approaching him. When David had gone to the battlefield looking for Christopher, he'd semi-deliberately given them the slip, but they couldn't be avoided any longer. Rather than speak amongst the dead and wounded, he headed over to meet them.

"A better life is what they want, David," Callum said, keeping pace with him. "Maybe I was right back at Trim when I said nobody would fight for Ireland, but you were wrong when you said that they hadn't. You've shown them what is possible. You have made them believe."

Comyn's disdainful expression rose before David's eyes. "You really think so?"

"I do." And then he grunted an amendment. "We all do."

"My lord." Hugh O'Connor came to a halt in front of David. "We were hoping to discuss the arrangements for your crowning at Tara tomorrow."

From slightly behind him, Callum added in a whisper, "See. I told you so."

David had to admit that the lords of whatever background who faced him were looking remarkably contented. Niall MacMurrough might have his arms folded across his chest, but the pose didn't imply defiance so much as self-satisfaction. Gilla O'Reilly, suddenly vaulted to prominence with the leadership vacuum created by Trim, was nodding to himself. Magnus Godfridson, whom David was already seeing as a staunch ally, was standing shoulder to shoulder with James Stewart, now the ranking member of the Ulster contingent.

David squared his shoulders. As when he'd taken the throne of England, it would be unconscionable—and unfair—to doubt the people's belief in him, or worse, to mock it. He'd asked for not only their armies and their lives, but their faith—and they'd given it. Comyn was free to nourish his anger, cynicism, and resentment. That didn't mean David had to.

"I'm ready if you are." He gestured towards his personal tent, which was doubling as the command center since the larger pavilion had been taken over by wounded men. "If you will," he took a stride in that direction, "follow me."

The End

Author's Note

Ten years ago when I wrote *Footsteps in Time*, before any of my books were published, I was fully aware of the difficulty Welsh names would present to readers. I spoke no Welsh at the time and merrily pronounced everything incorrectly. Nonetheless, I decided, given Wales's history of oppression and rebellion against the English, that anglicizing Welsh names would be the wrong thing to do. I still feel that way.

That said, I could not, in good conscience, use the unanglicized Gaelic names in *Outpost in Time*. While I mean no disrespect to Gaelic speakers and people of Irish descent (me included!), the names were so different and spelled in such a way that I felt they would be a barrier to enjoyment of the story.

For example, rather than Hugh O'Connor, a Gaelic version would read *Aodh Ó Conchobair*, while the ruler after him would be *Ruaidri mac Cathal Ua Conchobair*. Auliffe O'Rourke would be *Amhlaoibh O Ruairc*.

Yeah, I couldn't do it.

I would also like to make note for clarification of my use of the ethnicities, *Norman* and *English,* in *Outpost in Time*. To recap, in 1066 the Normans, led by William the Conqueror, crossed the English Channel from Normandy (which *his* ancestors had conquered) to conquer England, defeating the Saxon King Harold at Hastings. With that conquest, Norman rule replaced Saxon rule, and few Saxon nobles were allowed to maintain their lands and power. These Normans spoke French, first and foremost, and few initially bothered to learn English or anything at all, for that matter, about the people they'd conquered. But as much as Normans liked to conquer, they also were culturally predisposed to intermarriage and assimilation. They'd done it in Normandy. They did it in England and Wales. And when the time came, they did it in Ireland too.

Thus, as the decades passed, rather than transforming the Irish, who enormously outnumbered their Norman overlords, into Normans, the Normans became more Irish than the Irish themselves (which is an actual saying in Ireland today), and many lords cared more about their lands in Ireland than those belonging to their families in France or England. As when William the Conqueror had sailed to England, when Strongbow sailed to conquer Ireland, many of the men who sailed with him were landless younger sons. Their destiny became Ireland's destiny.

Furthermore, talking about the conquest of Ireland in terms of English and Norman is important but confusing. The leaders of the conquering army were of Norman descent, but the common men who fought for them and who settled in the towns around the new castles the conquerors built were English or even Welsh, since Strongbow was the Earl of Pembroke and his lands were in South Wales. Identity was further complicated by intermarriage and assimilation. Strongbow's first act, once he achieved power, was to marry the daughter of the King of Leinster. A hundred years later, the Normans had intermarried with the Irish, spoke at least some Gaelic, and many had little connection to England or Wales any longer. Does that mean they were still Anglo-Normans? Or perhaps calling them Anglo-Irish would be better? Or Norman-Irish? Or maybe a combination of all three?

Meanwhile, for the native Irish, everyone who arrived from Britain was a foreigner, be they English, Welsh, or Norman, and they were referred to as *Saxon*.

Finally, I'd like to say a little more about the second conquest of Ireland by the Tudors, beginning with Henry VIII. By 1500, the descendants of the original conquerors were almost completely assimilated into the native Irish clans, to the point that Henry VIII offered amnesty to all lords in Ireland regardless of ethnicity, provided they surrendered their lands to him (to receive them back immediately by royal charter).

Unfortunately for Ireland, after two hundred years of being mostly ignored by the English crown, the Tudors decided that the time had come to 'pacify' and 'Anglicize' the island to bring it under more direct English control. The country's offenses were remaining Catholic while England had gone Protestant, and the continued existence of clans and kingdoms outside of the standardized English system. The "Old English" families, as the former Anglo-Norman families were called, were viewed as no better than the native Irish. All were stripped of power and forced off their lands by new rulers and imported settlers from England, Scotland, and Wales, who were, of course, Protestant as well.

From Wikipedia:

"The first and most important result of the conquest was the disarmament of the native Irish lordships and the establishment of central government control for the first time over the whole island; Irish culture, law and language were replaced; and many Irish lords lost their lands and hereditary authority. Thousands of English, Scottish and Welsh settlers were introduced into the country and the administration of justice was enforced according to English common law and statutes of the Parliament of Ireland.

As the 16th century progressed, the religious question grew in significance. Rebels such as James Fitzmaurice Fitzgerald and Hugh O'Neill sought and received help from Catholic powers in Europe, justifying their actions on religious grounds . . . Under James I, Catholics were barred from all public office ... the Gaelic Irish and Old English increasingly defined themselves as Catholic in opposition to the Protestant New English ... By the end of the resulting Cromwellian conquest of Ireland in the 1650s, the "New English" Protestants dominated the country, and after the Glorious Revolution of 1688 their descendants went on to form the Protestant Ascendancy."

https://en.wikipedia.org/wiki/Tudor_conquest_of_Ireland

Far more than the initial Norman conquest of Ireland, it is in the Cromwellian conquest where the roots of the deep resentment of the Irish people towards the English lie, as well as the source of the campaign for independence that marked the eighteenth through twentieth centuries.

All of which, of course, David was trying to avoid.

Acknowledgments

First and foremost, I'd like to thank my lovely readers for encouraging me to continue the *After Cilmeri* Series. I have always been passionate about these books, and it's wonderful to be able to share my stories with readers who love them too.

Thank you to my husband, without whose love and support I would never have tried to make a living as a writer. Thank to my family who has been nothing but encouraging of my writing, despite the fact that I spend half my life in medieval Wales. And thank you to my posse of readers: Lily, Anna, Jolie, Melissa, Cassandra, Brynne, Carew. Gareth, Taran, Dan, and Venkata. I couldn't do this without you.

About the Author

With two historian parents, Sarah couldn't help but develop an interest in the past. She went on to get more than enough education herself (in anthropology) and began writing fiction when the stories in her head overflowed and demanded she let them out. While her ancestry is Welsh, she only visited Wales for the first time while in college. She has been in love with the country, language, and people ever since. She even convinced her husband to give all four of their children Welsh names.

She makes her home in Oregon.

www.sarahwoodbury.com

Printed in Poland
by Amazon Fulfillment
Poland Sp. z o.o., Wrocław
01 December 2020